TOO LATE!

TOO LATE!

A STORY OF BULLYING AND PERSECUTION

Thanks for spreading the message.

Pamela Hoffman

PAMELA HOFFMAN

iUniverse LLC
Bloomington

Too Late!
A Story of Bullying and Persecution

iUniverse books may be ordered through booksellers or by contacting:

iUniverse LLC
1663 Liberty Drive
Bloomington, IN 47403
www.iuniverse.com
1-800-Authors (1-800-288-4677)

ISBN: 978-1-4917-0721-0 (sc)
ISBN: 978-1-4917-0722-7 (hc)
ISBN: 978-1-4917-0723-4 (e)

Library of Congress Control Number: 2013916943

Printed in the United States of America

iUniverse rev. date: 10/04/2013

For all the children God gave me the privilege of teaching to read.
You've filled my life with joy and fulfillment.
This is for *you*!
Be safe and confident.
Be proud of who you are and who you are becoming.
You and I both know you're wonderfully made by God.
Believe *his* words about you and never the lies of Satan.

Walking in the Light

This is the message we have heard from him and declare to you: God is light; in him there is no darkness at all. If we claim to have fellowship with him yet walk in the darkness, we lie and do not live by the truth. But if we walk in the light, as he is in the light, we have fellowship with one another, and the blood of Jesus, his Son, purifies us from all sin.

—1 John 1:5–7

CONTENTS

CHAPTER 1

OKLAHOMA—LIAM'S NEED TO

FOLLOW THE NIGHT

Evil resides in the night,
comfortable in its anonymity.

Tiptoeing to the back door of the trailer house, I turn the knob quietly. The television in the other end of the house drones on with the late-night news. I picture my folks snoring in their chairs. I open the door, and Dad calls down the hall, "I thought I heard something. Liam, where do you think you're going?"

Schnap! I think as I open the door and swing it back and forth, pretending to fan the hall. "I'm hot, and I just thought I'd get some air before turning in for the night."

Tall and stern with unsmiling eyes, Dad answers, "Close the door and come in here with us."

I don't want to deal with one of Dad's lectures on how decisions are black or white and choices are right or wrong. I arrive at the hall doorway. "What do you want?"

His glare tells me I've overstepped my bounds with my curt reply. "Sit down for a minute and watch the news with us. This affects you too."

Mom hushes us.

The overly dramatic news anchor states, "We are experiencing service interruption of all cellular phones globally. The major communications companies across the globe are joining together to resolve the issues of what has been termed *potluck dialing*. No matter what country or phone number is dialed, no one is getting through to the correct person. Businesses are sending out merchandise to people who didn't order them and charging nonexistent persons for the merchandise. It's possible that identity theft is the underlying reason for this disruption. Our weather department has researched some interesting phenomena that could offer one explanation. Gary, do you have any meteorological reason as to why this is happening?"

The weatherman responds, "Solar flares can cause the disruptions we're experiencing. They can interrupt pretty much all things electronic and impact electrical grids. In 1859, a white solar flare was witnessed, and within hours the night's northern aurora lit the Earth with a light bright enough to read a newspaper as far south as Hawaii and Jamaica. The electrical surge sent through the telegraph lines of the day shocked the workers, even setting their telegraph papers on fire. They disconnected their telegraphs but could still send messages across electrically charged lines.

"Flares are normal and almost never hit the Earth head-on. In fact, we were sideswiped by a flare in May 2013; this one caused minor disruptions. Today, we monitor the sun carefully and we have surge protectors in place to help alleviate the pulse of energy. When these flares hit or sideswipe the Earth's magnetic protective bubble surrounding us, it causes it to quiver and ripple. A nuclear device detonated high in the atmosphere over the Earth would have the same effect. It would temporarily disrupt GPS navigation, satellite communication, and power grids worldwide. We're much more vulnerable to these disruptions because of our heavy dependency upon electronics. There was a ten-minute disruption to satellites communicating with air traffic controllers and ship navigation systems years ago. This doesn't sound like a very long disruption of service, but I wouldn't want to be on the plane landing by this network or on the ship docking using these measurements during a temporary navigation blackout.

"Now to answer your question of *if* it could happen, yes. But we've not had a flare directed at us that would cause these problems. We're in an active solar pattern. But we've not experienced an abnormal amount of solar flares in the past month."

The television programming goes to a commercial break. Sitting on the arm of the chair, I start to ask if I can go to bed, but Mom speaks first.

"I've noticed on the landline that it sounds like lots of people are talking at the same time. Sometimes I'm sure they can hear my conversation, because they answer me. There's always a ghost of a person listening to my conversations. It's spooky!"

Dad sits back in his chair. He has been leaning in toward the television. "It looks like another way to keep an eye on everyone to me. You mark my words: The day is coming when the government will know our every move. They'll be able to track us all and know our thoughts and opinions before we express them."

I stand as the news returns to the screen. "Can I go to bed?"

Dad is preoccupied with the breaking news; he's forgotten that he called me in for a lecture. "Sure. Go on. We'll talk in the morning."

The news anchor is back on the screen: "Identity theft is on the rise, and no one is immune to the reach of these ghosts that sweep in, wrecking our once-secure lives. Merchants are losing monies that they can't collect, leaving them vulnerable to bankruptcy."

I close my bedroom door quietly and calculate whether I'll make my rendezvous or not. If I'm not at the meeting place at the lake in thirty minutes, they'll leave without me and I'll have no choice but to return home and suffer another boring weekend at home. *It's Saturday night, for pity's sake! I'm going for it.*

Slipping the screen off my bedroom window, I silently slide it to rest against the side of the trailer house. My brothers are sleeping their lives away. The night sky is black, clouds blotting out all light from the stars. I turn to see my brothers sleeping soundly in the dim light of the digital alarm clock. I step out the window one leg at a time until I'm standing on the top of the lawn chest below the window. I bought the chest for Dad for Father's Day, knowing all along the real reason I got it was because *I* needed something to stand on as I made my weekly rendezvous. I'm the shortest kid in the family. Every family member is at least two inches taller than me. Some are almost six inches taller.

Disillusioned with the circumstances in my life, I find it easy to lay all the blame for my disappointments at the feet of my family. I can't come and go as I please, and I have to sneak out on Saturday night because I'm grounded, again! *It's their fault. I'll never measure up to their expectations. They disapprove of my friends, my hours, my attitude, my language, me! They all think that following examples from the Bible should come easy. It doesn't! The idea of turning the other cheek is just stupid.*

Evil resides in the night, comfortable in its anonymity. It calls to me. Its voice is calm, sure, and confident as it pulls me onward. I feel confident in my decision to sneak out. I wonder if I'm the only one to feel this kind of connection. I jump off the chest, and it bangs against the side of the house, waking my sixteen-year-old younger brother, Eli.

He exclaims in a hoarse whisper as he pokes his head through the window, "Liam, get back here!"

He's already four inches taller than I am, and it ticks me off. I look past him to the top bunk on the wall opposite the window. I see Fuller, my younger brother by three years, roll over and face the wall. *He* ticks me off with his puritan attitude. Disdain fills my heart, as dark as the night. Two years ago Harrison convinced me I was adopted and that my family didn't care. I don't have the same place in their hearts or our home as the rest of the kids. The night voices tell me it's okay to lie to them; they're not my real family. My family is Harrison and the guys.

I have my angelic facial expression on when I lock stares with Eli. My older sisters used to get so mad at me when I was little because I always looked innocent and they couldn't convince Mom that they had nothing to do with the quarrel. My short slight frame, round face punctuated with deep dimples, and large oval deep green eyes resembled a cherub, Gram would say. My dark walnut-colored hair and long eyelashes screamed sincerity. Mom would look at me and see her little boy and believe every word I said.

The warm breeze of early summer plays with Eli's long sandy-blonde hair. I lie to him in a whisper. "I'll be right back. I'm just going for a walk. Where can I go in the dark, on foot, and in the country? Come on. Think, pea brain! Don't tell anyone and go back to sleep before you wake Gus. If I don't take a walk, I'll explode."

I give him a trust-your-big-brother grin that displays my dimples. "You know I'd have your back, Eli. I just need some air. Please cover for me?"

His hesitation over waking Gus assures me that I'm getting to him. We'd all like to protect our baby brother. Eli knows Gus and I are tight. Gus is eight and idolizes his big brother. I like being worshipped. I deserve it.

I doubt my family's love *is* true, but Gus accepts me for who I am. He's beginning to see things the way I do. My family declares their love for me, but it's more likely some sort of Christian service project kind of love.

They're big into missions. *That's it. I'm a mission of theirs.* The dark affirms the idea. I feel better about lying to them.

Every time I sneak out I know I'll repeat it. I must be on the right track. This must be what growing up feels like, making your own decisions and being so sure they're the right ones. I'm becoming my own man. I'm no longer the boy who is told what to do. I'm a man deciding my own destiny.

Eli frowns and begins to withdraw his head. "All right, but if you get caught, you're on your own. You know how I hate lying, and it's unfair for you to ask me to do this."

I check my watch and see that it's already midnight. I whisper, "No one is going to ask us questions. Go back to sleep. See you later."

I jog to my motorcycle, which is hidden in a ravine of our pasture next to the house. It's full of gas. I push it to the dirt road, and within minutes I'm flying down the road toward another adventurous Saturday night.

Once I'm speeding away down the highway, the early years of my life come hitchhiking on the wind and into my thoughts. I should've never resisted the gang's advances. I see Harrison's dad treat him with the same words and actions that Harrison treats me. Now I see it as love, not as a way to control. Some people call it bullying, but my friends are training me. The torment and belittling isn't done because the gang is mean. It's my family's fault for being so unyielding in their views of good and evil, right and wrong.

Harrison, my leader and now my mentor, did me a favor helping me see that I must've been adopted. I don't look a thing like the rest of the family. I'm a stray. Harrison says even the simpleminded will pick up a stray cat or dog, but sooner or later the strays' wanderlust will empower them and they'll take off. He encourages me to make my own choices if I'm to follow him. I can't listen to my conscience. I need to take off. That feeling becomes stronger daily, and the decision to follow that pull becomes easier.

My thoughts return to power and the appreciation from others it brings. Harrison commands that everyone bow to him. If they don't, they pay the price. I like that feeling of total control over someone. In eighth grade, I was a target of Harrison and his leaders.

I turn off the paved scenic drive and onto a sandy road. When I'm halfway to the primitive camping area, a dark navy pickup rounds a corner and almost plows into me. My headlight illuminates the driver's side of the truck. The darkened window recedes slowly into the door panel.

Harrison's dark-blue eyes flash red when the light of my motorcycle reflects on them. He looks at his watch. "Liam, what took you so long? You're late! Let's go. Hide that piece of junk in the bushes; we'll bring you back later."

I turn off the motor, push my bike deep into the overgrown brush, and set the kickstand. The pickup's lights illuminate the abandoned campsite. My bike tips over in the sand. I start back to pick it up, but I act like it's no big deal. The motorcycle may not be much, but it's all I have. It's my only means of transportation away from the captivity of rural Oklahoma, where it's thirty minutes to a town big enough to have more than a gas station. It's an hour to anywhere large enough to have a freakin' Walmart.

CHAPTER 2

OKLAHOMA—LIAM'S NIGHTLIFE

I want my own gang.

I climb into the truck and sheepishly say, "I'm sorry I'm late. I almost got caught."

Harrison peels out, fishtailing in the soft sand. We come onto the paved scenic road that meanders along the edge of the lake and across the dam. Steering the pickup toward town, he looks in his rearview mirror at me. "Shut up! You moron! Liam, you know I hate whiners. There isn't room in this world for whiners. I'd be doing us all a favor if I got rid of the whiners one by one." His veiled threat isn't lost on any of us. George and Steve, who are also in the truck, continue smoking and laugh at the verbal assaults thrown in my direction.

I hate disappointing Harrison. He can be brutal when he's dissatisfied. I might be the object of his venomous attacks for weeks depending on the infraction. The bruises are always placed somewhere they can remain hidden until I come into line with his way of thinking. I never tell anyone about them because I'd get twice as bad of a beating the next time. Harrison's parents always back him up and give him the excuse he needs. They turn the tables on any parent or child who claims to have had a confrontation with him. It's always, "Not my boy," when they're pressed for answers. They've won enough lawsuits that they've cost many families a lot of money in legal fees. My family doesn't have any money to fight them, so I just go along with whatever he says to do.

I know being quiet is the best choice when he gets like this. As the music raps out its words, I listen closely. I used to ignore the words and enjoy the beat, but lately I like to have the words fill me with hate and violence. It's my way of using that emotion to direct invisible strikes against Harrison or my family.

Thunder vibrates through the seat and reverberates up our spines. The music is interrupted with a news bulletin: "All rail systems have come to a grinding halt! The government is unsure at this time if the shutdown is terrorist related. All of the Western Hemisphere has reported problems. All computer management systems are in lockdown, and the safety measures have automatically shut down the rails. So all trains, including passenger and freight trains, are stopped. Countries without automatic safety measures have experienced head-on collisions of an apocalyptic nature. The computers seem to have overridden all manual attempts to stop the trains. All communications are still faulty, adding to this widespread catastrophe."

Harrison pops a CD in, and rap music fills the cab of the pickup. I look out across the lake. My mind entertains how each one of us is so different. Harrison's family is from old money. Appearances are everything to Harrison's dad. He makes sure they have expensive clothes and cars. Harrison looks like the all-American boy next door with his short, neatly trimmed blonde hair, clean-shaven face, and true blue eyes. Why they look red sometimes in the dark is a mystery to me. His dark lashes seem to add to his sincere pleadings of innocence when the police stop us occasionally. His parents go about their merry way and leave Harrison at home with the servants. Harrison behaves like the ideal son when they're present, and only the closest staff members know the truth of the late-night hours he keeps on the weekend. George, the bodyguard of our group, has threatened to get Harrison's staff deported if they betray his best friend.

George is the perfect contrast to Harrison. He's heavier and taller, with black hair and small close-set dark eyes. His beard grows so fast that he always looks like he needs a shave. George never knew his dad. Rumor is his dad took off as soon as he found out George's mom was pregnant. George's mother is on disability and dying from lung cancer, so he'll be lucky to ever have wheels. George needs the money from our weekly rendezvous. Unlike Harrison, who has a super high IQ, George isn't too smart. He has failed high school twice already and grade school once, but he has to stay in school in order for his mom to receive her government checks while she's sick.

Steve's parents are divorced and hooking up with different partners every other weekend. Steve spends most of his time at his eighty-five-year-old great-grandmother's house. She's nearly deaf and rarely gets out of her chair. Neither parent ever checks to see where Steve is spending the night. They divorced themselves of any concern for him when they separated. Steve's grateful to his grandmother, but she's distant toward him even though they live together. She does a different kind of preparing him for life. She ignores and neglects him. She treats him as if he doesn't exist, forcing him to make his own decisions. She's never struck him and never gives him rules. He fixes his own meals and takes care of his own clothes. He comes and goes whenever he feels like it. If his grandmother knows of his absences, she doesn't say anything, or she doesn't care.

My mind spends a brief moment on my great-gram in Kansas. She is the complete opposite. She lives on her farm alone and does the chores to care for the farm animals. I used to spend my breaks on the farm with her, but that was when I was a child. I have to focus on the gang, so I push the thought of her from my mind. I think about my role in the group. I'm the illegitimate son of a druggy, adopted by a family trying to make me believe I'm their child. I'll never forgive my family for lying to me. I'll never ask them about it because I know they'll just come back at me with more lies.

I'll create my own family of followers like Harrison did years ago. There've been sets of three or four minions following his directions since he was twelve. Some of those kids have moved away or dropped out of school. George, Steve, and I are the only ones left of this gang. We're all going to be leaving high school this fall except Harrison, who left last year. I'll go to a small local college. Harrison is transferring to a Texas college this fall because he flunked out at Oklahoma University. He blames it on the university, not the fact that he never attended class. I've heard Harrison talk to Em, a cousin in Texas. They plan on rooming together.

I want my own gang. I know how to pick the weakest ones. I'll never waste my time with the ones who stand up to me. They can be trouble. If they show some bravery, you leave them alone. They refuse to be intimidated. My brothers and sisters are bold and don't submit to any pressure. In fact, they're all up in my business, telling me about how much God cares for me. There isn't a single private moment there. At least my two older brothers and two sisters are out of the house now. They escaped by going to college or getting married.

I've got to get out of here because since they left, Mom and Dad are on my case all the time. They're constantly harping about the way I wear my hair and my clothes. I look down at a tat on my wrist that matches my street brothers. Mom made me read Leviticus, chapter 19, from the Bible. Then I had to write a summary of what it talked about. If I hadn't respected her so much, I would've walked out then and there. I'm sure she was expecting me to say something about verse 28 and tattoos, but I didn't say a word. The whole stinking chapter was about archaic laws that don't mean anything anymore. I knew then my days living at home were numbered. No one talks about my homeboys, and I told my folks so. Then they grounded me from everything. Big woo! I'm not missing anything but the use of the ancient Atari, dial-up landline Internet, and a lame antenna television. Most of my friends don't even know what an antenna is, let alone what it does.

I ask, "What's up tonight, Harrison? You said something about a big score. I need all the money I can stash away if I'm going to be on my own in three months. School isn't for me, so as soon as the folks find out I'm not going to class, I'm sure they're going to cut off any financial support."

Harrison answers with a crooked grin, "We're going to that big church your family attends to relieve them of some of their electronics. If you'd have been here on time you could've brainstormed with us and come up with something better. *You always do.* Unless you think thunder and lightning will rain down on our heads."

Throwing his head back in a fit of laughter, he bares his teeth as he looks in the rearview mirror at me. In the dark it looks like he is snarling instead of grinning. Then he erupts into another evil deep-throated guffaw. The boys join him in laughing at me.

I flashback to when I was tormented. I hate to be the butt of jokes. Laughter seems contagious. When others join in laughing, they add strength to the comment. I see it as the crowd's way of saying they agree with what's said and done. A jagged bolt of lightning rips the sky open, sending out smaller streaks of lightning, cutting deep into the clouds and illuminating them while others skirt the outside of the clouds. It brings me back to the present.

I laugh too. After all, I made the choice to join the gang years ago. I tried bargaining with God. I told him I'd believe in him if he'd send a legion of angels to strike my tormentors dead, but nothing happened, so there must not be a God. The devil, on the other hand, whispered in my ear to not fight them and join in on the fun. I did, and the tormenting subsided.

Harrison knows I've been steering the group clear of that church for two years now. I always have to come up with bolder, more daring stunts to divert them. I wonder why Harrison chose this church. I bet it's a test to see if I've got the grit to be a leader. I'll prove myself. I'll show them where all the good stuff is, and that ought to win me some points with the gang. After Harrison goes out of state this fall, we'll need a new leader, and I plan on filling that position. It'll be easier for me to come home on the weekends and hook up with my gang than for Harrison to drive in from Texas.

I give directions toward where to park at the church. "There it is. Turn off your lights and coast into the back parking lot. There's a light broken. No one will see us as we carry stuff out."

Harrison gives the next orders. "Okay. Everybody put your ski masks on just in case. No one knows my truck yet, so if someone sees us, I'll just tell Dad I want to trade for a different make and color. We always lease anyway."

The navy pickup is Harrison's third new truck since he turned sixteen. Harrison is two years older than me, but he graduated this past May with my brother Coda. Coda never liked Harrison and even had a fight with him once because he wanted Harrison to leave me alone. I really paid for that stupid move of Coda's. The boys caught me in the bathroom and the showers during sports. They spread all kinds of rumors about me to the girls in my class. I never told a soul. I'm so glad I don't have any big brothers interfering in my life anymore. I make my own decisions about who'll be my friends. It has become comfortable, familiar somehow.

Harrison has never worked a day in his life. He has life figured out, how to play the game and not get caught. He's a night man, and the aimless underclassmen think he has life all figured out too. Harrison loves to boss others into doing his bidding. Some call it bullying. He needs to always be in control and loves to elicit fear in others. He manipulates the younger underclassmen into doing his dirty work, and he just watches humanity suffer around him. I admire people of power, no matter how they invoke it.

CHAPTER 3

OKLAHOMA—LIAM'S DECISION

*I can't go back to being held prisoner
by the vast pastures between me and town.*

We jump out of the truck and approach the church. I lead them to the nursery drop-off door because sometimes it's left unlocked. The parents are so busy with toddlers that they forget to check the door. Sure enough, it's unlocked tonight. A fluorescent memory verse hangs on the wall, illuminating the room: *Be alert and of sober mind. Your enemy the devil prowls around like a roaring lion looking for someone to devour (1 Peter 5:8).* I shudder.

We silently walk through the dining hall. I point to the high-dollar items in the offices off the main room. Then we begin to disconnect things and carry our haul to the truck. The first load goes fine. When we're gathering our second load of booty, I hear the familiar rattle of Preacher Bob's work truck. *What on Earth is he doing here after midnight? Has the church installed an alarm?*

The preacher pulls up to the front foyer doors. He leaves the headlights on to unlock the door. The boys step back into the shadows as the pickup lights shine into the foyer. They're all on one side of the entry hall, and I'm on the other. I don't have time to join them, and the nursery exit is at the other end of the building from where I am. Harrison, George, and Steve step back one step at a time, moving toward the nursery door where *our* pickup is parked.

Harrison holds a big brass vase over his head. He is ready to crack open the preacher's skull if he turns down that hall toward his office. I

12

have to make sure the preacher doesn't go down that hall. The guys might hurt him. When the preacher comes in, he reaches for the light switch. I flip the breakers, keeping us in the safety of darkness. I buy the others enough time to round the corner to the nursery door. I try to mentally will the preacher to go home, but *no*, the preacher has to see what's wrong. He heads for the breakers, which is where I'm standing. There's nowhere to hide. My only chance is to catch the preacher off guard and tackle him. I'll get up and run away before the preacher knows what hit him.

I can just imagine the celebrity I'll be among my gang. I already think of them as *my* gang. We'll have to recruit some younger kids to train the way we want them, but first things first. I tackle the preacher harder than I mean to because I'm excited. The preacher is lighter than I expect. He instinctively grabs the neck of my hoodie and holds on as we fly through the air. He groans like a granddad when I hit him in the stomach, knocking the air out of him. I hear his head hit the pew with a crack. He goes limp.

I'm on my feet and out the door as Harrison pulls away. I run as fast as my legs will carry me and jump onto the back bumper. In one motion, I leap into the bed of the pickup. I know we're to leave anyone behind and deny ever knowing him if anyone is caught. It's the first thing we learned from Harrison. Always look out for number one.

I lie in the bed of the pickup, feeling an overwhelming need to get to my cycle and get home. If Preacher Bob isn't hurt badly, he'll call my dad first thing because my dad is an elder of the church and lives the closest to town. Maybe he'll call the police first but probably not. Then the city police will be looking for any vehicles that seem out of place. In this sleepy town at this time of night, *any* vehicle is out of place. I don't even think about the evidence in the pickup bed. I just think of how this will impact *me*. The folks can't find out about the motorcycle. I can't go back to being held prisoner by the vast pastures between me and town.

I stare into the starless heavens. Then I hear the deep rumble and feel the electricity in the air before I see lightning. Briefly, I remember the earlier laughter at Harrison's comment about God's wrath. I shiver and keep my eyes glued to the light show above me. Just as big raindrops fall from the sky, we drive into Harrison's uncle's old barn outside of town.

Harrison stands in the middle of a horse stall. "The equipment ought to be safe here until we can find a buyer. Uncle Ed doesn't live around here anymore. He sold all of his cattle, and no one ever comes to this barn."

The thunder rolls over us. The wind whips in through every opening of the old barn, grabbing and snatching at our hoods, slapping them against the back of our heads. Then torrential sheets of water fall from the sky.

Harrison turns to Steve. "Have you got some buyers lined up?"

Steve's part of this group is fencing the merchandise quickly and quietly. "Of course. It'll all be gone within forty-eight hours."

George joins them. "When do we get paid? I'm strapped and need some cash quick."

George is our bouncer in case of emergency. He's quiet and usually doesn't ask questions. He tries to stay under Harrison's radar. George is happy to be on this side of the torment, kind of like me a few years ago. Back then I was too scared to buck the system. I remember a time when I used to think about separating myself from these guys, but now I want to be their leader. The adrenaline is still pumping through my body, and I like the feeling.

Finished, we kick the mud off our shoes before getting into the pickup. Steve climbs in the backseat behind Harrison. "I'll have the money day after tomorrow. We can meet up again at the lake."

Harrison stares at me through the open doorway. "Remember, if you can't make it, you forfeit your share. The more we're seen together the more likely it is for someone to put two and two together. I'll find *you*. *I* decide when and where we meet."

I defend myself, "I know. I can't always get away, but give me a little time and I'll be there." I hate it when Harrison leaves that threat hanging in the air, implying that he can reach out and screw with my life whenever *he* chooses. No one has that ability.

It's after four in the morning when I get home. I can't believe I made it ahead of the phone calls that I'm sure will come from town. I slide the window open and crawl back inside the bedroom. I slip off my muddy shoes and wet clothes and shove them under my bed. I hear the rhythmic breathing of my brothers and know they didn't hear me return. I'll shock Mom tomorrow and throw a load of clothes in the washer.

Eli rolls over but doesn't wake up. I lie down on the bottom bunk, thinking about all the things I'm going to buy when I get my cut of tonight's job. Then the phone rings. Content with the dark, I'm *home free*.

CHAPTER 4

OKLAHOMA—LIAM'S HOSPITAL VISIT

Dad fishtails down the dirt road
like there's no tomorrow.

I hear a muffled one-sided conversation. Mom and Dad are talking as they hurriedly walk to our room. I cover my head and roll toward the wall. My hair is still wet. I throw a blanket on the floor toward the window to cover any water that might still be there.

Dad opens the door and shouts, "Boys, wake up! We've got to get to the hospital as quickly as possible. Preacher Bob was injured in a break-in at the church and isn't expected to live. Hustle now!"

I jump out of bed and run to the bathroom. I've got to be in the shower so no one will notice my wet hair.

Eli pulls the shower curtain back. "Mom says no shower. Just get dressed and out to the car now!" Eli looks down and sees that in my haste I hadn't taken off my underwear.

I yell at Eli and turn red, knowing he can probably guess the truth that I just got home. "Get out of here, you little pervert!"

I'm the last one in the car, and I hardly have the door closed when Dad fishtails down the dirt road like there's no tomorrow. As the sun begins to lighten the eastern sky, it sinks in what Dad has said: not expected to live. I guess maybe there might not be a tomorrow for Preacher Bob. I begin to feel a little guilt, but I shake it off. A good leader can't dwell on things he can't change.

We walk into the hospital's emergency entrance, and my cousins are already in the waiting area. Jordyn comes running up to me with her face all wet from blubbering. She grabs me and tries to sob on my shoulder. Her long, curly strawberry-blonde hair flies across my face. I'm at least six inches shorter and two years younger than her. I feel like I look stupid. I start to shove her away, but Mom is staring at me and shaking her head. So I stand there and pat Jordyn on the back, telling her, "It'll be all right. I'm sure he'll be fine."

I steer her toward a chair while she hiccups. "He's so good—*hic*. I don't know why—*hic*. It's so senseless—*hic*. He didn't deserve this." She shakes her head and takes a breath. "Who will do—*hic*—my wedding?"

I understand only a few words, but it doesn't matter because I'm not paying attention. Everyone is overreacting. The preacher will be fine.

Jordyn's wedding is set for next month at our family's old red barn. She's probably worried that the preacher won't be out in time to perform the ceremony. The barn was used as a dance hall when my great-grandparents were alive. It sits on Highway 58, about a mile outside of a little spot in the road called Longdale. She thinks it'll be cool to get married where her Great-Great-Uncle Clarence once held dances. Girls can be so dingy some times. It probably smells like cow manure. Country life is not romantic; it's isolated from the world. I wonder what her fiancé from the air force thinks of getting married in a *barn*. He seems worldlier. At least he's from a town.

Masen and Jathyn approach next. I don't know why my aunt and uncle couldn't have just named him Nathan; it sounds like it anyway. I never understood why they needed to tack a *J* on the front instead of an *N*.

Jathyn, two years younger than me but taller, slaps me on the shoulder as if we're on the same side. "If I could catch whoever did this, I'd cream him! I'd just cream him!"

I smirk, thinking, *I'd like to see you try.*

Jathyn blows off more steam. "Preacher Bob doesn't deserve this. He's constantly giving and doing selflessly for others. Those bums are too lazy to go out and get real jobs, so they think they can just steal from others who do work."

Masen, who's my age but as tall as his brother, nods in agreement. "If they had told the preacher they needed money, he would've given them some."

I'm offended by their words. I defend my actions before I think. "Preacher Bob didn't work for that stuff either. It's all donated or bought with donations."

Masen may not say much, but when he does, it's with conviction. He looks at his brother in disbelief. Jathyn is speechless.

Masen pulls himself up to his full height in his chair before speaking for the both of them: "You're right about the donated items and the money given to the church, but that's so the preacher can minister to the people in the community. It's given back to those in need. He visits the widows, works with the youth, feeds the hungry, and just finished remodeling the bathroom of our neighbor who lost his leg and is in a wheelchair. We're to help him by giving what the Holy Spirit moves us to. The people who gave money for the things taken didn't have much money, but they gave what they could. It says in the Bible that's what we're supposed to do. No one is entitled to someone else's things!"

Normally I don't give these boys the time of day, but I guess I'll put up with them this one time. I stare at them like I'm bored.

Jathyn has regained his composure and turns to nod in agreement as they both stare with disgust at me. I don't need this, so I move away from them to a remote chair down the hall in front of the television. There are some adults watching the news, so I try to act interested.

The news anchor is reporting on the breaking news: "Major government secure websites have been compromised by hackers. They've breached United States firewalls. Our government is assessing the extent of the damage. CNN is reporting from countries in Europe and Asia, where they're experiencing the same things. The countries are sure that the anomalies experienced these past few days are the work of a terrorist cell. The United Nations is meeting to brainstorm their options to combat this dangerous threat. Homeland Security is on high alert. None of the systems can be trusted to be accurate."

Jaylie hurries down the hall. I pretend to be totally engrossed in the news program. Undeterred, she sits her little twelve-year-old self beside me in one of the five chairs available outside the surgery unit. Masen and Jathyn move as far away from me as possible.

Jaylie leans closer. "Did you hear what happened?"

I ignore her.

Her fourteen-year-old sister, Malorie, takes a seat as well. She looks younger than Jaylie because she's short like I am. Little ten-year-old Lia sits as well. The girls lean out, looking at me, waiting for a response we all know I won't have to give because just as soon as Jaylie catches her breath, she tells me everything she knows about the events of the night.

"There was a break-in at the church. Preacher Bob walked in on him, and he knocked the preacher out. He just walloped him for no reason. Can you believe he struck a preacher?"

I make no eye contact and sort through the magazines on the table. "How do you know it was a he? Maybe it was a *she*. Maybe no one slugged him. He might've tripped."

I choose a man's magazine, *GQ*, noticing right away the beautiful girls promoting the products. I thumb through it, hoping my rudeness will silence her, but she keeps going like the Energizer Bunny. Malorie and Lia are bobbing their blonde heads up and down in unison with their agreement of what is being relayed to me.

Dad walks over, reaches for my magazine, and closes it. "Come with me, son." He slides the magazine from my hands as I look up.

I figure he is going to lecture me on the scantily clad women in the magazine. I think about protesting, but I'm grateful to be away from the girly girls. I stand immediately and follow him. We walk down the hall toward the intensive care unit. I begin to sweat. I don't want to be here. Does the preacher know it was me under the ski mask? *What'll I do? Will I go to jail? What if Preacher Bob dies? Will I get the electric chair?* Every muscle in my body tenses, and I'm ready to bolt when Dad says in a whisper, "Liam, Preacher Bob wants to talk to you alone. I won't go in with you, but I'll be right outside." He keeps his arm around my shoulders as if he needs to comfort me.

I shake his arm off, ready to run. "Why me? I hardly know the man." Based on Dad's expression, I'm sure I'm scowling.

He calmly looks me in the eye. "Liam, he's not expected to make it, and I don't know why, but he has something he wants to say to you and you alone. So only you can find out. Now go on in, son. Don't wait any longer. You have to go now. He's getting weaker by the minute."

I hold his gaze a moment longer, and then I look at the door to the intensive care unit. I can't believe this. Preacher Bob can't be that bad, and he couldn't have guessed it was me. I had on a ski mask. I can't panic now and give myself away, so I take a deep breath and step through the door.

CHAPTER 5

KANSAS—GRAM'S RESTLESS NIGHT

It reminds me that evil could be lurking nearby.

Awakened from my sound sleep, I look at my companion for a clue as to why we're awake. At times like this, I feel all of my ninety-plus years. *Why am I still here, Lord?* I can't see, hear, or move as well as I did just ten years ago. But something most definitely woke us, a sound perhaps. My hearing is getting worse. I don't notice the sounds of the night. I see my ever-faithful and protective cat, Streak, sitting at attention. He's an Egyptian Mau; his turquoise eyes glisten in the moonlit room as he stares at the open window.

Streak's kneading of the blanket with his paws ceases as he listens intently. My eyes are drawn to the open window as the sounds of the night reveal themselves to me. The gauzy curtains billow in the breeze. In my fully awakened consciousness, I hear a lone motor running, which is out of the ordinary. My Centennial, Kansas, farm is so remote that to hear anyone driving down the highway is an oddity. I roll my aging body onto its side, and with effort I push my four-foot-ten frame into a sitting position. I reach over and stroke Streak's soft, healthy coat of fur.

"Streak, it's just a chainsaw or maybe one of those motorcycles. It'll be gone in a moment."

Streak's eyes stare into mine, telling me he's going to investigate. I'm lucky to have such an alert, intelligent, and protective cat. Since my Henry died six years ago, Streak has been my eyes and ears. Streak looks like a feline of the wild. His tabby coat of spots and stripes gives him the perfect camouflage. After I slip my legs over the side of the bed, my feet automatically seek the pair of house shoes that is waiting like an ever-faithful pet.

The sound draws us closer to the window. Shuffling in and out of the shadows through my bedroom, I know every seam in the carpet and what each shadow hides. These shadows are as familiar as an old friend's face, each line and blemish memorized. I know my home better than anyone. I was born here in this farmhouse. I was married and moved in with my parents for what was to be a short time. A month later, my parents died in a car accident. My husband and I continued to live here.

My older sister lived in the home in Boulder, Colorado. She received her degree and became a professor at the university in Boulder. She hated country living. I took the farm, and she took the home in Boulder the folks had purchased while she went to school there. We shared equally in the royalties from the oil and gas wells each month until her death a few years ago. I'm so ready to join her and the rest of my family in heaven, but I guess my work here on Earth isn't finished.

Standing next to the open window, I hear the motor cease about a mile away on the highway. Streak begins checking the perimeter of his domain. He loves any and every opportunity to play hunting games. I follow.

"Streak, you're the craziest cat I've ever had. You don't act a bit like the old mousers."

I follow him on his rounds of checking each room on the ground floor. He ends at the west door, the one closest to where we last heard the motor. With his turquoise eyes glistening up at me, I grant his request to go outside.

Admiring his sleek body, I can't help but think what a beautiful animal he is. The perfect *m* on his forehead almost earned him the name Milton, but the great-grandchildren named him Streak because that's what he does every time he sees them coming. I think Streak suits him and his cautious disposition. I watch my alarm system disappear into the shrubs surrounding the yard. I trust Streak explicitly. He has a sixth sense that tells him how much I rely on him to retain my independence. He takes the lead when we go for walks, searching out pitfalls that might trip me.

I take a moment to admire the beautiful May full moon hanging over the trees that line the banks of the Medicine River to the west. The evening is comfortable, with a slight northerly breeze. Standing on the west patio, I look north toward the highway, which is about a mile away.

The motor's sound came from that direction. It must've ridden on the northerly breeze. There's a weak cold front moving through tonight.

There aren't any neighbors near. The closest structure is an old one-room schoolhouse up River Road Highway about a mile. *Why would someone want to stop there?* Standing on the porch, gazing down the long driveway, I shiver in my thin ankle-length cotton gown, which billows in the light breeze. Feeling vulnerable, I'm startled when something moves over the stone wall to my right, causing me to jump, but it's only Streak carrying a mouse. I'm accustomed to his need to hunt.

"Okay, big boy, you stay outside with that thing. I'll see you in the morning." Streak lies down and enjoys his treat.

My nervousness causes me to look toward the schoolhouse. For the first time in a long time, I feel weak and alone, recognizing my frailties. For a moment, I swear I see a penlight, like a flashlight flicker, and then it's gone. I wish I'd thought to put on my glasses. After returning to the house, I lock the door and return to bed through the dark house. I don't need to turn on a light because I know my way around. There's an uneasiness in the air that wasn't here when I went to bed tonight. It's late before I can quiet my mind. I imagine the creaking of the boards in the hall upstairs.

The family thinks I shouldn't be living alone. I understand why on nights like this one. It reminds me that evil could be lurking nearby.

CHAPTER 6

KANSAS—GRAM RECEIVES NEWS

FROM OKLAHOMA

*I'm lonely for the familiar
in a suddenly unfamiliar world.*

The next morning, the only reminder of the night before is a smelly cat sleeping at the foot of my bed. I don't remember letting him in, but I must've because here he is. I mosey through the living room and turn on the television. I pause when I see that the normal programs aren't on this morning. A news bulletin has taken their place. I turn up the volume.

"Internet hackers have hacked into communication, transportation, and government agencies and now all credit card companies. Officials are alarmed at how quickly these infrastructures were breached."

I flip the television off because I don't understand anything about the Internet. Give me a pencil and paper any day. Young people today can't even make change if the electricity goes off. *What happened to good old math skills by hand?*

The wall phone beside the back door rings as I enter the kitchen. I pick up the receiver and notice the kitchen door is ajar. I close it absentmindedly. "Hello?"

Melissa, one of my granddaughters from Oklahoma, comes on the line. "Gram, how would you like some company today?"

I straighten the canisters on the counter. "That would be wonderful." My mood lifts at the thought of the family coming.

"We should be there in two hours, and we're bringing lunch. We'll see you then," Melissa states.

We say our good-byes, and I go outside to put food and water out for Streak. Young folks are so spontaneous. I look down at Streak as he weaves between my legs. "What if I hadn't been home? They would've traveled over a hundred miles for nothing."

Streak chortles as he sits squarely in front of me and scans the yard. Then his gaze returns to me.

"Point taken, dear friend. I never go anywhere, so they're sure I'll be here." Chuckling, I pet his head.

I scatter some feed for the geese in the barnyard. Malorie can feed and water the chickens. The kids love to gather the eggs. I turn out Wiley, my coonhound pup, to stretch his legs. Last month when I was delivering eggs to the neighbors, they were going to dispose of him. He was the runt of the litter, and the mother didn't have enough milk. Streak jumps on top of the corral fence to stay out of reach of the curious pup.

A few hours later, Melissa arrives with the look of doom upon her face. It's a good thing I have a batch of fresh homemade cookies coming out of the oven. This crew is in need of some sweet homemade love. She follows me into the kitchen. All seven children file by, give me a hug or a kiss, and then promptly disappear outside with warm cookies in hand.

Melissa takes a seat at the table with me as I wait for the next pan of cookies to bake. She reaches for my hand. "I need to tell you something before you hear it through the grapevine. The church was broken into last night, and the preacher walked in on the robbers. One knocked him down, and he suffered a fatal blow to the head. He remained alive for a few hours."

Alarmed and confused why this would be important to me, I say, "Oh my!"

Melissa clears her throat. "He wanted to talk to Liam alone in his ICU room. It was then that he died. Liam ran from the hospital, and in the confusion, no one realized for a while that he wasn't just in the park beside the hospital."

I retrieve my hand. "Why Liam? What did the preacher want with my boy?"

Melissa leans toward me. "We can only guess since no one was with them, but we think the preacher wanted to offer Liam the opportunity for salvation one more time. Liam hasn't found his way to the Lord yet, and we all feel the world is nearer to Christ's return. The preacher has tried to make a connection with Liam ever since Liam began bullying others."

"What? Liam is a bully? I don't understand." I shake my head.

I don't have a favorite grandchild, but if I did, it would be Liam. He seems to be the one who needs me the most. The timer dings, and Melissa takes out this set of cookies. She starts the next batch.

I'm deep in thought when she returns to the table. Liam spent his breaks from school helping around the farm when Henry was ill. He continued to come to help me after Henry, "Papa," passed away. Liam is a quiet boy, but during the past four years I haven't seen or heard from him. I thought high school kept him too busy. I miss him coming to the farm and staying with me. I could tell he was hurting on his last stay, but he refused to talk about it, so I didn't push him. The farm seemed to be the place he came to escape, and we all need a safe haven at one time or another in our lives.

Melissa continues. "I need to explain something. I said that Liam is a bully, and he is. But sadly, Liam has been bullied badly over the past few years and has become one of the many statistics. They say two-thirds of the children who are bullied become bullies. The preacher always felt he'd failed Liam somehow. Liam holds God responsible, and Preacher Bob tried to get him to see that God doesn't cause the bad things in life. God helps us through the bad things. I love my nephew, but the bullying changed him, and none of us can reach him. He became secretive. We were worried he might consider suicide. In the last five months, there have been seven deaths nationwide because of bullying."

"No! It's not that bad is it?" I ask, tormented by the very thought.

Melissa holds my hand. "It was bad enough to form a mentoring group of sorts to help these children. The young adult Sunday school class began mentoring bullied children after school with their homework. It is an opportunity to show them that they can have God on their side. We offered this service to the families of the bullies as well. That is when we discovered from the school system that Liam was classified as a bully. He was on that list."

I squeeze her hand. "Go on. Is this intervention helping? It sounds like a wonderful way to help the victims and to reach the bullies."

The bullying would explain Liam's visits whenever he came to the farm. And why he was so withdrawn. An enormous wave of guilt sweeps over me as I think of the many times I felt led to inquire deeper and didn't. I thought a teenage boy should be allowed his privacy, but when the Holy Spirit nudged me, I should have known better. I knew to act upon it.

Melissa finishes taking up the last of the cookies. "It helped some of them, but it's the age-old problem. You can witness to strangers easier than to your own family. The bullies were relentless on the passive children who just happened to be the Christian kids for a year or so. The main bully graduated a couple of years ago, but there's always another one to step up and take his place. Most of the time the new leader is from the little gang of kids who were abused into submission."

I pause my rocking. "You said earlier that Liam was friends with the bullies. Has he become a part of such a gang?"

Melissa pauses as she holds the spatula. "Maybe. Gram, he's often with them. Liam has changed. He's harder. He doesn't see anything wrong with laughing at others' expense. He says and does hurtful things to others, even his family."

I whisper, "I just can't believe it."

Melissa leans forward. "Gram, we're only guessing at this point why the preacher wanted to talk to Liam. I just wanted to tell you what's happened so you'll be informed. Liam didn't leave in a car, so we expect for him to turn up at someone's house soon. I'm sure he is just in shock. We'll find him, and he'll be all right, but if you should hear from him, we'd like you to tell his folks. And we'll tell you as soon as we see him. He may contact you before anyone else in the family. He has severed ties with most of us."

I mutter, "Of course I'll tell you. I can't believe what I'm hearing."

Melissa excuses herself to check on the kids.

I step outside to my rocker and rock in time with the wheat as it waves to and fro. I watch Streak make his way to Spring Creek. How will I cope without my crutch to hear and see for me? Loneliness envelops me amidst the chaos of my thoughts. I'm lonely for the familiar in a suddenly unfamiliar world. A lump comes to my throat because I feel the wind has been knocked out of me since I heard the news of Liam.

I close my eyes and remember the constants in my life. I visualize Liam and his brothers scaling the cedar trees on either side of the west porch, the ceiling of which is the floor of the balcony above it. My own children had done the same thing. I remember the many sunsets I've watched from that balcony, first with my parents and then my husband, our children, our grandchildren, and now the great-grandchildren. I send up a prayer that I might be able to remain in this old house until God takes me home. I need to be surrounded with memories of happier times now more than ever.

CHAPTER 7

KANSAS—JATHYN'S NARRATIVE: ATTACKED!

Jathyn, what did you do to the geese?

Out of breath and with my heart pounding in my ears, I fly by my older brother at a dead run. "Run! Run, Masen! Run for your life!"

Masen looks up. "Jathyn, what the—"

Before I can explain, Masen looks past me to see the geese trotting and squawking close behind. Masen turns and with the speed of a cheetah zips through the barnyard and the open doors of the barn ahead of us. He may be a year and a half older than me, but even at sixteen, I can usually outrun him. When he's scared, he can flat out make those muscled legs of his move. The old gander is leaning forward, flapping its five-foot wingspan and squawk-talking, closing the gap between him and me. The two females are close upon his webbed feet.

Wiley, Gram's coonhound pup, joins me in the race as I skitter around the corner of the porch to head for the barn. Wiley is a good pup but doesn't know the first thing about birds. First, his frantic barking alarms the geese. I guess he figures he'll get in on some of the racket. He usually gets in trouble for yapping in the yard. As he comes scrambling out from under the porch, he looks at me with his head cocked, and his long floppy black ears hang there as if to say, *I got your back.*

He makes another yap, nodding his head, and winks at me with his left eye, the one surrounded by the small patch of brown. He ends up directly in the line of the pursuit, between me and the gander and his two ladies—the gander's ladies, not Wiley's.

Wiley is standing there, hair bristled high on his back. I hear a thud, a yelp, a squeak, and a squawk, and I turn long enough to see Wiley on the ground. The big gander has run headlong into him. They're still rolling toward me from their momentum when Masen grabs my arm, drags me inside the barn, and slams the door shut. We peek through the cracks in the door and see the gander limping off.

The two female geese each grab an ear of Wiley's and take off with that little bewildered pup between them. He pitches and yanks free but not before losing part of his left ear. Wiley snaps, and the two female geese take flight, crisscrossing in the air. Wiley's eyes cross while trying to keep his sights on each of them. They alight about ten or twelve feet away from him. Wiley takes off after the one we call Marauding Maude. She likes to plunder everyone else's feed when they're not looking.

The gander bears down on the pup. The huge old gray cranky gander is on his tiptoes, wings spread to their full width and flapping. His long neck extends straight up, with the knob on the top of his bill aimed square at Wiley again. Wiley isn't just a good coonhound; he's smart too. Wiley turns tail and runs for the safety of his porch, diving under it like he's a baseball player sliding into home. That gander stands his ground, giving young Wiley a squawking to before waddling off like he owns the whole farm.

Masen asks ever so calmly and just a little perturbed, "Jathyn, what did you do to the geese?"

I stand up straight, open the barn door, and venture out slowly, making sure the geese are gone. "Well, nothing really. I mean Gram told me if I wanted another pillow, I had to get the down myself. Do you know where down comes from?" Not waiting for an answer, I continue, "It's the small soft feathers on the belly of the geese, ducks, chickens, and I guess *any* bird."

We pick up speed, heading for the kitchen door of the house. After taking the stairs two at a time, we're up the steps and through the screen door in three strides. I look at the fresh-baked cookies on the counter, and I know my green eyes are dancing mischievously. Mom says they do that when I'm about to get into trouble. I glance through the kitchen door to the living room, where Mom is watching television with Gram. I grab two cookies in each hand and slip them into my shirt pockets. I always wear shirts with pockets. I like my shirts to button and have collars and pockets.

Grinning at Masen, I nod toward the door and call out to Mom, "Thanks for the cookies. We're going to gather eggs."

I bounce out the door before Mom has time to answer, and I head to the chicken house.

Masen catches up. "What happened to your pillow?"

Striding out to the chicken yard, I say, "You know that lariat Jax and I tied up high in the tree on the west side of the creek, stretching it over and tying it to another tree on the lower side? Well, that's what happened to my pillow."

Masen hates it when he can't understand the clearest explanations, so he stops dead in his tracks in front of me, causing me to run into him. "What? That doesn't make any sense, as usual. You have to tell me the whole story, not just pieces. I'm not a mind reader."

I hand Masen a cookie and take a big bite out of mine. Then I say, letting my frustration show too, "I tied my pillow to my butt."

Masen sits down outside the chicken coop and begins to eat his cookie. "I still don't get it. How does this answer my question about what you did to the geese?"

I get out the second cookies for both of us and let out a big sigh. "I tied the pillow to my butt so when I reached the other side of the creek bank and landed, it wouldn't hurt. There wasn't enough room to come in for a landing on my feet. I glided down the rope in a sitting position. When I did that, my pillow caught on a jagged rock." I look up. "By the way, thank you, Lord." I never take God's name in vain, but I acknowledge his presence in my day at least once a day.

Then I continue, knowing Masen's patience is paper-thin. "The pillow ripped open, sending feathers floating down Spring Creek in all directions. I came home and asked Grandma for another pillow for tonight, explaining what happened to her other one. I told her I couldn't sleep without a pillow. She told me I had to get the down feathers and she'd make the pillow."

Masen shakes his head but doesn't say a word.

I slip the catch on the gate and step inside the chicken's pen with Masen behind me. I turn to latch the gate.

"Did you know geese aren't real fond of you pulling their feathers out of their bellies? Alice was easy. I tackled her and had a handful of feathers before she ever knew what hit her, but that Maude was another story. She may enjoy plundering Alice's feed, but you try to borrow something of hers, and she becomes all unglued. I only got two feathers. Look at what she got! Just look at my hair."

I remove my Stetson cowboy hat from my head and hang it on a post. "She snatched beaks full of my hair several times before I turned her loose. Hair for feather, she came out ahead probably ten to one. That's when the chase was on. I took off after the geese, and then the gander decided he'd turn the tables on me. He knows I'm scared of him, so I lit out like my pants were on fire. That's when we ran past you."

Cookies finished, I venture slowly toward the chickens. I eyeball a nice fluffy hen. "She looks like she's hot with so many feathers. I better relieve her of some."

I tuck my shirt into my jeans to make a kind of sack area to put the feathers. I begin to move slowly across the yard. I stalk her slow and easy, arms out at my sides, fingers extended and ready. Masen heads into the chicken house and begins to gather eggs. There're two doors; Masen goes in one, and the chickens leave the house by the other.

This is going to work out great. While he's inside, I gather some feathers for my pillow, stuffing them in my shirt. Some quills are sharp and scratch my chest and belly. Chickens aren't any fonder of giving away their feathers than geese. The rooster dive-bombs me, but I've almost got my shirt full of feathers. I can't quit now. I head for the flock, which is now making laps around the chicken pen. With each squawking, flapping lap, they gain speed. I lunge and catch Fluffy.

The others head for the chicken house just as Masen arrives at the door. He has gathered the eggs in his shirt like I gathered the feathers. His shirt is full of eggs. He stands there grinning at the abundance of eggs he collected. The flock hits him all at once, some running, some flying, but all squawking. They knock him off balance, and he stumbles back under their roosting bars, where they sit and poop at night. After the last chickens pass the door, I see Masen slowly reappear at the doorway. He looks at me with chicken poop all over his backside from head to toe. The eggs can't take as much rough handling as feathers, so their insides begin to drizzle out of the fabric of his shirt and run down into his jeans.

I stand up and offer him a hand. "I've got enough feathers. We can go now."

Masen looks at me with the same look as that gander. I'm no fool. I take off for Gram's bedroom to drop off my feathers as fast as I can. I almost make it to the house when I'm tackled from behind. We're wrestling in the dirt just outside the kitchen door. At least we're making an effort at it. I think Masen would like to hold me down, but the egg whites have made us both so slick that every time Masen swings, his hit just slides off.

I yell at him, "Stop it! You're ruining my feathers!"

We hear laughter that begins as a small giggle and then blossoms into a full-blown guffaw. We both know it's not us, so we stop long enough to look up, and we see the entire family gathered around us in a circle. They're chortling hysterically. I look at Masen, and he looks at me, and we both realize at the same time that we must be quite a sight. I begin to snicker first, and then Masen hoots until he's doubled over. By this time, most everyone is sitting on the ground because their legs are too weak to support them. They're snorting with laughter, and tears run down their faces. Grammy doesn't laugh out loud much, but even she is standing there hiss-laughing through her broken front tooth.

The evening is a little less exciting, but the mood is lighter. After Liam's disappearance, I'm glad we can distract everyone, even ever so briefly. We take baths, long baths with lots of dish soap to wash the egg slime away. Masen and I come to the supper table with our faces covered in small scratches from the geese and chickens. My hair has tuffs pulled out of it here and there, leaving it looking like I have mange. There's another round of laughter at the table, and we all retire to bed that night with smiles on our faces. We give Gram extra hugs tonight because we'll need to leave tomorrow, and I already miss her. Our heads barely hit our pillows before we're sound asleep. That is, those of us that have pillows. For those without pillows, it takes a little longer to doze off, maybe two or three minutes.

CHAPTER 8

KANSAS—GRAM FINDS MONEY MISSING

Lord, please watch over us
and lead Liam to someone who knows you.

Streak jumps into my lap and scares me to death. I must've dozed off rocking this morning. Yesterday was so eventful that I'm tired this morning. I set him on the ground and return to the kitchen. I wipe down the counter and notice my money jar is missing. I check all the cabinets, and there isn't a sign of it. I shake the fog from my brain and try to remember the last time I saw the jar. It was day before yesterday. I put more than twenty dollars in it because everyone at the Senior Center needed eggs since it was Friday. I remember seeing it the day the motorcycle woke us. I had left Streak outside with the mouse, *but* that morning he was on my bed. There was so much excitement yesterday that none of these little clues added up for me. I didn't think about the fact that there was an empty space on the counter.

I feel dizzy that perhaps someone has come into my house and may return. I step into the dining room to retrieve my purse and keys. I keep my eyes on the many open doorways of that room. One goes outdoors, and the others go to the bathroom, the living room, and the den leading to the upstairs. I have to concentrate on breathing because I feel light-headed. I back across the kitchen toward the door to the east porch. I turn to grab the doorknob, and I remember the door being ajar yesterday morning before the family arrived. The hair stands up on my neck, resulting in goose bumps up and down my arms. My hand trembles as I turn the knob. *Do I stay or go?*

31

I step out and look at my beloved farm, and I see danger everywhere for the first time in my ninety-three years. I make my way to the car and back out, watching the rearview mirror the whole time I'm driving down the half-mile dirt driveway. I hurry the next two miles to Tom's as quickly as I dare in my shaken state. Tom Washburn is outside watering his garden when I arrive. He waves, lays the hose down, and walks over to my side of the car. I roll the window down and suddenly feel very foolish. *What if I just misplaced the jar? Maybe I put it away in the cupboard? But that wouldn't explain Streak being in the house.* I smile and realize my lip is trembling. "Hello, Tom. I was wondering if you could come over to the house with me."

He looks alarmed. "Sure, what do you need?"

"Well…" I begin, shifting in the seat. "I misplaced my egg money jar. I last saw it for sure on Saturday. I put the cat out Sunday night and locked the door, but Streak was on my bed when I woke up. I know he was outside when I went to bed because he'd caught a mouse. Monday morning the back door was partially open." My throat becomes so tight that I can't say another word.

He says, "I'll be right back, and we will go." He slips into the house and comes back with his pistol. After hopping into the front passenger side, he states, "Ready. Let's go check this out."

Remaining in park, I look at him. "Oh, I don't think we'll need a gun, Tom."

Tom reaches over and places his hand on my trembling fingers. "I'm sure we won't, but if we do, I'd rather have it. Now would you rather I drive? You seem a little shaken. Did you tell me everything?" His leathery face is marked with worry.

Barely above a whisper, I answer, "Streak and I heard a motorcycle or something stop on the highway Sunday night. I think I saw a pinpoint of light in the trees by the railroad track."

"Hattie, you know to call me. Or better yet, you're to get me immediately. I don't mind going with you at all. I'd be devastated if something happened to you," Tom responds, appalled.

Head down, I can't bear to make eye contact. "I noticed my money jar wasn't on the counter just now. Then I backed out of the house and came straight over here." Now for no apparent reason I start to tear up, not cry, but the tension of the Liam incident seems to set in, and I'm afraid I'll crumble.

Tom gets out of the car and comes around to my side. Then he helps me out and into the passenger's side. He drives to the house without saying another word. He's very serious as he searches the ground for tracks, but there are tracks everywhere from my company. He doesn't see any car tracks except those of Melissa's SUV and my car. His crystal-clear blue eyes scan the windows of the house as he walks around checking each door. I stay at the car and watch Tom and Streak check the area around the house. Streak knows something is wrong. A chill passes over me as I realize Streak saw the intruder! Streak runs from strangers normally. *Why would he go inside with a stranger? Perhaps he thought I was inside and came to my defense.*

Tom is back. He opens the kitchen door and enters. Streak darts inside before the screen door closes. They're gone fifteen to twenty minutes, and then Tom comes to the door and motions me to come inside.

He says, "I've checked every room and closet downstairs and upstairs. All doors were locked except the balcony door. Do you normally leave it unlocked? I've locked it to be safe. You just can't trust anyone."

I feel safe and secure as soon as I come into the house and hear that Tom found nothing. I tell him that the boys might've used the balcony yesterday. I go to the cupboards and begin looking for the money jar. I don't find it, but I don't say anything. Tom sits with me and has a glass of lemonade. He tells me I probably moved the money or forgot I emptied it to go to town. He also blames the cat's appearance upon my not seeing him dart in, because he didn't notice him until they were in the living room. All of this could be true; I choose to accept it, for now anyway. Tom checks the outbuildings. The chickens are skittish. He tells me it looks like something has bedded down in the barn on some old hay.

I say, "Streak never lets me near the barn."

"Smart cat!" Tom exclaims as he gets into the car again. "You listen to that cat, dear friend. I'm sure he'd be a formidable foe for anyone. I know I wouldn't want to tangle with him. I want you to call me if you hear or see anything out of the ordinary. I can be here in minutes."

With my eyes on the road, I pull into his drive and manage a thank-you. "Tom, thanks for believing me and coming over to check the house. Please don't tell the family. They want me to leave my home, but I refuse to be a burden in their homes. I don't want to live in an assisted living center. I may need to one day, but I can still care for myself. I'm in relatively good health for my age. Could you keep this just between the two of us, please?" I look up with my best sad-lady face.

Tom blushes a little as he steps out of the car. He says, "All right, I won't tell anyone this time, but I think they should know. It would be best if you told them. Promise me you'll think about it."

"Okay, I will," I say as I wave good-bye.

When I'm making my evening snack, I notice that the Spam, crackers, and cheese are all missing. I look more closely at the groceries in the kitchen, and I think some pop is missing too. I could be wrong because I'm having my drowsy spells more and more often.

Streak has settled down and is already sleeping on my bed by the time I turn the lights off. I check the doors for a second time today. I lie on the bed and turn my head to watch the open window and say a prayer. *Lord, please watch over us and lead Liam to a friend who knows you.* I know the Lord is taking care of him and making sure he has what he needs, and one of those things is a deeper understanding of God. The gentle breeze blows the curtains back and forth, hypnotizing me into a deep, peaceful sleep.

CHAPTER 9

KANSAS—GRAM AND THE STORM

Is it really you?

Monday evening, Streak and I sit on the upstairs balcony to watch the sun set behind a bank of clouds. "We need rain so desperately. I hope that bank comes across us." I rock gently, and Streak lies at the edge of the balcony with his paws curled over the edge.

Before we retire, lightning begins to light the night sky. The wind switches, and I can tell the storm is building because it's pulling the air into it. Rain begins to fall in huge drops. I make sure I pull the chairs inside to the hallway so they won't fly away in the increasing wind. The storm approaches faster than I thought it would.

I hear a vase crash downstairs and the curtains rustling in the living room. I rush downstairs to close windows and lock the downstairs doors. After picking up the shattered vase, I sit down to watch the weather on the television. It says we may have bad storms tonight. I try to stay awake, but I fall asleep in my rocker.

I wake up to a loud clap of thunder. The lights flicker and go out. The television goes off. I reach into the pocket of my apron for the flashlight I always keep with me when I know a storm is brewing. The electrical lines coming to this old farmhouse are old, and the power company doesn't want to invest in new poles and lines. Sometimes it takes them more than a day to get the electricity back up and running.

Streak and I make our way to bed. I don't realize how much light the yard light brings into the house until it's off. Amidst the rumblings of the storm, I think I hear footsteps upstairs. Old houses creak and moan on

35

nights like this, so I can't be sure. It's probably the wind rearranging the old girl's boards and nails. She has stood solid and firm for more than a hundred years. I have no doubt she'll withstand the gusts tonight, but if it gets worse I can step outside to the cellar.

Streak is already on the bed, curled up and sleeping. If I'd heard something earlier, he wouldn't be sleeping because he would've heard it too. I stretch out and let my old bones creak and pop before I drift off to sleep. A question comes to mind: Did I lock the balcony door? I fearfully watch the bedroom doorway in the dark. The only time I can see into the next room, or this room for that matter, is when there is lightning. Every flash reveals a sleeping cat and a peaceful house. I've not heard another peep or creak out of these old walls, so I scold myself for my foolishness and decide I must've locked the door. Besides, who would be out on a night like this?

My eyelids heavy, sleep visits me again, only this time there are dreams. I hear footsteps on the kitchen linoleum. I shift my position in bed, and I smell a damp, earthy aroma. I wiggle again and hear the deep guttural growl of Streak. In my dreams, he morphs into a dog, and I smile. Then he hisses his warning of, *Come no closer*, like he does with the grandkids. I wake to find someone standing in my doorway.

The lightning flashes just as I open my eyes. I think I see a man of medium height. I lie perfectly still, waiting breathlessly for the next flash. A crack of thunder sounds, and then the room lights momentarily, but no one is there. I am fully awake this time, and I look around the room on the next flash. Everything seems fine except for Streak. He is kneading the covers and staring at the doorway. We couldn't both be seeing the same dream. I slowly reach out and get my flashlight from the nightstand. I try to decide if I should get up and investigate or stay quiet. If there's someone in the house, he or she isn't interested in an old woman.

Lying perfectly still, I decide to let the person take whatever he or she wants. Then Streak and I both hear it this time: footsteps upstairs. Then it's quiet again. Streak races for the stairs and comes back in a few minutes, twitching his tail as if to say all is well. He curls up on the bed but doesn't close his eyes for the rest of the night. I know because neither do I.

The house awakens to the sun's slow march upward. "Streak, I don't know about you, but I'm skipping the walk this morning. It'll be too muddy anyway. We'll get our exercise vacuuming the house."

I no more than get the word *vacuuming* out of my mouth, and Streak runs for the door. He hates the vacuum. I chuckle and start a pot of coffee. I normally fix a cup of instant, but I think I'll need more than one cup to get me going today. I pull the coffee canister out, and behind it on the corner of the cabinet is my money jar. I never keep it there.

I open the door to let Streak out, and relief floods over me. Now maybe I can put these suspicions that someone has been in and around my house out of my mind. No sooner than that thought gives me peace, doubt raises its evil head, questioning how Streak came to be in the house. I immediately embrace the explanation Tom gave me the day I dragged him over to the house. He said Streak probably entered unnoticed.

I'm so embarrassed for acting like a helpless old woman. I'll be certain next time and not call Tom unless I'm sure there's danger. I put the money jar back in the corner, hiding it with the canisters because I realize it would be smarter than out in the open. As I ponder this, I make a mental list of groceries I need when I go to town. Then I reach for my money jar. I decide to count my money and take it with me to the bank when I go to town today. The jar only has coins; all of the bills are gone. Most of my customers pay in ones and fives. I know I had at least twenty dollars from Friday. Dread and fear fills my soul. I turn, half expecting to see the intruder from the apparition the night before. No one is there. I step out the back door, carefully scanning the farm. It all looks so familiar and yet so menacing this morning. The shadows seem deeper, the foliage denser, the air heavier.

I address Streak: "I can't seem to breathe. This missing money deal has really shaken me."

I suck in air; I was holding my breath and hadn't noticed until now. I fall into my wicker rocker on the porch, feeling all of my ninety-some odd years. For the first time in a very long time, I seriously think it may be time for me to move from my beloved home. I have never really given it much serious consideration before. I have always felt that I could care for myself and didn't need assistance. Now I realize it might not be assistance that I need but protection. The calamities of nature I can withstand, but I never entertained the thought of someone wanting to harm me.

I shiver at the thought just as Streak leaps into my lap. Startled, I swat him off before I realize it isn't someone or something dangerous. I apologize, "Oh, I'm sorry, Streak. You frightened me. Here, kitty, come back up here." I pat my lap.

After careful consideration, he jumps up one more time. His penetrating stare tells me he sees the change in me as well. He begins a conversation of chattering chortles and meows as if to ask what's wrong. I feel old, frail, vulnerable, and defenseless. My trembling hand stroking Streak causes me to give way to the emotions welling up inside of me, and I begin to cry. Streak begins his nervous habit of kneading his paws on my lap. Each time he extends his claws, it pricks my legs, so I gently place him on the ground as I continue to sob.

Then I hear, "Grammy, don't cry. It's me."

Streak takes off like a shot, and standing outside the porch's half wall is Liam. He waits for me to answer.

I collect myself and dry my eyes, making sure I'm not seeing things. "Liam? Is it really you? Where did you come from? Are your parents here?" I look to the drive, expecting to see a car.

CHAPTER 10

KANSAS—GRAM'S FAMILY TRUTHS

*It seems as though two men live within one body:
one man who's hostile and distant and the other
who's vulnerable and hopeful.*

Liam replies, "No, Grammy, no one is with me. I'm all alone. I didn't mean to scare you. I'm sorry!" Then he begins to visibly tremble.

I notice his clothes are dirty, and he isn't much cleaner. I try to process his appearance, and it comes to me that he had to have traveled all the way from Oklahoma. I stand and open my arms as I say, "Come here, boy. Come in the house. You look awful."

He jumps the half wall and is in my arms, hugging me as if his life depends upon it. He trembles uncontrollably, muttering something.

"Grammy, I'm sorry. I didn't mean to do it. I'm sorry," he chokes out, pleading his defense. Raw emotions choke off any other words he wants to say. I've never seen him this vulnerable.

Leading him through the door, I direct him to a chair at the table. "What are you sorry about? I'm so glad you're safe and sound. Your parents are frantic with worry over you. We must call them straight away." I head for my phone.

This statement about calling his parents seems to shake him considerably. He becomes extremely distraught and holds me back from going farther.

"No! We can't call them, Grammy. Please! Not yet! You don't know everything. I can't have them know."

Liam begins sniffling softly with a heart so obviously burdened that my own heart begins to break. I scoot a chair closer and place my hand upon his. His hand is ice cold, and his clothes are damp. No wonder he's trembling.

I begin again slowly, gently this time. "Liam, I won't call your parents yet, but let's get you into some dry clothes and warm you up, okay? You go to the bathroom, and I'll bring you some sweats and a T-shirt I kept here for you when you worked for us. I just put on a pot of coffee this morning, and you can help me drink some. Then when you're warmer and feeling better, we'll have a little breakfast and talk."

I can't imagine why Liam would react so intensely to the death of his preacher. I guess the sight of someone dying can be traumatic. He heads for the bathroom. I follow him, pulling out a T-shirt and sweatpants from the chest outside the bathroom.

Liam turns and hugs me fiercely. "Thank you, Grammy. I don't deserve your love." Choking back obvious tears, he adds weakly, "But I can't imagine living a life without it."

He must think we're all going to hate him for running away. Now that he's had time to think about it, he is probably embarrassed and doesn't know how to face his folks. I put on a cheery smile and say, "It's all right. Why don't you take a warm bath while I cook breakfast? You can call your folks after we visit. Would that be okay?"

He relaxes noticeably. "I'd like that, Grammy." He gives my hand one last squeeze and closes the door.

As I return to the kitchen, I try to remember if this is the great-grandchild who likes gravy. Liam has stayed at the farm more than any of the other great-grandchildren. He likes large breakfasts if I remember correctly. It has been a while since he was here. Once the kids are in athletics in high school, I don't see them much anymore. I begin to gather the ingredients I'll need. I don't have any meat thawed out because I don't eat much. I have a small package of sausage in the freezer. I begin frying the frozen meat slowly. I pour myself a cup of coffee and gather the ingredients I need for biscuits.

Forty minutes later, Liam emerges looking like a thinner, paler version of his old self. I can't help myself. "You are such a handsome young man. Your medium height, short brown hair, and hazel eyes could be the spitting image of your great-grandfather. You take after his side of the family, you know."

40

Liam recoils like I'd slapped him. "Grammy, I don't look like anyone in *this* family, and I don't think like them either!" He's hostile in his response. His emotions and reactions are all over the place. I choose to ignore the venom in his reaction. I try again, saying tenderly, "Sometimes when I look into those eyes I swear my beloved Henry is looking back at me." Motioning to the table, I say, "Sit down and I'll bring the food to the table. Do you want creamer for your coffee?"

Liam remains standing, his chin stuck out in defiance. "What if I was to tell you I know the truth about *my* family?"

Liam isn't tall, but he's a few inches taller than me. I move past him on my way to setting the table. Gathering things to bring to the table, I think about this last comment. I decide not to respond, and pretend I didn't hear him. Then Liam's mood lightens as his stomach growls.

"Let me help you, Grammy. No creamer for me. I'll carry the skillet of gravy. This smells so delicious. Thank you. It all smells great, and it looks like you made all of my favorites."

We sit down and begin to eat. Liam eats as if he hasn't seen food in days. He hardly takes a breath between bites, so I don't press the issue of conversation. I do excuse myself from the table. When I return, the meal comes to an end, and Liam clears the table. I start to protest, but he insists. We move to the living room and sit across the room from one another. I sit on the couch, thinking he will join me, but he sits in a chair across from me. I get up from the couch and walk to him, carrying a photo album. I open it to my favorite picture of Henry.

"Liam, you said you didn't look like any of the family. I want to show you something. This is your great-grandfather when he was about your age. He's a couple of years older because it's when we were married. I want you to tell me who you think he looks like."

The silence is awkward and long, but I don't say a word.

Liam looks shell-shocked as he says, "This could be a picture of *me*." He utters this barely above a whisper. Then he looks up into my eyes for confirmation of his own disbelief. "I'm really from this family?" His eyes fill with tears.

I smile and nod. I've never seen this boy so emotional, and I can't imagine where in the world he would come up with the notion that he didn't belong in the family. Normally he is pretty detached from emotional displays but not from logical thinking.

Liam squeaks out, "I don't remember Papa looking like this. I remembered him as a taller man."

I say kindly, "He appeared tall to you because of his confidence in himself. He was getting sick by the time you started coming to stay with us. You were much younger, and young kids don't notice details. Papa was thin and pale, and even his eyes were fading. The man you remember was but a shell of the original. You're so very much like him. Remember that!"

Liam looks at the picture, mumbling, "They told me. I believed them. I was such a fool. So many choices made because I thought…"

I ask, "Who told you what? What are you talking about, son?"

Liam shakes his head. "Never mind, it's not important. It's *too late* now. I've lived my life in the reality they created for me." Then Liam sits a little straighter. "Grammy, I have something I have to tell someone. Do you remember when I was little and I had nightmares when I spent the weekend here alone with you and Papa?"

"Yes, I remember," I answer.

Liam continues. "I had the same dream over and over. I wouldn't stop crying because I couldn't stop thinking about it. I'd go to sleep, and the dream would be there again, and finally I refused to sleep for fear of the dream. You told me to tell you my dream as if I were dreaming it again. I told the dream to you, and I never had that nightmare again. I need to tell you something now so a nightmare will stop." He pauses, drops his head, and then looks up pleadingly and asks, "Do you think it will work with real-life nightmares?"

I answer hopefully, "I don't know, but what can it hurt to try?" I settle back into the couch. "I'm all yours. Take your time. You're safe here. You know I won't say anything to anyone. We've shared many secrets over the years." I smile and nod as if to say, *Now, go on, boy. Tell me what's on your mind.*

He stares out the window behind me. "First, Grammy, I owe you an apology." Liam's gaze moves from the window behind me to make eye contact with me. "I'm sorry, Grammy, for not coming the past three years when the folks came to see you." His eyes seem to carry the burden of the world.

I shake my head, dismissing his comment. "There's always a few of you missing. It's hard to coordinate visits when everyone is available. There's always someone involved in something at school or studying for something."

Liam's mood seems softer when he looks at me. It seems as though two men live within one body: one man who's hostile and distant and another who's vulnerable and hopeful. *That's odd. When did I stop thinking of him as a boy?* Something about him tells me he's seen and lived more than a boy of his young age should have.

Liam slumps a little, and his gaze leaves mine, bringing back the vulnerable boy I once knew as he stares at the floor. "Grammy, I wasn't too busy. I chose my friends over you. At first I was afraid to tell them no because they were brutal when I didn't do what they wanted me to do. Then I was too embarrassed about how weak I was, and they told me daily I was weak, worthless, and stupid. I couldn't tell anyone about the torment at first. My brother suspected it, but I handed him the excuses they told me to say. I'm a terrible, weak, worthless person; everything they've said about me is true. Well, almost everything."

He looks down at the photo album still on his lap. He places it on a table before continuing. "I decided long ago that it would be easier to go along with them and join in with them tormenting others than be the one tormented. I've done terrible things, and I've not done things I should've, which is equally horrible. There's no hope for me."

His words are spoken with the full emotion of a person unburdening his soul before leaving this world. Fear begins to grip at my heart and squeeze.

I start to get up and come across the room to him, but he stops me by saying forcefully, "No! Stay there. I won't be able to finish if you're too close. I have to come to terms with who I am and what I've become. I'm not good for anybody."

I stay on the couch, but I remain leaning forward, ready to go to him if he should change his mind. I feel this thread that connects us as a very fragile thing. I'm frightened for his state of mind and that he might hurt himself if he doesn't feel he has any other alternative.

I risk saying, "It's never *too late*, Liam. You said they've already told you one lie. Don't you think they could be lying about other things as well? You always have the Lord. You can earn back trust, and God offers forgiveness to all who sincerely ask. Remember Papa's favorite verse?"

Liam looks bewildered, so I go on, reciting Philippians 4:13: "You can do all things through Christ who strengthens you."

CHAPTER 11

KANSAS—GRAM HEARS ABOUT THE FATEFUL NIGHT

God would give me everything I needed to stand firm and endure their bullying, but I would need to clear a space in my life for God to reside.

Liam, voice full of emotion, says softly, "It's *too late*, Gram. My sins are unforgivable. Even God can't wipe my slate clean. I know what I've done was by choice. I could've chosen to stand firm and endure, but I didn't. I can't go back now. Preacher Bob gave me the tools I could've used to stand firm. He said I could rely on God's promises, that God has *never* broken a *single* promise. God would give me everything I needed to stand firm and endure their bullying, but I would need to clear a space in my life for God to reside. He said that meant I needed to confess my sins and clear them out of my heart, mind, and soul. I couldn't do it, Gram!"

Liam is obviously exhausted from his ordeal. His hands hold his head, and his shoulders shake from the release of emotions that have been pent up for far too long. I stay on the couch, praying, *Lord, give me the words that might penetrate his soul. Use me to tell Liam what he needs to hear.*

I begin slowly and quietly, "Liam, there's no expiration date on accepting God's gift. There's nothing so terrible that it would keep you from God's love. You said you were scared and that made you weak, but it doesn't. Everyone is scared sometimes, but you can hand over the scary times to God when you are his child. I'm sure that's what the preacher wanted you to know."

Liam stands and turns to blow his nose. He looks out the screen door. "A part of me liked being a part of a group. I was relieved when the bullying subsided when I followed their directions. I even found pleasure in watching others being made the butt of jokes. It somehow made me feel more important. I learned words are powerful weapons. When they're hurled at someone, they make puncture wounds, but when they're written and shared for the world to see, the wounds become gaping holes. A person either bows down to you, submitting themselves, or their raw insides will be exposed for the world to devour on the various social medias. I found being the one using the words felt thrilling and powerful."

Liam turns, and his hostile side is back. He defiantly makes eye contact. "I didn't want to listen to the preacher and be the one submitting to his words. Even if those words were God's in the Bible. My way just seemed easier and faster to get the torment to end for me personally. I wasn't worried about anyone but myself." He walks over to the screen door and strides through it. He sits in the chair on the wraparound porch and stares south into the distance. He leans forward, resting his elbows on his knees. The muscles in his jaw flex.

I think back to what Melissa shared with me about Liam being bullied. What if he believes his life isn't worth living? She told me that since the first of the year seven children in the United States had decided suicide was the answer to their tormented lives.

I follow Liam outside and sit in a chair a distance away from him. "Liam, I know people have said things in the past to make you feel bad about yourself, but don't listen to them. You're a good boy. You're a good man," I quickly add because I want to treat him as the young adult he is. Then I continue quietly, "You shouldn't let someone else define who you are, but I know in the midst of warfare that is easier said than done. If a man tries to stand against this world as a mortal man without the divine promises of God, it seems hopeless. Remember the words of Eleanor Roosevelt, 'No one can make you feel inferior without your consent.' Tell me what has happened."

Liam's eyes flash with a fury I've never seen before. His tongue becomes as razor sharp as a sword, and his words slice across the porch at me. "You don't know what you're talking about! I have friends who tell me the truth about myself."

Without thinking, I recoil to the far corner of my chair, and he notices. He pauses only to note my reaction and goes on, "They make me see that I am worthless in the eyes of the world. They may say things that aren't positive, but they're on my side. They're helping me find ways to be good at something. They never expect me to be perfect. I'm only worth as much as I make of myself. This world is the one that's dumped me into a goody-goody family. I'll never live up to their expectations. They expect me to believe by faith, and I know I never will. My friends have shown me how science says that God can't possibly exist, and I agree. How can a loving God exist and there be so many inequalities in what people can and can't have in life? There's nothing after this life!" Liam stands, drops his eye contact, and looks out across the southern fields again. "It was a mistake coming here. I should've known you wouldn't understand."

I'm afraid he's going to leave. That fragile thread disappears with his gaze, which no longer holds mine. I remain seated when I beg him to stay. "Please, Liam, help an old narrow-minded woman to understand. Tell me about your friends. Tell me how you see them. How does it make you feel to know you have someone so special in your life? Let me see them through your eyes." I try to sound submissive and in agreement with his arguments. My submissive action is obviously from God, because my anger is boiling over. I know I can't help him if I don't know what is residing in his soul.

Then Liam stares at me for what seems like an hour. There's a wall firmly in place this time. I feel he judges me to be sincere because he seems to go into a trance of determination as he declares, "I need to tell you what happened. That's all I need from you. Then maybe the nightmares will stop, and I can be on my way. If not…" His eyes well up with tears, but not a one falls because he visibly steels himself.

Terrified at the unfinished sentence, I remain quiet as panic forms a lump in my throat. I wish not for the first time today that I had called Liam's folks while he was in the bathroom. I'm not equipped to deal with this alone. Then Philippians 4:13 rests upon my heart. *You can do all things through Christ who strengthens you.* I think, *Yes, that's it. I'm not alone.*

As peace resides in me, Liam stares out across the fields and stands as straight as a soldier. His narration continues as if I'm no longer here. "I sneak out of the house at least once a week. My gang and I help ourselves to things that are left unattended."

Appalled, I can't help myself, and I interrupt. "You steal?"

My interjection doesn't seem to deter him because he continues as if he didn't hear me. "Last weekend, we took some things from the church.

The preacher showed up, and I tackled him to keep him from seeing me or my friends. He hit his head pretty hard, but I thought he'd be all right. I only meant to delay him from following us. I didn't mean to…" He chokes and can't finish his sentence.

Frightened, I listen spellbound and send up a prayer for my grandson.

Liam breathes deep after his incomplete sentence. He raises his chin an inch as if to see something more clearly. Then he continues his account. "We hid the stuff and returned home, and then there was a call from the hospital. The preacher was dying, and the family went to the hospital."

CHAPTER 12

KANSAS—GRAM LISTENS TO LIAM'S NIGHTMARE

Do you still feel like taking your life is the only way out?

The breeze picks up, blowing Liam's unruly dark hair across his forehead. It seems to propel the thoughts from Liam's mind for a moment. He looks around as if he hadn't noticed where he was, but when he sees me he checks his emotions. He turns back to the open fields, leaving me to stare at his back.

I wish he would face me so I could see his expressions, so I ask weakly, "Liam, could you look at me as we talk?"

I realize he feels personally responsible for the preacher's death. He *is*, if what he's telling me is accurate. He *is* responsible but not with intent. My heart goes out to the preacher's poor grieving family. The preacher was a husband, father, son, and friend to many.

Liam stiffens his back and says a defiant "No!" He takes another cleansing breath and proceeds. "We got to the hospital, and the preacher wanted to talk to me." Liam turns and looks at me as if in disbelief, and then he restates, "*Me!* I didn't want to go in to see him. My gang and I had worn dark clothes and ski masks. I was sure he couldn't identify me as the one from the church. Can you guess why he wanted to see me? I couldn't. If it wasn't because he knew it was me, then what reason would he have?"

I don't recognize the man in front of me. He is a stranger. "Liam?"

He looks at me, and his frozen expression melts. "Gram?" His new expression is one of disorientation and fear. "Gram, I can't keep reliving these next scenes. Help me!" He crumples before me, puts his head in my lap, and sobs.

I stroke his hair to comfort him. "I'm here. I'm listening." Liam stares at me, pleading with his eyes to take this burden from him. "Do you want to go back inside?"

I shiver, and he must realize it might be too cool for me. He hesitates and collects himself. "Sure, let's go inside."

He holds the screen door open as I enter, and then he follows. I sit on the couch. He sits across the room, and then as if not to be deterred any longer from his goal, he continues. "This is where my nightmare begins, as Dad comes to the waiting room and takes me to the intensive care unit. The preacher wants to talk to me alone. The nurse leaves, and I go inside. I'm thinking, *What am I doing here?* Then I hear someone call my name. It is the preacher. He's motioning me to come closer."

Liam's demeanor changes. He narrates as if he's a spectator. "'Liam, come closer,' Preacher Bob says barely above a whisper. His gray eyes search my face, but I keep my stone face in place as I step to the edge of his bed. The heart monitor is beeping, and the monitors around his bed are flashing their numerical data constantly. I let my eyes linger on all the machines and tubes to avoid looking square into the face of the man who did absolutely nothing to me. Nothing but love me enough to share his faith with me every chance he got.

"I smile my fake smile. 'You need any water or anything?' The preacher answers, 'No.' He pleads with me one last time, 'Accept who Jesus is, Liam. None of us are guaranteed tomorrow. Don't wait. God loves you and wants to forgive your sins so you can spend eternity with him.' It's all the preacher can do to complete his sentences, and I don't know for the life of me why he chooses to waste these breaths on me. The preacher quotes Acts 26:18: 'To open their eyes and turn them from darkness to light, and from the power of Satan to God, so that they may receive forgiveness of sins and a place among those who are sanctified by faith in me.'

"I'm ashamed, but I know my face reveals nothing. I've become so accustomed to lying, it's second nature now. I have the mannerisms down pat to go with any mood. Hanging my head gives me the opportunity to not look into his eyes and still look remorseful. I tell the preacher that we've been over this before. I know God doesn't want me. I'm not even sure I believe in God. Each time I make that affirmation of belief, it seems to stick tighter to my soul. Each time I say God doesn't want me, I'm more and more sure of it. The same voice that calls me in the night affirms it.

I used to feel like it was me not wanting God, but now I'm convinced it's the other way around. God doesn't want me!

"Preacher Bob raises his fist up from the bed and fist bumps my hand. Lying there helpless and frail, he opens his fist. He's holding my necklace. I reach instinctively to my neck with my other hand as he tells me that he knows my sins and none are too great for God not to forgive. His breathing becomes slower and his voice fainter. He pleads, 'It isn't *too late.* Nothing is worth your soul.'

"Then with his last breath, he begs me to repent. He tries to grab my hand, but I jerk away. The necklace falls to the floor, and I scoop it up. Then I step away from him. I'm scared. My heart pounds out the words, *He knows!* I stare at him, and the last thing he says is, 'I've told no one. I forgive you.'

"My eyes lock with the preacher's as tears stream down my face. I hear the monitors beeping one continuous beep! I see nurses rush in. The preacher's eyes close, and his hand goes limp. I rush out as more doctors arrive at the doorway. I step aside, sliding through the crush of people and machines moving quickly down the hallway to the preacher's room. As I move farther away, I see the exterior door to the building, and I pick up speed. I run for the door and daylight. I can't breathe. I have to get air. Fresh air, outside, where I can't hear the sounds or smell the stench of death. I relive this moment over and over. This is my nightmare, awake or asleep!"

Liam sits perfectly still while recounting this horrific nightmare. Now he walks through the open doorway again. I think, *If only I can keep him here until he heals. Then I know he'll be strong enough to do what he has to do.* Liam seems to know my thoughts and continues his narrative from the porch.

"I run and run! I hide in an abandoned barn by the highway and try to catch my breath, but the monitors are screaming, 'Repent, murderer!' And they follow me. Their continuous screeching pierces my brain with excruciating pain. My head throbs, and I begin to vomit. I stay in the barn until I empty my stomach of everything, including the bile. I race across the countryside, staying close to trees, scrubs, ravines, and structures. I arrive home before anyone else and know they'll be there within minutes since it's taken me so long to get home. I throw a few things in my backpack, grab some money, and leave. I take my motorcycle and head north.

"It isn't until I come to Medicine Lodge that I realize where I'm going. I sleep in your barn, or try to sleep when the nightmares recede. The alarms are with me always whenever there's a quiet time. I stole money, food, and something to drink when you went to sleep. I know one thing for certain: I can't go home. I can't face my family or friends. By now, I'm sure the police are after me. I'm going to disappear. If the nightmares will stop tormenting me, I'll leave, but something keeps me here."

I answer softly as I go through the screen door to stand beside him, "The Lord has brought you here to me. I've been praying that God would surround you with his servants, but instead God has brought you home to me. The preacher was right. God will forgive you anything. He is God, and he keeps his promises. He loves you and is giving you another chance to accept Christ's gift of salvation. Don't wait! Do it now! Don't let your heart harden and your opportunities pass. Christ is real and coming again, and you must be ready to go with him!"

Liam's eyes fill with tears, but not a single one escapes. Then he says, "No, I can't ask God to forgive me when I can't forgive myself. I'm worthless and shouldn't even be here."

I am fearful that he means he shouldn't be here on Earth instead of my home, so I rush to assure him, "Liam, you are worthy, and I think we should have more than one visit. The police aren't looking for you, but you'll have to tell them at some point in time. You aren't in any hurry to leave me, are you?"

He cautiously answers, "No. I'll miss you most of all." Then he returns to the living room, and I follow him.

I rush on with an alternative for him. "Liam, stay with me. I won't tell anyone you're here, and you can sort out your thoughts. You know I love you, and the worry alone will drive me to my grave. Please stay, and when the time comes, I'll go with you to the police." I plead as if my life depends upon it, but I'm thinking it's his life, his soul, that depends upon his answer.

Liam hesitantly says, "I don't know. I should sort this out on my own. I shouldn't have shared it with anyone. I should've kept it all inside and never told a soul. That's the first thing we learned in my gang."

He walks to the west window. I can tell there must be a cloud bank building, because the light is dim for this time of day.

I join him at the window, but I don't touch him. I believe the presence of Christians will bring strength to prayers. I begin quietly, "No, I disagree with you, Liam. You should've trusted the preacher, and I'm sure your family didn't tell you to harbor these secrets of abuse by the bullies by keeping them locked inside. Who are the *we* you refer to?"

He doesn't take his gaze off his focal point on the horizon. I can feel the fragile state of his emotions and mind as he answers, "The others who were disciplined for their weaknesses. They all watch. They all snicker and laugh when the girls are playing you and the tormentors surround you. They pretend to be your friends to reveal to the world your innermost thoughts."

He turns to face me and looks into my eyes as if he's boring a hole into my soul. Then he continues. "They didn't just tell their friends or family. It isn't the fact that the whole school knows your weaknesses. It's plastered on the Internet! Literally the whole world knows. You are either one of them or one of the chosen to be sacrificed."

I latch on to the word *sacrifice*. "That's an interesting way to look at what's happened to you and others. Sacrificed, you said. Do you believe God requires sacrifices? You know, offering something of value as payment?"

Liam looks at me, bewildered. "God? I suffered at their hands. It's *not* heaven-sent! It's far from it. As for offering something of great value as payment, I'd say a person's soul and very life are the most valuable things one has. I didn't choose to endure the suffering. I had that choice, but I chose the easier way. I gave in, and now my soul is dead."

There it is. The elephant is recognized as being in the room, so I pounce. "Liam, do you still feel like taking your life is the only way out?"

He reaches out and places his hand on my shoulder. "No. If I'd thought I could do that, I'd already have done it. I've made my choice. It's to become like them. It's all that I know now. Are you sure you still want me to stay?"

I walk into his arms and hug him around his waist, resting my weary old head against his chest. I can hear his heartbeat. "Of course I want you to stay, my precious boy. I want you to find rest in my arms and peace in my home. I want you to heal and to understand the true meaning of a love so pure that no one could ever earn it. Don't leave. Give me this chance."

I look up into his eyes and finally the tears that refused to fall earlier slide down his cheeks. I continue to hold him, as he does me, and we allow the bitter hopelessness to leave us on the evening breeze.

CHAPTER 13

KANSAS—GRAM'S PURPOSE

You've left me here for a reason, Lord.

The next morning, I sit in the living room, sipping a cup of coffee as I watch the morning news. Liam is sleeping in this morning. I think, *Poor boy. He's been through so much, but he has a tall mountain yet to climb in going to the police.* In the middle of my thoughts, the news station's alarm beeps across the airwaves with breaking news. Before I can turn it off, they begin their news feed, and I sit watching it, spellbound.

"Breaking News from KWCH-DT in Wichita, Kansas. We're breaking into your regular programming to inform you that the financial institutions around the world have been compromised by a cyber attack. Currently, North and South America are totally off-line. The markets plummeted around the world before closing. Countries are defaulting in record numbers in Africa, Europe, Russia, and Asia. The one thing they have in common is the fact that they all have substantial loans to countries in the Western Hemisphere. Most of the smaller countries have no way of repaying even the interest.

"The Eastern Hemisphere closed all markets one hour after opening this morning in an attempt to stabilize the financial integrity of all countries. All governments are pooling their resources to battle the constant bombardment of the cyber attacks. It'll take a miracle of all countries uniting together for them to remain solvent.

"It's unclear exactly how much money has been transferred and lost in these faulty transactions. The FDIC would like for all persons with monies in the banks of the United States to be patient, allow the dust to settle, and not panic. A panic would surely send the country over the brink. So in the best interest of all citizens, the United States government has made the decision to immediately close all doors to the banks of all states, including the American territories and the District of Columbia. We'll keep you informed as details become available."

I wonder why I'm still alive to see this tragedy. I send up a prayer. *Dear Lord, help me to set this news out of my mind. I must be strong and focused for Liam. You've left me here for a reason, Lord. Your work isn't finished yet. I pray it's to bring Liam home to you. Please let me live long enough to see that happen.* I'm dizzy. I'm going to have one of my sinking spells, so I lie down on the couch for a while longer.

CHAPTER 14

KANSAS—GRAM INTRODUCES THE WORD

I won't be here much longer, and he'll have to be able to stand firm in the face of Satan.

Days fill with menial tasks of gathering eggs and fixing loose boards and broken wires. The clutter that accumulates on the porch is cleared, trees trimmed, and the lawn cut. Now if I can just mend the mind, heart, and soul of Liam.

Each morning I receive a call from Oklahoma, giving me an update on Liam. "Hello, Gram. I don't have any news on Liam. The local news stations have picked up on the story, so don't be alarmed if you read something in a newspaper."

I ask, "What news? Have they caught the burglars?"

She answers, "No, but everyone is being more vigilant. The police are following up on leads. The news media wants to sensationalize the tragedy by interviewing Liam if they can find him. They want to ask him about the last words of the preacher."

I gasp. "Oh my, I'm sure he's just staying with a friend and is all right. He'll be so embarrassed to find out that they've made such a fuss. I'll continue to pray. Keep me posted."

I call Liam into the house and tell him about the phone call.

"You can't tell them, Gram. They'll arrest me, and if they don't, I'll be eaten alive by the knowledge of what I've done. I can't face any of them, especially nosy reporters. You're the only person I can trust. Do you understand?"

I nod, but I want to scream, *No!*

Each morning after their call, I beg Liam to let me tell them that he is with me and all right, but he refuses. "I swear to you I'll leave, and no one will ever find me. I'll never trust anyone again."

He is very good at using guilt to make someone do his bidding. I can see that these kids have done quite a number on him. But I've lived longer, and I have the wisdom of the Spirit on my side. I have a few things up my sleeve to get him to do the things I want him to do. I haven't lost him completely, and I'm not going to if I can help it.

"Liam, I need you to do something for me tonight," I say.

"Sure, Gram. What do you need me to do?" Liam asks. I'm sure he thinks it's another chore, which he approaches as if it's his penitence.

"I'd like you to read Ephesians, chapter 4, tonight. Would you do that for me? Please!" I ask with my heart on my sleeve.

He stands there glaring at me. "Sure."

I keep his secret and lie to the family. The next day, I fill him in on the phone call. "The police have found the stolen items hidden in a barn. The local people began their own investigation of searching every abandoned structure on their properties."

Liam asks, "Have they made any arrests?" He doesn't make eye contact and keeps his eyes diverted.

I answer, "Not yet. They feel they're getting closer to solving the case." Then I ask him, "What did you think about Ephesians?"

Liam closes his eyes, breathes a sigh of relief at the first answer, and pretends as if it doesn't bother him. He answers my second question, "Well, there were a couple of places I really liked. The verses that said, 'Instead, speaking the truth in love, we'll grow to become in every respect the mature body of Him who is the head, that is, Christ. From Him the whole body, joined and held together by every supporting ligament, grows and builds itself up in love, as each part does its work.' Another verse I liked was, 'You were taught, with regard to your former way of life, to put off your old self, which is being corrupted by its deceitful desires; to be made new in the attitude of your minds; and to put on the new self, created to be like God in true righteousness and holiness.' I especially liked the way it ended: 'Get rid of all bitterness, rage and anger, brawling and slander, along with every form of malice. Be kind and compassionate to one another, forgiving each other, just as in Christ, God forgave you.'"

I'm so pleased that he read it. I send up a prayer. *Thank you, Lord, for being with him last night.* Then I add, *Please let him stay long enough to realize he needs to go to the police.* I ask Liam, "Will you read chapter 5 tonight for me?"

He hesitates.

I fuss with my apron. "I lied to your parents, and I've done what you asked me to do. Please do this for me."

Without the hesitancy this time, Liam smiles. "Sure."

The call from Liam's folks comes the next day. I try to comfort them the only way I know how. I tell them I'm sure he is fine, safe, cared for, probably in hiding, embarrassed, and will soon contact them himself. The news media drops the story after a week or so. The police don't seem interested in him as a runaway or as a suspect in the death of the preacher. They are convinced it was some transients who were in town that week. The authorities say he's eighteen and probably decided to take a vacation by himself or with a friend.

I realize Liam needs a birthday cake. I find some candles and balloons. I inflate the balloons and place them on the table with the cake. After fixing Liam's favorite supper of brats with macaroni and cheese, I tell him I have supper ready. He quickly arrives, announcing that he's starving as he reaches for the handle of the screen door. Upon entering, Liam takes in the room with one glance, grabs me up, and twirls me around while exclaiming, "Gram, I love you so much! I'll clean up and be right back. It looks great! I'd forgotten I turned eighteen last week." He exits the kitchen en route to the bathroom with a bounce in his step.

I call out, "I love you too. Happy belated birthday!"

I open the Bible to Romans 8:28–39. I can't imagine a more uplifting, encouraging passage to give a man hope and optimism for the next year, and the rest of his life. I know he's stronger inside and out, regaining an awareness of God while here on the farm, but my weak spells have been coming with greater frequency lately. I've been able to hide them from him, but I know I won't be here much longer, and he'll have to be able to stand firm in the face of Satan. I'm sure evil will try to reclaim his soul, or at the very least lead him away. I pray it's not *too late.*

Liam returns freshened and with a smile on his face. He sees the open Bible, and his smile fades. I quickly say, "I didn't have a card, so I picked a passage I thought appropriate for a young man about to face the world head-on. I'm so glad you came here and decided to stay with me. I would like nothing better than to keep you with me forever. You must conquer this world so I'll see you in the next one. Now blow out your candles before there's nothing left of them."

I sit down at the table, and Liam closes his eyes, blows, and gives me a smile. He sits down, picks up the Bible, and asks where he should start. It's my Bible, so almost every word is underlined with notes in the margins.

I point to verse 28 and say, "Read this section, *More than Conquerors*. You're stronger and braver than you were two weeks ago when you arrived. Pretend verses 28 through 30 are on the outside of the card and the rest on the inside." I smile broadly and nod to indicate that he should read it aloud.

Liam clears his throat and says, "'And we know that in all things God works for the good of those who love him, who have been called according to his purpose. For those God foreknew he also predestined to be conformed to the image of his Son, that he might be the firstborn among many brothers and sisters. And those he predestined, he also called; those he called, he also justified; those he justified, he also glorified.'"

Pretending to open a card, he then begins again with a mischievous grin. "'More than Conquerors. What, then, shall we say in response to these things? If God is for us, who can be against us? He who did not spare his own Son, but gave him up for us all—how will he not also, along with him, graciously give us all things? Who will bring any charge against those whom God has chosen? It is God who justifies. Who then is the one who condemns? No one. Christ Jesus who died—more than that, who was raised to life—is at the right hand of God and is also interceding for us.'

"'Who shall separate us from the love of Christ? Shall trouble or hardship or persecution or famine or nakedness or danger or sword? As it is written: "For your sake we face death all day long; we are considered as sheep to be slaughtered." No, in all these things we are more than conquerors through him who loved us. For I am convinced that neither death nor life, neither angels nor demons, neither the present nor the future, nor any powers, neither height nor depth, nor anything else in all creation, will be able to separate us from the love of God that is in Christ Jesus our Lord.'"

Liam remains upbeat and says, "Let's eat! It looks great. I can't thank you enough or tell you how much this means to me." He pauses, grins, and says softly, "The card was perfect."

I breathe a sigh of relief that I haven't pushed too hard. We have a wonderful meal and lively conversation. I decide I'll tell him the news of his parents' call tomorrow because I have one of my sinking feelings. I excuse myself from the table. Liam says he'll clear the table. I only get as far as the doorway before things go black. I wake up to Streak licking my face and Liam standing over me, looking terrified. I sit up and ask Liam to help me to my bed. After I lie down, he starts to call for an ambulance.

I stop him. "No, you can't! Liam, they'll find you. I'm fine. I have these spells once in a while. The doctor tells me everything is wearing out. You know what I want more than anything is to die right here on this farm. So if I go tonight, I will die a happy woman."

Liam's voice is full of emotion as he sets the phone down and sits on the edge of the bed. "Gram, I can't lose you. Please let me call the doctor."

I smile and say, "Now you know how helpless I've felt these past two weeks when you wouldn't let me at least tell your folks that you were okay. If you will phone home, I'll go to the doctor. I don't want you to go to the hospital with me though. I think it would be too soon since your trauma. Stay here at the house. I'll be right back. I can get Tom, a neighbor, to take me."

Liam answers quickly, "Anything you say. Just get help." He picks up the phone and hands it to me to call Tom.

I know this time my episode has taken quite a bit out of me. "I can't see to dial. Can you do it for me? You have to promise me not to tell your folks about these episodes. If I get to come home again, it's going to be to the farm, not the nursing home."

"I'll promise anything. What's the number?" Liam's finger is poised over the number pad.

While we wait, I ask Liam to read Ephesians, chapter 6, tonight, and he agrees. My breathing is labored, so we don't talk much. Tom arrives in minutes. I'm carried to the car, and Liam closes the car door.

I roll the window down. "Don't forget you promised. I'll be home in a few hours or in the morning for sure. Don't worry! I love you and my farm. I will be back to both of you."

I look over to Tom. "Liam is one of my grandchildren. He has come to stay with me for a while. After the doctor checks me out and releases me, you can take me home and my grandson will look after me." I give him a weak smile. Tom returns my smile, nods to Liam, and speeds off.

CHAPTER 15

KANSAS—LIAM PHONES HOME

I will instruct you and teach you in the way you should go.

Alone on the balcony, watching the sunset, I reflect on my life. I love my family, and that's a sign of weakness. Bullies can get to you through what you love. When I was young, I wanted to look and act like my brothers. I never thought a thing about being shorter or my eye color until Harrison gave me a reason to question why I looked different. I was probably in sixth grade when Papa died, and I never noticed what color eyes he had. But that picture of Gram's confirmed beyond a doubt that I'm a part of this family.

My folks took us to church, taught us from the Bible, and tried to make sure that each of us was equipped with the information we needed to make our own decisions about eternity. I've felt pressured to believe a certain way because of my family, but now I realize my friends applied the same pressure. Their pressure was to make sure I believed as they did, that I'd act and think like them. I'm ready to decide for myself what I'll believe and do with my life.

There was a moment in the ICU room in Oklahoma with Preacher Bob when I wanted to make that confession of faith. I'd almost believed that God did love me that much. How else could the preacher plead so convincingly except by the love of God? But in the twinkling of an eye, the opportunity was gone. I know now I can never go back to pretending to be something I'm not. Now the same thing has happened again. After Gram's so-called birthday card, I made up my mind to ask God for forgiveness. The moment was snatched away again.

The sun has set, and the night wraps its darkness around me. It whispers on the wind, *You'll never be worthy of asking for that forgiveness.*

I sit here with the muggy warm breeze buffeting me with reasons for my unworthiness. I once believed it was wise to listen to the darkness, but now I'm not so sure. I notice Gram's Bible on the table next to me. She has a passage bookmarked. I go to my bedroom, flip on the light, and sit on my bed. I open her Bible and begin to read.

Psalm 32:8 reads, "I will instruct you and teach you in the way you should go; I will counsel you with my loving eye on you."

I pick up Gram's cell phone, and I make the promised call. "Hello, Mom. It's Liam. I'm okay."

She squeals, "Liam! Oh thank you, Lord, for finding my boy! Where are you? I'll come and get you!"

I begin the familiar lying. "I hitchhiked to Gram's. I was pretty messed up when I got here. She's been helping me. I made her promise to not tell anyone I was here. She made me promise to make this call as soon as I felt strong enough."

Mom says, "You're at Gram's? We've been talking to her, and she hasn't said a word to us. I can't believe she would lie to us. I can't believe she would let us worry and imagine…" Mom begins to sob, but she continues. "I want to talk to her."

I rush to talk over her words. "I'm so sorry I couldn't call before now. I was kind of a wreck when I arrived. I haven't been here where Gram was aware of my presence for that long. I slept in the barn and stole food and water when Gram wasn't looking."

Mom's tone changes. "Are you sure you're okay, son? You've had an awful shock. Your Dad and I are just sick that we allowed you to go into the ICU room alone. We had no idea the preacher was so close to death."

I answer for the first time completely truthfully, "I've got to be honest, watching him die blew me away. I had nightmares for days. I know I wasn't thinking clearly. I'm sorry I worried you and Dad."

I can tell Mom is crying again. Dad's voice comes on the line. "Liam, it's Dad." I can hear him choke back the lump in his throat.

I pick up the conversation. "Dad, I'm better than I've been in a long time. I'm sorry I caused you to worry. I just had to sort things out for myself, and I need you to understand that I can't come home. I can't! I want to stay with Gram this summer and help around the farm. She needs me, and I need her. I'm healing here. Gram and the farm have always been good for me. You know that."

Dad is in control when he answers, "Sure, son. Whatever you need. We're so thankful that you're okay. Liam, I'm so sorry I made you go in the ICU room alone. I didn't realize." He chokes up again.

I quickly say, "It's not your fault, Dad. I needed to hear what Preacher Bob had to say to me alone."

Preacher Bob must've not told anyone about the necklace, just like he said. Unless the other guys get caught, no one will ever know. I try to end the phone call. "Dad, I'll call again soon. I can't talk about this, okay?"

Dad calls out before I hang up, "Let me talk to your grandmother."

I have to do some fancy lying. "Gram is outside feeding the chickens. She doesn't know I called. Give us tonight to talk about it. Please don't rush me. She'll call you back in a day or so. It's a deal Gram and I have. I take one small step at a time when I'm ready. I was to make this call and then we talk about it. Please don't come! I'm making some headway in getting my head screwed on straight. Gram will call. I've got to go."

Dad quickly adds, "I love you, Liam."

We hang up.

CHAPTER 16

KANSAS—LIAM IS REUNITED WITH HIS FAMILY

The action of this little guy
I'd tormented rips at my heart.

I'm holding the cell phone when it rings. I hesitate before answering. Then I see it's Tom calling.

"Hello. How's Gram?" I answer the phone, my words running into each other as they tumble out.

Tom says, "They're keeping your grandmother. She'll be fine. She has had these spells before. They are more often lately, but she wants to be at that farm when the end comes. Your grandmother is a stubborn woman."

"Yes, I know," I agree and then ask, "Is she going to come home soon?"

Tom says, "They usually keep her overnight. I'll come and get her first thing in the morning. Will you be okay tonight? You can spend the night at my house if you'd like."

I pace back and forth across the bedroom. Then I answer, "Thanks but I want to fix up a few things around here before Gram gets home. I'll see you both in the morning."

When Gram returns, she's slow and forgetful. Maybe she's always been this fragile and I saw only what I wanted to see. I needed her so desperately that I never stopped to think that she might need me. She doesn't ask me about Ephesians and what I think. I was ready too. It said we need to be imitators of God—careful, wise, patient, kind, obedient, and respectful. I learned that submission isn't a bad thing. There was even a section on putting on the armor of God. If I'd known God years ago, I'd have been ready for the bullies. I should've listened to the preacher. I wish I could tell him, but it's *too late* now. I can't go back and undo my past. My future is sealed.

Gram spends her day in bed, and I fix our meals. She doesn't talk much because she can't catch her breath. When she does say something, she's thanking me for staying so she can die at home. I hate to hear her talk this way.

The folks arrive by nightfall. They probably left as soon as Dad got off work. I hear the car drive up as the evening news is signing off the television. I don't normally watch the news, but Gram has made me more aware of the world around me. I personally can see a full collapse of our government, but there's a whole generation that thinks things will be fine. They'll tweak a few things and all will be well with the world. I leave the weight of the world and then step out onto the porch. My heart drops because I don't know what I'm going to say about Gram's declining health. Then Eli and Fuller come running through the gate.

I smile. "It's about time you guys got here."

Fuller gives me a fist bump, and Eli gives me a bear hug, lifting me off my feet. He has always been the more affectionate one. I take my hug like a man and even give him one back. I've changed, and I can feel it. I don't want to just participate in life; I want to make it better.

Mom sets down her purse. "Liam, you look so good."

More hugs. Streak almost trips Dad, racing through the gate as Dad enters.

Gustin brings up the rear, carrying his backpack because he's stuffed it too full to put it on. I meet him halfway across the lawn, and I start to grab him around the neck and put him in a headlock. I stop myself. I grab his pack to help him instead.

"What've you got in here? Bricks?"

Grinning, he grabs me around the waist. "I missed you." The action of this little guy I'd tormented rips at my heart. I'd practiced all of my bullying techniques on him. I'd done almost everything to him that Harrison had done to me. I had put my own flesh and blood through the unimaginable.

Dad glides past me into the living room. "Where's Gram? Has she gone to bed already?"

I take the opportunity to say, "Yes, she turned in a little while ago. She's beat. We've been busy today. I guess I could wake her, but I think it'd be great if you'd wait to surprise her in the morning."

We talk for a while in the living room. Then they make their way to the bedrooms upstairs. I sleep on the couch. I don't feel like answering my brothers' questions, so I let them have my bed upstairs.

CHAPTER 17

KANSAS—GRAM'S PROPOSITION

I'm feeling weak.

The next morning, Lucas and I are having coffee and discussing Liam.

Lucas sets his cup of coffee down and holds my gaze. "Are you sure, Gram? He can be a handful. I think he should come home."

My reply is steady and sure. "No, Lucas, you don't understand. He's helping me as much as I'm helping him. When he arrived, he was a shattered boy, weary from the nightmares. Please know that I need him. Without him, I don't know what I'd do." Truth be known, I feel that I'm still here on this Earth to give Liam another chance to repent and be saved. His soul is worth everything, and I appear to be the only one who can talk with him about such matters.

Liam rounds the corner. "Morning." He pours himself a cup of coffee and sits down at the table.

His dad sets his cup down. "Your grandmother and I were just discussing your plans to spend the summer with her."

Liam replies, ready for a fight, "I'm eighteen. Legally, I can do whatever I want." He sees my warning glare and softens a bit. "But I'd like you to want the same thing for me. I know there's too much history back home. I can't go back there. I should've graduated last month. I'm sure my grades were high enough, and even with the last week's absences, I didn't have enough absences for the year to keep me from graduating. Surely with the circumstances they'll give me my diploma. If not, I'll just take the GED classes and get my high school diploma that way. I've thought it through, and I'm needed here. Gram needs me, and I need her."

Liam looks in my direction. I nod and smile at him. Jennifer and the boys drift in and seat themselves around the table with us.

Lucas looks at both of us. "I can see your minds are made up, and I can't change them. Liam, I must say this is the best I've seen you in quite some time. The farm agrees with you. You may stay with our blessings on one condition."

I see Liam clench his jaw. "What condition?"

Lucas reaches over and places his hand on Liam's shoulder. "You must call us once in a while and let us know how you're both doing. Also, if you decide to go to college later, you'll let us know. We'd like to help you."

Liam grabs my hand and squeezes it. "It's a deal."

Lucas needs to get back to work, so they leave shortly after breakfast.

I return to my bed. Liam asks if there's anything he can do. I smile and pray that God will touch his heart. "Liam, would you read to me from the Bible? I love to hear God's promises. They give me a peace of mind that isn't found anywhere else on this Earth."

Liam smiles, for he knows I've chosen this for his peace of mind as much as my own. "Sure, Gram. I'd love to read to you. I'm so glad you're home recovering and that I get to stay with you this summer. I wish it could be longer."

My hand goes to my chest. "Would you like to stay with me longer?"

Liam pulls up a chair beside the bed. "Gram, I'm thinking about taking a few courses at the junior college in Pratt. I won't be any trouble, I promise. I'll go to school and straight home. I can do the chores this winter for you. I can make the repairs around the house."

I put up my hand to stop him. "Liam, I'd love for you to stay with me as long as you'd like."

He leans over the edge of the bed and kisses my forehead. "What passage would you like to hear today?"

I'm feeling weak. "John, chapter 14. It's where Jesus is trying to prepare his disciples for his physical death. To die isn't the end, you know. For a Christian it's just the beginning."

As he reads the chapter, I draw strength from its words. Then I ask him, "Read from verse 25. This time I want you to think about how those words can help victims of bullies. They'd know that when they accept Jesus as their Savior they'd know his presence, because he'd dwell within them. Jesus resides within us through the Holy Spirit. He enables us and equips us with what we need when the bullies' assaults are aimed at us.

God the Father, God the Son, and God the Holy Spirit are all one in the same. Without God, this life can be terrifying. You must believe in order to claim these promises."

Liam reads the passage again. "'All this I have spoken while still with you. But the Advocate, the Holy Spirit, whom the Father will send in my name, will teach you all things and will remind you of everything I have said to you. Peace I leave with you; my peace I give you. I do not give to you as the world gives. Do not let your hearts be troubled and do not be afraid.'"

I hear Liam flip on the television. I remain in bed but listen intently.

"The government's Social Security office is on highest alert. Everything has been shut down and disconnected physically, but the satellites that are the usual routing source have been nonresponsive since yesterday afternoon. The financial institutions are in a free fall. We're going live to the World Conference."

The president of the World Conference is at the podium. "Ladies and gentlemen, we're experiencing complete shutdowns of finance, communication, and transportation sectors. We're setting aside all political, regional, and cultural differences to join together to battle this unknown enemy. Our staff of the brightest minds across the globe is working round the clock to get ahead of the imminent crash of governmental structures. We'll be broadcasting on all channels in all languages on a repeat loop. There will be one message from one central location with one voice so that you can trust the transmission. Please stay tuned, and we'll keep you advised of the decisions of this conference."

CHAPTER 18

KANSAS—GRAM'S UNITED STATES?

*My fellow Americans, this will be the last time
I address you as your commander in chief.*

Liam and I rush into the room when we hear the alarm. We leave the television on all the time since governments are crumbling daily. We take a seat and watch, mesmerized.

"This is not a test. Repeat, this is not a test of the Emergency Broadcast System. This is an important announcement by the president of the United States."

A banner scrolls across the screen while the announcement is made, and we view an empty Oval Office in the White House. There's nothing but silence for what seems like an eternity. Then the president comes from the left and sits behind the desk, and the camera zooms in for a close-up. The president looks exhausted, as if he hasn't slept in days. He appears less than his immaculate self. He looks straight into the camera.

"My fellow Americans, this will be the last time I address you as your commander in chief. You know that the fiscal state of the union has been in jeopardy for a few years now. This latest attack has placed us perilously close to *total* collapse. I come to you with an oppressively burdened heart and mind. In order to remain solvent, we've had to make the same difficult decision as our allies, becoming one of the many nations under the newly formed One World Government. This One World governing power was formed during the cyber attacks. The creative, bold steps taken by the new government have saved our world's stability in many areas. We're safer and more mobile and have more secure communications because of their ingenuity.

"Nations that have at least 51 percent of their government's assets may choose to join the One World Government. The One World Financial Institution will be determining these ratings. Nations below this level are immediately absorbed under the default ruling of the nations holding their debt. If the defaulted nation is absorbed, it does not have voting rights. Those votes will be given to the nations holding their collateral. The amount of votes will be dispersed among the various nations that are floating their loans.

"The citizens of the nations in default no longer retain the right to live in their homes. They may be relocated, and all city, state, or federal buildings become the property of the new government. They may restructure using them as the new government sees fit. Land may be confiscated to be used for the good of the world. Homes may be bulldozed to make everything from cornfields to airstrips. The deciding factor will always be whatever is most beneficial for the new government. Individual rights are terminated. As of today, the absorption of those countries has begun. The reason for the absorption at this time is to bring stability to the regions. Nations joining the One World Government, accepting its policies before falling below 50 percent, retain their right to vote. Their people and their buildings will go through a less aggressive reconstruction. Most people will be able to stay in their homes.

"I just signed our allegiance to the One World Government. We'll begin this week with town hall meetings at your state's capitol building. I'm sure you have many questions concerning our reconstruction. We're providing a link at the end of this broadcast where you may ask questions. Ask as many of them online as possible because I'm sure there are many people with the same questions. There'll be a militia present at these meetings. They'll be dressed in black-and-white uniforms like the ones you see on these men and women behind me. Do not be alarmed or afraid. They're there to protect you should anyone become aggressive and pose a threat to this united peace-keeping effort."

The camera pans to the United States flag of red, white, and blue. The lens then zooms out to take in the entire Oval Office. Military personnel in black-and-white uniforms remove the United States flag from its stand while others are at attention. Another soldier with the same uniform replaces it with a flag that looks similar except it has a huge world of blue and green sewn across both sides of Old Glory. The only thing remaining is three corners of red and white stripes and one corner of deep blue with a few white stars peeking out from under the edge of the huge world. The camera pans back to the president, and he's visibly shaken, but he wipes his eyes and regains his composure. As the camera zooms back in, he looks directly into the lens.

"We must make this work. Our lives and livelihoods depend upon it. Do not resist or mistakenly believe you have a choice, because you do not. Our military no longer has the capacity to be our protectors as the United States military. Those men and women in our military branches will complete their service under the One World Military. The alignment of militaries for the world's security against terrorism is the world's goal. Our great nation has been weakened beyond repair. We'll be a part of the One World Military now. We're accepting the protection of the coalition forces of the One World Government at this time until all of our armed forces can be absorbed and reassigned.

"I repeat, please do not resist or try to fight this change. The One World Government owns our country because of our indebtedness. We retained our vote; most of you may remain in your homes. Continue going to work at your normal jobs. The One World Government will pay your salaries for any United States government agency. This includes the state and local levels. The one exception is public school employees. Formal schooling at all levels is over for this year. All grades, even higher education, are included. Advancement to the next grade level will be automatic this one year only. All students will advance no matter if they were in jeopardy or not. All students in higher education courses will be given credit for the classes they are currently attending. If these student's current grades are a D or higher, they'll not have to repeat this class.

"All families will be given a three-day minimum to secure other arrangements for child care before returning to work. Those not having children will go back to work today. There'll be more updates to follow. To keep you informed on your government's progress, the One World News Broadcasting Company has taken over the airwaves. Regular programming will continue, but news updates will override all transmissions on the televisions, radios, and the Internet."

The camera zooms out. The president hurriedly ends, "I leave you now and *pray* that *God* will help you with this transition."

Pamela Hoffman

The military men standing closest to the president take a step closer to him when he says the word *pray*.

He takes a breath, picks up a paper, and reads his closing in a monotone, completely without emotion. "We'll be a stronger nation as we work together with the One World Government, eliminating all lines of race, religion, fiscal worries, and cultural difference from our lifestyles. We'll embrace one another's differences and appreciate our diversity by accepting everyone's unique views."

There's another pause as the president stares into the camera and says nothing. The tension of the room is so thick that we can almost see it ooze from the walls. The president continues to stare directly into the camera. He seems to enter my living room, willing me personally a silent message.

Then he looks down and reads with choked emotion, "Peace is with you, along with all the blessings the New One World Government brings for you."

He immediately stands and then strides quickly and quietly from the room.

CHAPTER 19

KANSAS—LIAM'S LAST OPPORTUNITY

*Your heart is hardened a little more each time,
until one day it's too late.*

That evening, I come into the house to find Gram deeply engrossed in her Bible. She looks up, acknowledging my presence in the room. She thinks for a moment before speaking. "There are passages that tell us we'll suffer for Jesus. They're usually followed by a call to stand firm in our faith so that at the end of time Christ will return for those of us who know him personally. Evil will have to stay and pay along with the undecided. We'll win in the end, Liam." Gram's smile is tired or weary looking tonight.

She always includes me in her pronouns that refer to Christians. She ignores the fact that I haven't chosen to accept Christ. I speak up. "Why would anyone want to voluntarily follow Jesus if they knew it meant suffering? If he's not going to take the evil ones out until the end, that doesn't do us any good now."

Gram shakes her head. "No, Liam, we're weakest without the Lord. The sufferings are going to be there whether you believe and accept him or not. He gives us strength, endurance, patience, and discernment to know right from wrong. If we are to physically defeat someone in his name, he'll provide the strength. If there's a trial to make us stronger, he'll help us endure. If we're to wait and not react immediately, he'll give us many opportunities to practice patience. Most of us know what's right and what's wrong. Take for instance to kill someone. A person is bound by the law of the land, but God's forgiveness is paramount."

She pauses, watching my reaction. "If a person commits murder with malice in his or her heart, it's wrong. But what if someone threatens to murder your baby, and you protect him at all costs? Let's say an accident happens and someone dies. Then there's war and those deaths. What's in your heart is what makes the difference. The intent is what God looks at and judges, but when we repent of our sins, he's just and forgives us our sins. The Bible is full of God's promises. He calls the sinner, not the righteous, to repentance. When God looks at us, he sees his Son and none of our sins. Jesus's blood washes away our sins. That's the *good,* as you stated, it does for us."

I shake my head. "Gram, I've gotten along fine without any major declarations. I'm going to think about this some more. There's plenty of time." Old folks always think decisions need to be made right now when it comes to religion. I think they're so close to the end of their own lives that they fail to see that the rest of us haven't lived yet. They pressure a guy too much.

I notice for the second time tonight that Gram looks old and worn out. She gets up to walk past me.

"You can wait too long. Each time you are offered the opportunity to accept Christ as your Savior and you don't choose him, you allow Satan a foothold. Your heart is hardened a little more each time until one day it's *too late.* Remember, God isn't moving away from you. You're the one choosing a path that takes you farther away from him, and with each step away, you're more vulnerable to attack." She pats my arm and continues. "You can be as good as gold but come up short when it comes to going to heaven. You know what decision you need to make. I'm going to sit out on the balcony for a while tonight. It should be a beautiful sunset with these clouds."

I hear her make her way slowly up the stairs. Streak rushes past me to join her. I stay behind, thinking about what she's said about my heart becoming hardened. Suddenly my life seems to flash before my eyes. I thought about making this decision when I was young but decided I'd be more popular if I didn't. Then the bullying escalated, and I decided it wasn't worth the risk. I thought about it when Eli and Fuller were baptized after the rattlesnake episode with Braden and Coda. I'd just been chosen to play on the junior high and high school football teams. I was popular and too busy. I thought about it when Coda and his friend Feather were baptized, but everyone was watching and expecting me to do it. I wasn't going to be pressured into anything I didn't want to do. There was the time at the hospital with the preacher. I was going to do it then, but I think it was guilt that stopped me. Then he died. There have been a couple of times here with Gram this summer. I don't think I have to make a decision one way or the other yet. I'm young. There's plenty of time.

A scream comes from the balcony. I run up the stairs, taking them three at a time. As I race down the hall, I see the door standing wide open, and the railing is missing. Gram's slipper is caught on the door's weather strip along the floor's doorjamb, which is pulled loose from the frame. I can't find my voice to call to her. I'm scared to go to the edge of the balcony, but I leap over the loose weather strip and stand at the balcony's edge. Gram is lying still on the ground below.

I bail off the balcony and into the tree and am at her side in moments. I gently touch her face. "Gram, talk to me. Please be all right. I don't want to live without you."

Her eyelashes flutter. A peaceful smile spreads across her dear face. "On my farm. I get to stay on my farm." Gram holds up a fist and places it next to her heart.

As she becomes limp in my arms, her fingers uncurl, and dirt falls across her chest. I feel for a pulse, but I can't find one. I kiss her face and sob like a baby. Collecting my wits about me, I call Tom. I have no idea what I tell him; I just know he's there when I look up from crying. I can't move, and I hold her close until the ambulance comes to take her away.

CHAPTER 20

KANSAS—LIAM AND THE WILL

Hope you find what you're looking for in Colorado.

After the funeral, the will is read. Gram's amount of property ownership is surprising.

Listed are the farm and gas and oil minerals in Kansas. There is the car; a house in Boulder, Colorado, near the university; and numerous stocks, bonds, and CDs at the bank. Gram's sister was a professor at the university and never married, so all of her property went to Gram. It is that property that is to be divided among the great-grandchildren. We all get a little money and the use of the house rent-free while in college if we behave ourselves. I grin at that statement.

The lawyer says that Gram specified her expectations of behavior in the appendix. I'm about to leave when the next thing read is that I'll get the house as my own after the last great-grandchild is finished with college. I also receive the 1999 Buick.

The lawyer reads a personal note from Gram: "I hope that Liam will be the first to live in the house and receive his degree. I expect you to set a high standard for the rest of the children to follow you to Boulder. The house has three bedrooms and should accommodate all of you. Liam, take care of Streak for me. I trust you'll know what to do with the rest of the farm animals. Find them good homes. Take care of my home. Prepare it if it is to remain empty. You know better than anyone that farmhouse is a part of me."

I am so honored that I have to leave the building before I break into tears.

Masen walks up to me at the back of the building. "Congratulations. You made quite a haul."

My first instinct is to walk away and blow him off like an annoying fly because I'm still mad at the world for Gram's death, but I stop myself because that isn't what Gram would want. Instead I say, "Thanks. Do you want to go look at the car?"

This is the first time I've been decent to my cousin in years, and it shocks him speechless. He doesn't answer, but I notice he's following me around the corner. We approach the Buick.

"It looks like an old lady's car, but it's a sweet ride. It has heated leather seats and a heads-up display on the windshield so you can see the gauges and speedometer without looking away from the road. It has the same engine as the Camaro. It can get up and go when you're passing someone. It has ports to plug in a cell phone charger or DVD player all over the car. There are three in the backseat and four in the front. There's a CD player in the trunk that holds ten CDs and plays them through the radio. It didn't sport XM radio, but it was pretty sweet in its day. This old car even has a moonroof. Gram says, I mean *said*, it gets great mileage. I checked it once, and I got thirty-four miles to the gallon." I finally stop my nervous chatter and give Masen a turn to talk.

Masen nods and says, "Yep, she's pretty sweet."

He is always brief with his comments. I smile and wonder if that is because he is afraid at any moment I'll make fun of something he might say.

I walk slowly around the car to the driver's side. "Are you planning on college this year?"

Masen rounds the car to the passenger's side. "No, I've got one or two courses I need to finish before I can graduate. I wasn't able to finish this year."

I look him in the eye. "Well, when you're ready, you can stay with me and go to the University of Colorado in Boulder."

I sit down in the car, turn the key, and begin to run through the car's features until I come to the odometer. I want to see how many miles this old car has on it. I've driven it off and on over the past year, but I never noticed.

Masen responds cautiously, "Sure, that might be okay." He sits on the passenger's side.

He stares at me like I'm a stranger, and I guess I am. In the past I picked on him every chance I got. So I say sincerely, "Hey, I'm real sorry for the way I've treated you in the past. I was a tyrant, and I know it. I'm trying to do better."

He shrugs. "That's in the past. How many miles does she have on her?"

I look. "This can't be right. It reads 63,437. Do you think that's all it has?"

"Yep, I suppose Gram's sister drove about as much as she did. Gram didn't drive anywhere," Masen answers.

I nod in agreement. "I wonder what will happen to the farm. I'll take care of putting Gram's farm in order if no one is moving in right away. If it's to be empty, there're things that need to be done to it, and I know how Gram would want it. Then I'm leaving for Colorado this summer, and I'll start college in the fall."

Masen examines the contents of the glove box. "That would be a good idea, and I know Gram would appreciate you preparing the farm and getting an education. Who knows, I might join you in Boulder one of these days." Then he steps out of the car. "Bye. Hope you find what you're looking for in Colorado."

I wave and think as he walks away, *What a strange thing to say. How could he know that I'm searching for the answer to life and death, freedom or imprisonment?*

CHAPTER 21

COLORADO—LIAM MOVES TO COLLEGE

I can work for the government while I go to school.

Streak and I secure the Kansas farm. I sell the chickens and geese to Tom. I spend one day covering the furniture with sheets, getting Streak out from under the sheets, and putting the sheets back on again when Streak pulls them off. Next I put extra locks on the doors and plywood over the windows. The last day, I take all the food and donate it to the food pantry in town. I keep a box of miscellaneous food items that were my favorites, and cat food, of course. I shut off the breakers, open the doors to the refrigerator and freezers, and turn off the pump to the water well. Then I turn on the faucets until the last drop is drained to keep the pipes from freezing. The gas is shut off to the heater and kitchen stove.

Finally, I turn to Streak and say, "Well, are you ready for a new life, my friend?"

Streak chortles his answer and leans into my leg with his body. I've learned it's his way of giving me a hug. I hate to give him the sleeping aid the vet prescribed for him for the car ride, but I don't know what I'd do if he runs off when I open the door of the carrier, which takes up most of the backseat.

The sun is beginning to break over the trees down on the creek. I want to leave early this morning and drive straight through to Boulder. It should take about eight hours or less depending on the traffic and the fuel efficiency of the Buick. I sit down on the ground and open a can of cat food, place the medicine in it, and watch Streak devour it. I stroke his beautiful coat of spots and stripes.

"This moving gives you an appetite, doesn't it?"

He twitches his tail, and I look around me.

A lump forms in my throat as I speak to the wind as much as to anyone. "Gram, I'll look after Streak, and I'll try to make you proud of me. I know now I'm from this family, so I need to stop trying to be someone else."

I look down at the last pile of books to carry to the car, and my eyes rest upon Gram's Bible. I pick it up, and it falls open to Psalm 32:8. I wonder if the promises in this Bible are only for those who believe or if they will work for everyone. I watch Streak's steady breathing, and I know he is sound asleep, so I can load him into the carrier. Gram's white Park Avenue turns onto Highway 14 in Medicine Lodge, and I head north with Streak.

Eight hours and twenty-three minutes later, I'm pulling into our new home's driveway.

I call the folks as soon as I park the car in the drive. "Mom, Streak and I made the trip fine. I drove directly to the house. It's overgrown with trees, but it looks like a very nice brick two-story home in a quiet neighborhood. I need to go to check out my new place. I'll call later in the week."

I'm carrying the carrier to the house as Mom replies, "Okay. We're glad you made it there safe and sound. I'll be looking forward to your call. Love you."

I smile. "Love you too. Bye."

I unlock the door to my new home and walk inside. I try a light switch and find that the electricity is off, as well as the gas and the water. I'll have to find out how to turn them on tomorrow. I return to the car and grab a flashlight. The mountains to the west and the thick overgrown trees have removed all that remains of the day's twilight. I let Streak out of his carrier, and he looks up at me as if to ask, *What happened?*

I address him by saying, "Let's check out our new digs."

I begin to look through the ground floor and see a basement staircase, but I think I'll leave that until there's electricity. I go upstairs and find bedrooms and a bath. Whoever took care of the property upon my great aunt's death did a good job. In fact, I couldn't have done better myself. Streak rubs my leg and purrs in agreement.

Returning to the ground floor, I'm sure Streak needs to relieve himself because I have the same need. We walk through the kitchen to the back closed-in porch. It is mainly walls of windows tacked on to the back of the house. There's a washer-dryer closet area, couch, and an antique game table with four chairs. I look out at the backyard jungle. I open the back door, and Streak dashes through it, disappearing into the wilderness. I sit on the steps. Shortly after vanishing into the backyard, he reappears to check on me.

My life has changed directions yet again. I put Streak on the back porch, lock the door, and hope he'll be okay until I can get back. I jog down the block to a convenience store I passed on our way to the house. It feels so good to stretch my legs. The store is fairly large with quite a few things that most don't have, like fresh fruit and fresh sandwiches. I visit the restrooms first. Then I pick up a few things, including a couple of candles.

I say to the cashier, "This is a very nice store. These sandwiches look delicious!"

She replies as she scans my purchases, "They *are* very good. My favorite is the chicken salad. We make them fresh daily, and we sell lots of them. This road is at the base of the hiking trail and not far from the university campus. Are you new to town?"

"Yes, I just arrived. I hope to attend your university this fall. My name is Liam," I reply, taking my sack.

She holds out her slender hand. "Hi, I'm Crystal. I'm a transplant too. I came to the university last fall. This'll be my third semester. I live on Sixth Street."

I switch the hand I'm using to hold the sack, and I shake her hand. "I live on Baseline Road. I remember seeing Sixth Street. Maybe I'll see you again. Thanks for the information. Have a nice evening."

I hadn't taken the time to really notice her when I came in, but now I find her blonde short pixie haircut and light green eyes mesmerizing. Her handshake is strong, like a girl I knew from the basketball team back home. Crystal is tall like her too, so count her out. She wouldn't want to hang around a short guy.

She begins scanning the next customer's items. "You have a nice evening too," she says as she finishes the next transaction.

I pause at the bulletin board notices as I'm on my way out of the store. There's a Help Wanted sign for the Servants' Center, a government-run social service for the homeless. I grab a brochure and head toward home.

I hear a mournful yowling a block before I reach the house. Sprinting the last block and heading directly to the back porch, I see Streak is frantic in his glass room. But as soon as I walk through the door, he hushes the yowling. Then he begins a half growl and half chortling as if cussing me out.

I pet him and put out some food and water for him. I never thought about doing this before I left. I guess it would be frightening to wake up in a new world and locked up without food and water. He didn't know if I'd be coming back. I apologize all evening long. I remove the sheets from the furniture. The house is completely furnished with furniture and appliances. I guess they work. I light a candle and venture through the rest of the house. I choose my bedroom. As I go back downstairs, I see a policeman through the window driving up to the house. Streak sticks to me like glue normally, but he makes himself scarce when a stranger arrives. I guess he thinks if I slipped off once, I might do it again.

Heading to the front door with my flashlight, I try to remember where I put Gram's will. I'm sure the officer wants to know why I'm at this abandoned house. Before I open the door, the thought travels through my head that someone in Oklahoma has told what I did to the preacher and the police are here to arrest me.

I open the door. "Hello, Officer. Can I help you?"

He looks beyond me into the house. "Who are you, and why are you here in this house?"

I respond, "I'm Liam White from Kansas, and I own this house. It was my great-aunt's house, and my great-grandmother, her sister, gave it to me in her will. Let me find the will for you." We enter the house, and his partner skirts the outside of the house.

I quickly find the will, and the officer examines it. "Why are you in the dark?"

"Well, I've never owned a house before. I should've realized driving in this evening that it would be without utilities." I scoot Streak out from under my feet and continue, "As you can see, I have a cat, and I didn't know where a motel might be that accepts pets. Besides, Streak isn't house trained. He's had his shots, so he's safe to be let out. He's familiar with the freedom of a farm." I know I've given the officer more than he probably wants to hear, but I'm nervous.

The officer's partner returns to the front door, and they exchange a nod.

"Well, welcome to Boulder. We hope you'll like it here. You'll need to get a collar and tags for your cat as soon as you can. Good night."

"Good night," I say, "and thanks for checking when things seemed out of the ordinary. It makes me feel safer. And I'll get Streak a collar tomorrow."

Streak meows a grunt and marches off into the other room. He's smart, but surely he doesn't know what I'm talking about. I close the front door, and the officers drive away. I lock up the downstairs again, and then I head upstairs to bed.

The next morning, I let Streak out as I jog to the convenience store to buy coffee and oatmeal with fresh fruit. After paying, I step out of the store and head home, but as soon as I cross the street, I'm joined by my favorite feline.

"Good morning, Streak."

He chortles his reply.

We finish our walk. I feed him and sit at the game table on the back porch with my breakfast and the brochure from last night. This windowed room lets in enough light to read. I tell Streak my plans.

"They're looking for workers at a place called the Servants' Center. It's run by the New World Government. I agree with the One World Vision that we need to help one another and be more inclusive of all the differences in religion, economic levels, ethnicity, and opinions of any kind. If we have a clear direction from our leaders, we can get behind them and make this country great again."

Streak meows as he sits erect and gazes at me, waiting for me to continue.

"The countries see that without the differences in money, values, military strengths, and religions, there won't be tensions great enough to cause world wars. Take away the catalyst to ignite those wars, and the people will live in peace. I believe in the government's new positions with the world, even if the new initiatives have to be enforced by the militias at first. I hope to be in some division of serving others and helping the government achieve these goals. Now an opportunity has presented itself. I can work for the government while going to school."

Streak chortle-talks several syllables and then waits for a reply.

"I don't make much money from this work, but I do receive college hours of credit in the field of humanities. Don't worry. I'll be able to buy cat food, my friend. I've got my nest egg to get us started."

Streak rakes his rough tongue across the top of my hand and purrs.

Streak and I visit the veterinarian, get the utilities turned on in the house, and head home to drop Streak off. I leave in the afternoon to enroll at the University of Colorado. After deciding on a major, I visit with my advisor and fill my fall semester with classes in linguistics and humanities.

My advisor looks over my selection. "Looks good, but you must take the New World Government's Harmony Objectives class because it is mandatory." He sets my work schedule for helping in the administrative office. I received a grant to be eligible to work on campus as I go to school. The hours available aren't many, but it gives me enough money to buy ramen noodles.

I think Gram would understand. I carry the thought of her with me throughout my day as if she were here. I miss her. I continue to think my choices through as if I'm explaining it all to her. I loved foreign languages in high school, and the teachers said I have an aptitude for learning other languages. Human behaviors have always intrigued me, so the pairing of linguistics with humanities and government seems a perfect fit.

Before returning to the house, I stop by the convenience store. Crystal is just getting off work, so I offer, "Can I buy you something to drink before you leave?"

Crystal places her purse on a table and takes a seat. "Surprise me with anything cold."

I return with a drink. "I need to talk to a live person. Streak is a great companion, but his conversation skills are limited."

We part ways an hour later.

CHAPTER 22

COLORADO—LIAM CONNECTS WITH GUS

Dad wants us to go into hiding.

I visit with Mom on the phone, and she fills me in on the guys I used to hang with back home. Harrison's dad and mom were arrested for embezzlement, and even though Harrison is twenty, he has gone to Texas to live with his cousin. Mom heard the cousin had a line on a job somewhere in Colorado.

I couldn't believe Harrison was going to have to work for a living for the first time in his life. George's mom passed away in June. He was arrested for breaking into houses and stealing food. Mom is so tenderhearted that she begins to cry. If she'd only known, she could've helped him. I ask about Steve, and she thought his grandmother had been put in a fellowship home. She wasn't sure what happened to Steve.

I realize I miss my brothers. It isn't their fault I feel like they're judging me. I know my past actions say I come up short even by my calculations. I have a family that loves me, and I know I'm a part of them. I've been such a fool, but I can't change the past. I decide I'll e-mail Gus.

Hey, kid.

You'll have to come to Colorado to see me. Maybe you can come next summer. I've been busy getting settled into my new life. The house is an older brick two-story maize-colored house. It has brown shingles and a porch with pillars on the front and an enclosed back porch. I have a small yard for Streak. Of course, he doesn't stay in it. He roams pretty much wherever he wants. I have an old lady on my left and an old man on my right. There're a bunch of kids across the street about my age. It might be a flophouse because different faces come and go. You probably don't know what a flophouse is. Well, it's a cheap room for the night. I bet you're excited about school this year. Tell Eli and Fuller hi for me. Be good and listen to them.

Fist bump,
Liam

I get home from work, and the first thing I do is check my e-mail. I suppose I should get on my Facebook account and get acquainted with some people out here. I log on and comment on my new home and my plans for attending the university. I exit my account and open my e-mail. Let me see what's up with my little brother.

Hey, Liam.

It's so good to hear from you. I'd love to stay with you next summer. Hope you have a good fall. Your house sounds cool. I mean, it's your very own. I'm glad you're getting the chance to go to college. I'm going to be in third grade and excited about that. Do you think you'll be able to come home for the holidays? I miss you. Things are tense around here. Dad is going to prayer meetings often, and Mom is jumpy and serious all the time. Got to go! Eli's hollering at me to come help him carry out the trash!

Bye,
Gus

I smile and I think to myself about how easy it is to communicate with home and not feel all the drama. I head to the kitchen for a snack. Streak is underfoot and wants a snack too. I guess it must be slim pickings for rodents in town. On the farm, Streak wouldn't be gone long at all, and he'd be back with a nice little mouse. I give him a can of food and take my snack out to the back porch to join him. I do this routine almost every night. If I wasn't so tired, I'd be depressed at how little I get out and about.

After my snack, I look at the couch on the porch and think about how it would be nice to stretch out. I lie down, and Streak leaps to the back of the couch. He lies down and promptly begins to purr. It's not long before his rhythmic purring has me wanting to close my eyes.

I wake up sometime in the middle of the night. I hear a low growl. For a moment, I'm disoriented and forget where I am. Then my eyes adjust to the darkness, and I look toward the growl. Streak is on the table between me and the back door of the porch. I try to focus past him as the hairs on the back of my neck stand up. I see movement as I sit up, and a dark figure runs away.

I tell Streak, "It's probably someone from across the street. Don't worry. We're locked up tight. Let's go to bed, my friend. I'm getting cold out here."

We make our way to the bedroom after double-checking that both doors are locked.

The next morning I sit down at the computer with a cup of coffee and fire off a note to Gus. There is an e-mail from him.

Liam,

I wish you were here. Mom and Dad are worried about this government deal. Dad wants us to go into hiding. We're having drills on where to go to hook up with our cousins. Oh! Here comes someone. Gotta go!

That is weird. He's probably playing one of his spy games with me. I respond with,

What's up, Mr. Mysterious?

Go into hiding? I bet this is one of your spy games. I can't believe my little brother is going to be in third grade. I'm starting classes next week, and I'll be working too, so I won't be able to e-mail much. Have a great year.

Your favorite big brother

I let Streak out the front door and flip on the television. The news banner is on the screen, so I turn up the volume.

"News update from the One World Vision news stations around the globe: The reunification of the world's nations is making great strides in securing the futures of its citizens. The One World Government has accepted all countries' entrances into the talks with the leading finance committees from around the world. The resolution made this Friday is that all nations will use the same currency. All monies will be printed and distributed from the One World Financial Federation League.

"Amnesty will be given to all nations willing to be a part of the One World Government. Their decisions must be made by the first of the year, but their indebtedness increases each day they delay. After the first of January, any remaining countries will be absorbed for the greater good of all. Representatives from all nations that had assets equaling at least 51 percent of their national debt will have a seat on this board. Any nation not meeting this requirement will be acknowledged as one of the minor countries but will have no voting rights at this time. The board will develop and promote the financial policies.

"The nations in the restructuring will need to meet the minimum requirements. Requirements will be in several areas. There will be zero tolerance for extreme religious views. The nation must sign an agreement to accept any and all religions as long as they recognize the One World Religion as supreme. They must pledge allegiance to the peaceful initiatives of the One World Order by not discriminating against anyone for their race, creed, gender, economic status, or social and sexual preferences.

"Programs already in place such as health care, food programs for the homeless, and charitable organizations that help feed and clothe our citizens will remain in effect until the government at large organizes the management of these programs. At that time, those working in those capacities will be the first ones considered for appointment as heads of the departments they've served.

"The goals of the World Board will remain in force until every nation is in compliance. Military will be trained in each voting nation, with all resources of weapons gathered and redistributed from minor nations to those major nations as the World Board deems necessary. All military will receive the same training and same goals to enforce. Any nation failing to instill the One World views within their military will be stripped of their voting rights and military status. If the nation believes any personnel is lacking in the needed conviction to carry out these goals, they are required by law to place those individuals immediately into the retraining facility, where they'll have the opportunity to learn the Peace and harmony objectives.

"The individuals are promised at least one more opportunity to pledge allegiance to the peaceful unification of all people before more drastic measures are taken. They'll receive the help they need to restructure their beliefs and become patriots of One World initiatives. The people have spoken as one voice and one world; they'll not tolerate anything challenging their peace. Any action or ideal that creates tension will be viewed as an act of terrorism."

CHAPTER 23

OKLAHOMA—JATHYN'S SURVIVAL TRAINING

There could be rattlesnakes, so be careful.

"Wake up, boys. You have five minutes to get dressed, get your backpacks, and meet me at the pickup. This is a drill. Use no lights. Make as little noise as possible. Your lives depend upon it. Ready, set, go!" Dad states in a robust no-nonsense voice.

Masen is out of bed and half-dressed by the time I figure out Dad is serious. I'm not more than thirty seconds behind Masen. I'm carrying my shoes, and I have only one arm in my shirt, but my pants are zipped. We look at the pickup, and eight-year-old Jax has beaten us both.

I ask Jax, "How did you get here so fast?" as soon as I slide into the backseat of the crew cab.

He smiles and says, "I've been sleeping in my clothes and shoes for three days, waiting on the drill."

Dad pulls away before the doors are completely closed on the old camouflage hunting pickup. The interior lights have been disconnected, and the brake lights have been blacked out with the paint job done on the pickup. When Dad needs to take the pickup on the roads, he hooks up the brake lights to the haul-bar that mounts on the tailgate.

Masen frowns at Jax and states the obvious: "That explains the stink of sweaty feet in our room." He looks out the side window as we pull away from the house in the dark.

Halfway across the pasture, Masen asks, "What's up, Dad? Where are we going?"

Dad answers cryptically, "I need to show you boys something. I want you to think of this as a real deal. Imagine you had to escape in a hurry. Where would you go? You can't go to anyone's house. Your only choices are hiding places in nature. Someplace no one else would think of or maybe even knows about except you boys."

I smart off, asking, "You need to show us at five thirty in the morning?" Then I yawn big.

Dad ignores my attitude and says, "I'm counting on each of you to protect our family in the event that your mother and I are gone. I've taught you to use your heads. You've relied on your big sister, Jordyn, all of these years because she was the oldest. She is now married, and you have to step up. She lives in Germany, too far to come help you."

Masen, always the serious one, asks, "Dad, what's wrong? You can tell us." Masen's very demeanor humbles me, and I wish I hadn't popped off.

Dad answers slowly as if he's measuring his words. "The time is coming when we may have to hide in order to worship God and live a life that affords us that freedom. The world is changing faster than I expected. We're okay for now, but I want you to practice and be ready for anything. I've taught you to use your heads. You're smart and quick in your decision making. I know you trust in the Lord, and I want you to pray every day for wisdom and guidance. Then give God the glory for your safekeeping. I don't want you to doubt yourselves. You start your day in that prayer, and you'll know God is the one guiding you. Listen to him and respond quickly. Don't argue with each other. Listen to each other's reasons for why you want to make the choice you have before you and weigh it with what your heart tells you God would want."

Dad pulls to a stop in a grove of blackjack oak trees a mile straight south of our house. We traveled through the wheat field and grass field to get here. This is the remains of the brush pasture. All the rest has been cleared from our land for farm ground.

He turns in his seat to face all three of us. "If you have a choice, leave at night. Do you think you could drive to this spot without your lights on?"

I answer, "Yes."

Jax looks around and then says, "Absolutely, Dad. I can do this."

I smile and roll my eyes at Masen. He smiles back and shares the pleasure of watching our little eight-year-old brother.

Masen nods. "I think I can." His head is probably full of possible catastrophes. He is the biggest worrywart I've ever seen.

Dad looks at me. "Jathyn, I want you to drive if the time comes. You didn't hesitate. You were positive. God wants you to be positive about his ability to lead you. Masen, you hesitated. Why?"

Masen defended his decision by saying, "Well, if it's cloudy or stormy, we maybe couldn't see. If there isn't a moon, we might drive into the little pond here in the corner. We might hit a fence."

Dad states, "Masen, I just told you not to rely on your humanness to guide you. Believe with all your heart and mind that God is real and he'll be there providing what you need when you need it."

Dad puts his hand on Jax's shoulder. "I like your attitude too. If Jathyn can't drive, you're next in line. Listen to Masen; he'll help you avoid things you're too young to realize might be a problem. Next, I want you to watch the horizon and make sure you don't see any lights—car lights or flashlights—that might be following you. Does anyone see anything?"

We all scan our surroundings.

Masen is first this time. "Not a single light that's moving, Dad, only the yard lights of the nearby houses."

Dad states, "Good. We're going to the cave at Uncle Luke's place. In order for it to be a safe place, no one must know where it is. Only the family knows about it. Don't tell a soul. Your cousins are preparing to rendezvous with us at the same place."

Dad opens a gate in the barbwire fence. It is hidden by a thicket. He holds it back as we come through. "Put the gate back like it was so the cattle won't get out and cause a farmer to check this fence and find your pickup."

We walk in silence straight east down a closed section line. We crawl through the fence, and Dad breaks off a tumbleweed. We jog across the dirt road. Dad goes last and brushes out our tracks just like in the movies.

My attitude gets the best of me again. "Do you really think that's necessary, Dad?"

His answer is firm. "Yes!" His tone tells me to keep my mouth shut.

We walk down the ditch beside the dirt road until we come to the railroad tracks. Luckily, we haven't seen a car this morning, or we would have to burrow into the overgrown weeds of the ditch. The gravel over the railroad ties allows us to jog because we don't have to be so careful about leaving tracks.

The sun is beginning to light the eastern sky. We follow the railroad tracks as they meander off toward the northeast. As we approach the next dirt road, we hear no vehicles, but Dad points to the lease road that's close to the railroad tracks. It has a camera mounted above it, recording who goes into the well site. Some of the oil companies have had trouble with thieves stealing diesel. We skirt to the far side of the tracks, opposite the camera, staying well out of range of the lens, and then continue around the bend in the railroad tracks to the back side of the pasture.

There's a pond upstream from the cave, and we crawl through the fence, winding our way down the streambed. It's light enough to see where we're going. There isn't much water today because of the drought. We approach the cave, but Masen and I both miss it, walking right by it. A cedar hides its entrance.

Dad warns us, "There could be rattlesnakes, so be careful. Your Uncle Luke and Uncle Nic and I have been catching and destroying snakes every year since the cave was found. We didn't catch any here last year, but that doesn't mean there might not be one this year. Later in the year is better. They hibernate and move slowly." He hands us flashlights and a snake catcher that's propped up behind the tree. Then he says, "I'll go in first, and you follow me when I say. I don't want you in my way if I want to get out fast."

We answer, "Okay."

CHAPTER 24

OKLAHOMA—JATHYN REALIZES DAD IS SERIOUS

Who might be after us, Dad?

I think, *No way am I going first!* Dad showed us last summer how to use snake catchers, but it was with bull snakes, not rattlers. We heard of the cave after Braden and Coda nearly died from rattlesnake bites when they entered. We've been threatened within an inch of our lives if we went searching for it. I can't believe Dad wants us to go in there.

We hear a call from inside. "All is clear. Come on in."

I look at Masen and bow to his entering first, and he does the same to me.

Jax gets on all fours and shimmies through the opening.

We hear another call. "Quit your screwing around and get in here, boys! It's safe!"

How my parents know what we're doing when they can't see us has always been a mystery to me. Masen begins to crawl inside as soon as he hears Dad's tone. I follow close behind. The entrance is snug. Then it opens up, allowing plenty of room to crawl. If a person is short, he or she can stand and stay crouched over. I shine my flashlight around and see evidence of where water once rushed by, leaving swirled-out cavities along the path. Each cubby is clear of any debris that can hide a snake.

I smell something like diesel burning and see the end of the hall come alive with a flickering light. I'm almost to the end of the short hallway, and then it opens up into a larger cave. There's a ledge, upon which Dad and Masen are already standing. Dad has a torch that's obviously soaked in diesel by the smell of it.

I say, "Wow! This is so cool!"

Dad smiles but shushes me. "*Shhh*, speak quietly anytime you're in the cave. It echoes, and the sounds drift down the canyon. On a still night, your cousin Coda said he could hear Feather playing her flute from the other side, and his house is a half a mile away."

Masen furrows his brow. "Other side of what?"

"Follow me, and I'll show you." Dad makes his way around the ledge to an aluminum ladder. We climb down into a pit that shows markings on the rock as if it has been chipped away.

Quietly I ask, "Was this a quarry? What's this darker colored rock?"

Dad answers as he follows the ledge around the pit to the opposite side. "The Native Americans used it for making arrowheads to hunt birds and small game."

On the far side, there's the original older rope and branch ladder that Coda described to us. Dad starts up. "Go up one person at a time. It seems in excellent condition, but you never know."

The rope ladder ends at a little higher position than the elevation we crawled through when entering the cave. We weave our way between and around tumbled gypsum boulders.

Dad stops as we observe at least two directions we can take. He points to the notches above his head on one pathway. "Watch for this marking. It will lead you to the quarry." Then he continues as if we're in a hurry and none of us have any questions.

Well, I for one have lots of questions. So many, in fact, that I don't know what Dad just said. We travel about a half a mile, angling to the left, which would be north and toward Southard and the United States Gypsum Plant.

We come out from behind a boulder into a large quarried room. Masen and I stop and take in the sight. Dad and Jax walk to the middle of the room. They stop, and Dad holds the torch out, showing the expanse of the room. Large pillars of gypsum support the ceiling. The first miners dug into this layer of gypsum from where it was exposed to the outside. They left behind these pillars as natural braces to support the earth above our heads. The layer of rock for this room is at least fifteen feet above our heads and forty feet back into the hill where our hidden tunnel entered. The opposite end of the room reveals sunlight. It is an exterior opening covered with thickets from the outside and an iron gate that has a padlock.

Smiling, Dad sprays the hinges of the gate. Then he unlocks it with a key that is kept on a rock shelf above the gate. He douses the torch in a bucket of water.

"This is one of the first quarried layers of gypsum taken from this area. Most all of the other mines have been sealed shut by collapsing the entrances. This one was missed or saved; we're not sure which. It doesn't show up on any of the United States gypsum mining maps, so we believe it was dug by George Southard. He was the man who owned this land and began the mining of gypsum in this area. We're on the property of USG's plant, so be careful not to be seen. We need to meet your mom now. We're a little late. It took us longer than I expected to make it to this point."

Masen asks, "How long did it take us, Dad?"

He looks at his watch and replies, "It took us just under an hour to get to this cave. When you have the girls with you, it may take longer. I want you boys to practice exiting as fast as possible. I don't want you to be exposed to someone seeing you. Your odds are greater of not being caught if your time of being out in the open is less. So try to limit your exposure to no longer than an hour at a time when you're escaping."

Jax asks his first question. "Who might be after us, Dad?" He looks alarmed.

Dad looks at Jax, and we all feel the tension in the room. "The government, Jax, and they may have helicopters to spot you. That's why I want you hidden in under an hour. If they have heat-sensing radars, you need to be underground, so don't be near the openings."

Jax follows up by asking, "What about the police? We could call the police, couldn't we, or tell our neighbors?"

Dad is outside the opening of the quarry when he whispers, "No police or neighbors. Trust no one! We can only be sure of our immediate family and your cousins—Uncle Luke, Aunt Jennifer, Eli, Fuller, and Gus. You can trust Uncle Nic and Aunt Holly and your cousin Zayne. You may have to get Zayne depending on whether he is here or at his grandparents' house. Your cousins are practicing how they can get here in a hurry too. Hopefully, you'll be able to band together until help can arrive."

I ask, "Don't we have time to look around?" I turn to look back at the now dark quarried room.

Dad shakes his head. "We'll be back. I promise. We have to go now. I don't know how long Mom can pretend to have a photo shoot along the side of the road."

We walk about three-fourths of a mile through a thick brush pasture before coming to a dirt road. We find Mom taking pictures of the trees about a quarter of a mile from where we leave the pasture. We climb into the car and head home without seeing anyone.

CHAPTER 25

Colorado—Liam's Friends and Neighbors

He sniffs, snorts, and hikes his leg.

I discover that my home has dark golden-brown colored bricks. The double windows on all corners of the house let sunshine in again after my ruthless trimming of the trees and shrubs. The windows in the upstairs master bath are stained glass of gold, cream, and burnt orange. I have some light through the basement windows. They'd been completely covered with tangled overgrown weeds and grass. I use a weed eater to mow the first time since I'm not sure what might be under the thick grass.

I find a water hydrant and a fence between my neighbors and me that is in desperate need of repair now that the weeds and brush are no longer holding it up. Behind the property is a large concrete drainage ditch that has a chain-link fence on either side to keep anyone from wandering into it. It is one continuous fence, probably placed there by the city.

My neighbor to the north is an elderly lady who reminds me of Gram. My neighbor to the south is a short stocky man who never makes eye contact and wears gloves and a baseball cap pulled down across his forehead all the time. He comes home midmorning and leaves before dark each day. There're four houses on my side of the street on this block. The old woman is on the corner, then me and the old man, and on the southern corner is an older box style two-story. I've seen no one there, but someone mows and trims around things.

I carry my trash can to the curb because Crystal told me that tomorrow is trash day for our side of the street. My neighbor lady pulls her car into the drive and struggles with a large grocery sack. She's trying to manage the large sack as she struggles to see around it to walk to her door. I jog over to help her.

I call out, "Excuse me, ma'am. May I help you?" I'm smiling as I approach her.

She looks scared, not just startled but fearful.

She says, clearly frightened, "N-n-n-o, get away! I don't have anything!" She backs into the bushes next to her house. She holds the grocery sack out toward me and adds, "Here, take this. It's all I have. Take it and go, please! Leave me alone!"

I stop and hold out my hand to her. "I'm sorry for frightening you, ma'am. You remind me of my great-grandmother, and I just want to help you. My name is Liam, and my great-grandmother's sister owned this house next door." As I talk, it seems to reassure her that she's in no danger, so I continue as I take the sack from her weary, outstretched arms. "I'm your new neighbor. I moved here from Oklahoma. I'm going to the university this fall. Did you know my great-aunt?"

She untangles herself from the bushes, looks around to see if I have any friends, and then walks up to the front door. She swallows. "Thank you for carrying my groceries, and yes, I knew your aunt. She was a very sweet lady, and I miss her very much." Her voice is trembling.

I can see the kitchen from the open doorway and ask before entering, "Would you like me to set the sack on the counter or table for you?" I remain on the porch, giving her time to decide. Immediately, my entry is blocked by three of the biggest cats I've ever seen. They line up in front of me, sitting at attention and staring at me like I might do for supper. They just haven't decided yet.

She looks into my eyes this time and smiles before saying, "Please, place them on the table. You aren't like the other young people I've met since the first of the year, and apparently my bodyguards have no objection; they're still in the room." Fear begins to raise doubts in her again. She fidgets with the back of the chair and then drops her gaze.

I feel terrible that someone has spooked her. She trusts no one.

"I'm sorry you've been frightened, but I want you to know you can call me day or night. I'll leave you now to put your things away. I'm writing my cell phone number on your phone book. I mean it when I say I'll help you."

The cats weave in and out between my legs, almost toppling me to my knees.

She remains in the kitchen with the table between us as she says, "Thank you, Liam. My name is Lena."

I pause and flash my famous dimpled smile. "It is a pleasure to meet you. Before I go, would you like me to carry your trash to the curb?" The striped yellow kitty continues to caress me by leaning into my leg. Streak does this when he wants to be affectionate.

Smiling as if privy to a secret, she answers, "Yes, that would be nice. The wheels don't work so well. You'll find it at the corner of the house outside. Yeller seems to be taken by you, Liam."

"Would you like me to fix the wheels tomorrow if I can?" I'm uncomfortable with the cat's affection, and I can't wait to get out of the house, but before I can exit, Yeller hikes his leg and sprays my leg.

She warms up to my presence. "I'd like that. It's getting harder to find a handyman I can trust." She hasn't noticed her cat's indiscretion because her back is turned while she puts the milk away.

I excuse myself and close the door securely as I leave. I hear her shuffling quickly to the door, and I hear the tumblers lock, all three of them. I smile to myself, walk to the corner of the house, and pull her trash to the curb. She's right; the trash bin might as well not have any wheels at all. I walk back to my house, slowly looking at my street through her eyes. I see what the old lady is talking about.

There are five small houses across the street. They all appear to be rentals. I see groups of young people gathered on the small lawns and porches. They're watching me. I wave. Some wave back. Most of them watch, and I feel as though I'm being sized up and have been found lacking somehow. I reach my own porch, and Streak joins me. He instantly smells our neighbor cat's message. He sniffs, snorts, and hikes his leg. I jump out of the way and head straight for the shower. I throw my jeans into the washer and add everything in the cabinet to get rid of the odor.

I check my e-mail before bed and find nothing from Gus. I log onto Facebook and upload a picture of my house now that it is visible. Then Streak and I rack out on the couch and nap.

CHAPTER 26

COLORADO—LIAM AND STREAK MISS GRAM

I can't believe I've done this to my own flesh and blood.

I return home from applying for jobs, and the old man's house on the other side of my house is dark with the shades drawn, and his old car is pulled up close to the house. I wonder if he's been harassed too. I could ask him, but he's probably sleeping.

I look at my home. It has all of the curtains wide open, along with my front door. I must've left it open when I left this morning. Streak appears beside me, and I voice my concern to my roommate. "The person who lives here must be very trusting to leave his front door open. Gram's Buick fits right in. Don't you think?"

I glance down, and Streak has stopped and is looking at me as if he wants to ask me a question. I sit down on the stoop, and he climbs into my lap, rubbing each side of my face with his.

"Whoa! That's enough loving." I smile as I think of how I've seen him do this with Gram. Then it dawns on me. "Do you miss Gram?"

Streak stops, looks around, and runs to the door of the house, chortle-meowing insistently while twitching his tail in Morse code.

I open the screen door, and he runs through the house, searching. I follow, feeling sad for him. I know he thinks we'll find Gram. When we're coming downstairs, I swear I hear the screen door close. I look all through the main floor, but I don't see a thing out of place. I close the doors after letting Streak outside, and I make a mental note to try to repair the wheels on the trash can for Lena.

101

I pour a glass of water and head for the office area, a small room at the front of the house next to the living room. I decide to e-mail my family. When I enter the room, my computer is on, which is odd. I don't remember turning it on, but I guess I must've. I check Facebook and send a few messages and e-mails. Then I shut the computer down for the night.

I step out the back door, and Streak bails out of the tree beside the house. He likes to climb as high as he can and remain on lookout until I call him in for the night. I wonder what he thinks of our new home. We go inside, and I lock the doors as Streak watches and chortles his approval. I think he appreciates the security of this action. We make our way upstairs and settle in for the night.

The next morning, I flip on the television to my one free channel. It's a continuous news and weather station. I guess since it's free, I can't complain. I pour a glass of water and sit in my great-aunt's tiny recliner. It's just right for a petite woman. I'm grateful for the furniture, even if it's old, but when I make some money, the first thing I'm buying is a recliner that fits me. I saw one at the thrift store off campus at a reasonable price.

I bump the volume up to hear the news.

"News update from the One World Vision news stations around the globe: The states aligning themselves with the mandated regulations by the One World Government are holding their town hall meetings. Those attending must attend all three days. They will be held at each state's capitol. The first day is for questions; the second day, questions will be answered; and the third day, votes on the compromises will be announced, with everyone having the opportunity to sign their allegiance to the One World Government and its peace initiatives. The government has given a three-day weekend to all citizens so that they may get to their state capitols and register as patriotic citizens of the new nation under the rule of the One World Government.

"When you pledge your allegiance, you'll receive a small symbol on the back of your right hand or your forehead, along with an implant as small as the end of a tattoo needle. These will help speed the process along in many areas. It'll assist our militia in identifying who has pledged their allegiance to the cause and who might be a terrorist. They'll be able to identify people with a swipe of their reader wand. This will link to their phone and alert them to any dangerous persons. These same implants carry identification numbers that will be used as a method to pay for purchases and receive free medicine and medical services provided by the government. They'll track all information about your financial spending.

"We promise to become contributing members of the new One World Government. Citizens age twenty-one and older will sign at their state's capitol. In order to man the new militias, all youth ages eighteen to twenty-five will be registered with the government by their birth certificate or Social Security records. You'll be sent a notice in the mail to appear at the nearest high school. Militia recruitment officers will be there to explain the next step in your illustrious career with our military.

"The only exclusion to immediate service will be a deferment given to students. If you're pursuing a college degree, you'll be given a deferment until you've completed your course work. If for any reason you fail a semester, you'll report immediately to the militia service. These individuals will be your police, fire, sanitation, and emergency workers. They may also fill the national level military to support your nation in cases of natural disasters or random terrorist outbreaks.

"All remaining citizens will be expected to pledge their allegiance at the end of their Peace and harmony objective course. The government has added five courses to every vocational and university level curriculum. It will be fifteen hours credit for theology training with the One World Vision in mind. This is bringing about record enrollments in higher education. The One World Committee has appointed their brightest and most passionate followers to teach the new courses.

"The principles set forth in the One World's constitution are simple: Peace and harmony to all. Anyone not living by these principles will be arrested and then evaluated as to their threat level. If it's believed that the individual can be salvaged, he or she will be sent to the retraining centers. If not, he or she will be terminated. Indefinite incarceration will not be an option. If noncompliant citizens refuse the Peace and harmony training, we will categorize them as terrorists. Terrorists will be handed swift terminal justice, no matter their reason for contradictory views to the established government."

I pet my cat, who is sitting at my feet. "I need to go by the government's city office and sign my allegiance to the new government." Streak leaves the room. Sometimes that cat acts so strangely.

I check the address on my computer, and I see I have an e-mail from Gus. In fact, I have several e-mails.

I begin to open them.

Hey, did you hear the news? I can't believe things can fall apart so fast. Dad and Mom talk in hushed tones all the time now. I wish they'd talk to us. I think Eli and Fuller understand more of what is going on than I do. I wish you were here. You'd tell me the truth. You always told me when I was stupid or dressing like a brainless dork. I listened to you, and I knew you had my back. You just told me what I needed to hear. I know when you embarrassed me at school by giving me wedgies or making fun of me that you were toughening me up, and I want to thank you. Well, have a good day, bro.

I sit there staring at the screen and see myself years ago staring back at me. Here was my own little brother stating the very things that had gone through my mind at that age. I'd tried to explain why I put up with the bullying of Harrison by convincing myself it was for my own good. I can't believe I've done this to my own flesh and blood.

I write back.

Hey, little man. I heard the news. I know it sounds scary. Just keep your head down, and you'll be okay. I want to apologize for how mean I was to you these past few years. I'm sorry for what I've said and done to you. It wasn't right. You don't need anyone to toughen you up because you're already one of the toughest little dudes I know. You're smart and darn good-looking. You look just like me. LOL. Later, bud.

PS: Don't let anyone tell you you're stupid, including me. You're smart. Use those smarts to stay safe.

I can't deal with all the emotions this is bringing up, so I delete the rest of the e-mails without opening them. I shut down the computer and go in search of Streak. When I find him, we go for a hike on Flagstaff Road. It's my favorite hike. It's not too steep, and it's close to the house.

CHAPTER 27

OKLAHOMA—JATHYN'S QUICK THINKING

Over the next week we begin
burying plastic bins of supplies.

We practice our drills on packing, loading, and exiting the house quickly and quietly.

Dad praises us, "Good job, kids! I'm so proud of you. You've beaten your last time by nearly three minutes. Those three minutes may save you and your cousins one day." This last sentence weighs heavily on us. Dad goes on like it's an everyday phrase. "Okay, what are you to remember and state daily?"

All six of us chorus, "We can do all things through Christ who strengthens us. We are strong."

Dad was never in the military, but he sounds like he's instructing soldiers. "Jax, get your mud boots. We're going to the hills to feed cows. We'll be back later, and I want the provisions ready to drop off at the cave under the pretense of a picnic at the pond when we get back at noon."

The girls head to the kitchen to begin packing food for storage and making sandwiches to eat at the picnic. Masen and I head to the computer to finish a short course we've started in electrical engineering. We're doing experiments on the side as we learn more about the generation of electricity.

Jax grabs his boots and a book he's been reading off the back of the couch. He and Dad head to the pickup.

After about three hours of reading and note taking, Masen and I surface from the bedroom. We have an idea of how we could piggyback on the connections of a solar power panel to generate enough electricity to recharge cell phones or other USB port devices. We have to be able to regulate the electricity, and we think we've figured it out. Uncle Nic's love for electronics has ignited our interest in the subject for years now.

"What's for lunch?" I ask. "It smells delicious."

Mom pours the last of the homemade spaghetti sauce and meatballs over the pasta. She adds three different cheeses and carries it to the table. "Thank you for the compliment. The girls made the pasta and salads."

Lia chimes in, "Don't forget the Jell-O and fruit dessert I made."

Masen sits down at the table. "Girls, it looks delicious, smells delicious, and tastes delicious!" He stabs a meatball and pops the whole thing into his mouth. The girls erupt at the same time saying things like, "Mind your manners," "We haven't prayed yet," and my favorite, "No fair!"

Masen asks for blessings upon the food and gives thanks for our health. We're just about to dig in when Dad and Jax come through the door. They join us, and Jax is so excited. Dad can't shut him up, so he lets him tell his story. "We found it! We really found it!"

I bite. "What did you find?"

Jax beams as he takes his seat. "We found the cave the outlaws used as a hideout. It's down in Salt Creek Canyon. We've been looking every time we go to the hills to feed cows. I bet you didn't know." He is so proud of himself for keeping this secret, but Masen, always literal and serious, has to state the obvious.

"I wondered what you were feeding in the hills since this time of year the grass is up to the cows' bellies and they don't need a thing." Masen stabs another meatball.

Dad interjects, "Go ahead, Jax. It was quite a find."

Undeterred, Jax jabbers on, "I've been reading up on the histories of Blaine County and some of the other counties. I found that outlaws came through here in the late 1800s. They used several places to hide out. Sometimes it was an abandoned farm, one was a dugout on the South Canadian River, but the one we found is a cave in Salt Creek Canyon. The Black and Yeager gangs used this hideout on Salt Creek near Hitchcock. They would go in one way with a high vantage point because of the bluff, but the cave is open completely through the bluff. They watched for anyone who might be following them."

Jax is so theatrical that he leans forward as he tells his story and then slams back in his chair as he finishes. "If someone came, they'd run through the cave to the other side of the hill, where they had their horses waiting. They'd get on and ride away, escaping to rain terror down on the area for another day." He takes a breath and pops a meatball into his mouth.

Dad asks, "May I tell of the significance of this find?"

"Sure, Dad," Jax says with his mouth full. Then, after he swallows, he adds, "Girls, the spaghetti is delicious, and that dessert looks great!"

Dad lays his fork down. He has his elbows on the table and his fingers intertwined under his chin. "We have to be ready to leave things behind and live on the run. This cave gives us one more place to hide. If the government comes for the adults in your lives, you have to find safe places to hide out. You'll only be safe if no one knows about these places. Your cousins are receiving the same instructions, and we expect you kids to stay together *if* at all possible and not to tell a soul. Be smart! Be strong! Believe that our Lord and Savior *is* coming back. Don't ever be talked into getting any kind of mark for the government or any religion. Don't let anyone implant a chip under your skin, no matter how small it is. Jesus will win the final battle. Stand firm in your faith."

After lunch, we load up and head to the pond with fishing poles and picnic baskets. If anyone sees us, they'll not think a thing about what we're doing. Once at the pond, we fish for a little while, and then we unload the pickup. While the family fishes, Masen and I carry the supplies to the cave, and we store them in the pit.

Masen looks around at the roomy cave. "You know, there could be some people who know about this cave. I know we weren't to ever tell anyone, but that doesn't mean someone in the family didn't spill the beans."

I ask him, "Do you have someone in mind?" We both are probably thinking about the same person, but I want him to say something first.

We crawl back through the opening, and Masen replies with one word: "Liam." It's the same name on my mind.

I say without hesitation, "I think we've got to store supplies in more areas. That way if we can't get to the house to restock, we can get to the stash. Is that what you're thinking?"

Masen says, "Yep. We need to plan where we might hide and where a good, safe place would be to hide things."

"Preparation, that's the key," I declare as we walk back to the pond. "We need to start to work on the tunnel in the gyp hills because I think the cabin would be a good place. We'd have the creek to escape down and heavy cedar tree cover. We could even mine our own salt if need be from the salt vats on Salt Creek."

When we reach the top of the dam, we encounter company—the game warden! I notice that he has the new One World symbols on his uniform.

"Where've you boys been, or should I ask what have you boys been doing?"

Without hesitation I answer, "Looking for arrowheads."

Then I walk past the warden and check my fishing pole. I have my back to the warden, and I see the scared expression on Malorie's face. I wink at her, setting her at ease.

I ask, "Did you catch my fish? You said you'd watch my pole while I looked for more arrowheads."

She relaxes and smiles. "Of course." She holds up a stringer with two fish, one small and one large. "Mine's the big one; yours is the small one." Giggling, she plops them back into the water and then returns to watching her bobber.

The game warden asks Masen, "Did you find any arrowheads?"

Masen answers, "No." He meets the warden's glare and doesn't look away.

The warden walks over to me and asks, "How about you?"

I ask innocently, "How about me what?"

The warden gets mad and says snidely, "You get smart with me, boy, and I'll haul you in right now! Did you find any of these fictitious arrowheads?"

Mom is marching our way, so I answer, "Yes, I did. Would you like to see it?" Mom halts.

He answers, "Yes, I would." His voice is smug as if he's caught me in a lie.

I reach into my pocket and pull out a rock I picked up in the pit. I show him, and he takes it and looks at it for a long time. Then he asks, "You found this?"

"Yes, sir, I did," I say sincerely. "I'm sorry I popped off a while ago. I thought we were joking around. I come here as often as I can. I've got a collection of arrowheads at home."

My abrupt change of tone disarms him, and he hands the arrowhead back. "You need to always address authority with respect. Our new government demands respect to be shown to all of us who are in authority." He walks off without a good-bye or a look back.

Masen comes up to me. "Where did you get the arrowhead?"

"The pit. Something told me to pick it up." I watch the warden disappear over the rise. "We've got to make more preparations and fast."

"Right," Masen says as we look around at the family we love.

Over the next week, we begin burying plastic bins of supplies. We bury some bins in the thick trees of the pasture, while we bury others near the cave and down in the hills near where the homestead rock cabin stands. One more site is near the outlaw cave Jax found.

It's late when we return to the house, and the landline phone is ringing.

Mom picks it up. "Hello?"

Jordyn says, "Mom?"

Mom says to us, "It's Jordyn!" Then to Jordyn, she says, "I'm putting you on speakerphone. We happen to all be here this evening."

Jordyn talks in hushed tones. "Ken has been contacted by the New World Militia. They would like him to use the remainder of his time in the military to work stateside and help with the patriot's pledge campaign. I'm so worried that he may have to accept their offer to keep us safe."

Dad responds first. "Is there any way he can leave the military early?"

Mom asks on the heels of Dad's question, "Are *you* all right?"

Jordyn answers, "Yes, I'm fine. I just never thought marriage would be this hard. You guys make it look so easy. You work together. Dad decides what should be done for the family, and you back him up to help his decision be something positive. If you argued at every turn and went against Dad's decisions, it would sabotage the success of what he'd planned. Mom, I don't remember you ever asserting yourself *over* Dad's wishes. You've been supportive in that you let Dad lead. You taught us at home, teaching us God's truths from his Word. Ken has never been as strong spiritually as I am. Ken isn't going to be allowed an early release because he's a pilot. I want to be a supportive wife, but I'm afraid of what I might be supporting in Ken."

Mom and Dad exchange glances. "Jordyn keep us informed, but you and Ken are the ones who need to talk to one another right now. These are big decisions that affect your lives. Your dad and I discussed these things. We did them in private, and you children were not privy to all the details before we arrived at our decisions. You've only been married for a few months. You both need to pray about this together."

Jordyn agrees. "You're right. I've not given this enough time to work itself out. I'm sorry I bothered you."

Mom states, "It's never a bother to hear from you. Call me when you can. I know God will tell you what you need to do."

Jordyn says, "You're right. I forgot to go to God first. The air force just asked Ken yesterday, and we really haven't had any time to discuss it. I'm just used to running all my decisions by you or Dad. I guess I'm going to have to make a few on my own."

Dad adds, "Not on your own, sweetheart. Don't forget the Lord. Keep him front and center in your life, and you'll be fine. We love you, and call anytime."

They hang up the phone. Mom and Dad exchange another look that means Mom wants to talk in private.

CHAPTER 28

RAMSTEIN, GERMANY—JORDYN'S DILEMMA

His kiss told me everything would be all right,
but his exit leaves me doubting.

"What do you mean you're afraid of what you might be supporting in me?" Ken asks from the bedroom door.

I jump at the sound of his voice. I thought he was outside cleaning out the car. I turn to see anger or painful disappointment on his face.

I take a deep breath, and I say, "Ken, we need to talk." I get up and walk over to the door facing him. "Let's go into the living room." The bedroom is a place I want to keep free from all tension. I want to always think of this room as our "escape from reality" room.

"Okay." He walks through the door and down the hall.

He purposefully chooses a chair positioned alone in front of the window. I'm forced to take a seat across the room from him.

His impatience is evident by his immediate demand. "Jordyn, explain what you meant! You act like you don't know me. What's wrong with you?"

I'm caught off guard by his attacking tone, and I stutter, "I… I'm sorry. I didn't mean it that way."

His temper is visible by his white knuckles as they grip the wooden arms of the chair. I begin again. "I mean we haven't had the time to discuss whether you'll take the job with the One World Government. I was worried that in your attempt to protect us that you might compromise your belief in God."

112

He looks at me as if he doesn't know me. I now know how he must feel. Then he barks, "Take the job! Believe in God! First, it's not just a job. I pledged the next four years of my life to the United States government as a pilot. The fact that the United States chose to merge with another entity for protection from total collapse and government failure is a part of that so-called job. It's my duty to uphold my nation's decision as a way of protecting its citizens.

"I am the first line of defense, and in order to do that, I have to trust that the country I serve has men and women in charge who are studying the situations, and I'm to act upon their orders. They have all the information, and they felt it necessary to make this move into the One World Government. I don't have choices of, *Okay, I'll do this part of my contract but not that!* I'll do it all! I'll do it with honor and to the best of my ability. Second, I believe in God. There's only one true and living God. The One World Government's chosen religion is to embrace all who claim alliance with that same one God. How's that compromising anything?"

I feel awful about viewing what he does so cavalierly. I start to go to him, but he stops me with an upturned hand. "Stop, we're talking now. Stay where you are. We're going to get to the bottom of this."

I return to my seat. "I'm so sorry, Ken. I never meant to belittle what you do. You offer your life for others on a daily basis, and I know how seriously you take that vow. I was questioning the intentions of the One World Government. I was afraid they might use those character traits of honor and service to tear us away from our belief system in God. I thought at the very least that they might succeed in diluting our faith. I know they claim to believe in one God, but the big difference is that they don't recognize Jesus as his Son."

He glares at me. "That doesn't explain what it is about me you might be fearful of supporting. If you believe what you just said, *you know me!* You know who I am and where I stand on things. Who were you talking to anyway?"

I answer, feeling foolish that I even called them now, "My parents. I called my parents." I know as soon as I've said it that I shouldn't have called. I need to work things out with Ken. I need to trust for the Lord to lead in our decisions.

His voice relaxes. "Your parents. You called to tell them what?"

I feel like a little girl getting disciplined. "I told them you'd been asked to work stateside with the militia. I told them I was worried you'd take it, and I alluded to the possibility that you might abandon your faith to save us."

Ken walks over to me and puts his hands upon my shoulders. I want to stand and go into his arms. I want to feel his warmth and know everything in the world will be set right side up again. When I try to stand, he applies just enough pressure to stop me. I relax, sit, and look up.

He asks, "You talked to them before your own husband? Do you trust me?"

In that moment in time I wanted to scream, *Yes, definitely yes!* But all I squeak out is, "Yes." My voice is full of emotion, and I love him so much I just want this confrontation to be over and for things to go back to normal.

He smiles, kisses me, and releases my shoulders. "I have to get back to the base. I'll be late tonight, so don't wait up."

Before I can find my feet or my voice, he's out the door. I watch from the window as he speeds away, spraying gravel across the lawn.

His kiss told me everything would be all right, but his exit leaves me doubting.

CHAPTER 29

COLORADO—LIAM'S VISITING AND VISITORS

*Hitler raised an entire generation to believe
as he did by governing the classes taught.*

Streak discovers a female cat in the neighborhood, which leads to many sleepless nights. He wants to go outside at least a dozen times each night. I hope this isn't going to be a problem. Lena's cats are all males, but they've been neutered. Hopefully, we won't have a marking of territories war between Streak and the neighbors.

My social life consists of visiting with Crystal whenever I catch her car at the store and watching for a freckle-faced girl on campus who keeps my mind preoccupied. I haven't talked to her yet because she is very illusive. I see her reddish-brown ponytail bouncing one minute, and it's gone the next. Sometimes all I notice is her perfume; it's very distinct. It seems to follow me some days. It's like she is always close but never quite within reach.

I stop by the store on my way home. Crystal is filling the cooler with beverages.

"Do you need some help?"

Her smile lights up her face, and she says emphatically, "I'd love to have some help. We're shorthanded, and these crates are heavy."

I immediately begin helping. We talk as we work.

"I got a job with the government's Servants' Center today."

She stocks a shelf. "Which building is the Servants' Center?"

I clear the empty box and rip open another. "It's a closed elementary school east of the university campus on Aurora Avenue. It has a big gymnasium on the east side where the tables are set up for meals. Those coming for meals can come through the front doors on the south side and make their way straight north to the cafeteria. Then they go to the right and eat. The classrooms have been converted to hold cots, and the gymnasium's locker rooms are open to the public for showers from eight to noon."

She gives me a teasing nudge with her elbow. "That's great. Hope that doesn't mean I'll be seeing less of you." She flashes one of her drop-dead gorgeous smiles in my direction, and I'm sure I blush.

I set the crate down before I drop it. "I doubt it, but I'll be busier once school starts. The Center is flexible and will let me work weekends and mornings. I'll prepare breakfasts most days. Two nights a week I serve the evening meal. When school starts I'll have class, and any of my hours between classes I'm to fill in at the Registrar's Office."

Crystal restocks the deli items. "I think the Servants' Center is a very worthwhile job. There are so many kids who are hungry. The sheer number of them blows my mind. Sometimes they come in here, and I know they're starving. All I can offer them is directions to the Dumpster out back. I have started wrapping the out-of-date food I throw away so the scraps are cleaner when they find them."

I agree, "That's a great idea, wrapping the food before throwing it out. Working in a service capacity to help others makes me feel good. Today I served food in the soup line and handed out coats. They were definitely needed! Some of these kids have migrated here with shorts and sweatshirts only. I think originally they were on their way to California, but after the restrictions to be enrolled went into effect, they needed to stop."

I finish carrying the last meat items from the walk-in cooler. "The news center is predicting a cold front to move through during the night. There are many young people living wherever they can in this city. I see more homeless all the time. Why do *you* think they're coming here?"

Crystal finishes stocking her last items and sits down for a moment before taking her shift at the register. She takes off the gloves she used while handling the deli foods. I notice the tattoo on her right hand, and the thought that I need to go get mine crosses my mind. She tosses the gloves into the trash.

"Rumor has it that the Rockies have the largest training centers for the Peace and harmony objectives. One school of thought is that they've flooded to Boulder because of the university, I guess. I understand the One

World Government reissued the use of the large educational buildings for youth training centers. The young people whose parents have refused to conform are sent here to help teach them how to be good patriots. They're taught the Peace and harmony objectives along with reading, writing, and arithmetic."

I'm surprised this is the first time I've heard of such a thing, except of course in history books. Hitler raised an entire generation to believe as he did by governing the classes that were taught.

I ask, "What age of children are you talking about?"

She answers with a shrug. "Oh, middle-school- through high-school-age kids are brought out here mainly. The elementary-or preschool-age kids are staying in their homes with foster parents assigned by the government. The displaced foster parents get a home out of the deal, and the kids get someone to feed and take care of them."

I try not to act shocked. "What's happened to their parents?"

Crystal stops and stares at me before saying, "Where have you been, boy, under a rock? The parents who refuse to submit to the new One World Government, religion, and objectives are arrested. If they resist, they probably don't exist anymore. If they appear willing to learn, they are sent to training facilities where they'll receive the same Peace and harmony courses you and I are enrolled in this semester."

Crystal's boss tells her he's leaving and that she needs to man the registers. I walk over and pick out a sandwich for supper, thinking about our conversation. I check out.

"Good-bye. Have a good evening."

Crystal is already checking out the next customer and calls out, "Bye now. Thanks for coming in today and pitching in to help me."

I look at Crystal, and I see her differently. I'm not nearly as attracted to her as I once was.

CHAPTER 30

Colorado—Liam Chooses a New Friend

I notice that, unlike Crystal's hand, Emily's has no tattoo.

I'm dazed by what I heard at the convenience store. Gus's cryptic message—*Dad wants us to go into hiding. Someone is here. Gotta go*—takes on a whole new meaning. I've got to read his message again. I need to try to retrieve my deleted messages from Gus that I didn't even bother to read. I'm probably becoming alarmed over nothing.

There's a pamphlets stand at the front door, displaying the Peace and harmony classes available at the university. I take a flier home with me to read tonight. This new government sounds like it'll be great if we all give it a chance. I like the idea of everyone pledging to not force their way of thinking down the throats of the rest of us. On the heels of that thought are my parents. They're so single-minded in their views of religion. Maybe I can get them to lighten up a little for the good of the family. It sounds like Dad has gone around the bend if he wants the kids to go into hiding. I think I'll call them tonight. If they don't conform, they could be some of the ones to be arrested. They have such strict black-and-white views of religion. It's either heaven or hell with them. There's no in-between.

I head to campus to pick up a few things at the bookstore before heading home.

On my way, I see a freckle-faced kid who has been staring at me from the television screen every time I turn it on. He's listed as a runaway, and his parents are asking anyone who sees him to please call the police.

I call out to him, "Hey, can I talk to you?"

He turns and looks around as if he's looking for the militia. "Sure. You're that guy who serves us food."

I grin, thinking about the way he categorized me in his life. "Yes. I think I saw your face on television last night. I think your folks are looking for you. Do you need a phone to call home?" And I hold mine out to him.

He looks panicked. "I ran because I don't want to trade one set of rules for another. You know, to be indoctrinated into the philosophies of the new government would be just like living at home, only someone I don't know is calling the shots. I'd rather leave home and have a choice rather than be told to conform. My folks are sold on the One World Vision and insist I go down to the polling center to register early. I'll be eighteen next month, and I want to make my own decision. My youth minister back home says this decision will affect the rest of my life. Don't you think I owe it to myself to read about that decision, think it over, and pray about it before deciding?"

I can relate. "I agree that we should be informed and not do something because everyone else is doing it. I've done that too many times in my life because someone made me, and even more because everyone else was doing it. I believed things and did things because someone told me it was the thing to do. You're secret is safe with me. I never liked the rules at my home either, but now I at least see why they made them. It wasn't to aggravate me. It was to keep me safe." I see another opportunity to help. "Are you safe? Where are you staying?"

He responds, "I hooked up with some kids who came from my state. We've lots of things in common. We've got each other's back. We have the Bible to lead us. I'm safe at their house. Thanks for asking. I gotta go. See ya at mealtime." He grins and jogs toward downtown.

As I watch him leave, a voice from behind me says, "Most of us don't have anyone looking for us. We're living on the streets, out of the reach of our parents, and they don't even care."

I turn to find *the* girl with the lingering perfume, the girl with the bouncy ponytail. I thought of her as Waldo. I feel like I scan the landscape to see where the mystery girl is hiding each day, just like the *Where's Waldo* books. "Hi, Waldo."

She smiles, and laugh lines appear next to her big brown eyes. "Who's Waldo?"

I'm so embarrassed. "It was a joke. Let me start again. My name is Liam. What's yours?"

She takes my outstretched hand and shakes it. "I'm Emily, but my friends call me Em."

I nod to the bookstore. "I'm going to the bookstore. Which way are you headed?"

She cocks her head and levels a look at me that tells me she is someone who's used to being in charge. "I'm headed that way too." She locks her arm through mine at the elbow, and we head for the bookstore.

I feel as though she is taking over, but I don't mind. I like her by my side. She is the same height as me, and stride for stride we walk together as if we were made for each other.

I ask, "I came here from Kansas. Where're you from?"

She says with a drawl, "Texas."

I feel pressed to keep the conversation going. "I'm shooting for a major in government and a minor in linguistics. Where do your interests lie?"

She snuggles closer, making me feel uncomfortable somehow. "My interests lie with you at the moment, but if you're talking about classes, I attend them all."

We step through the doorway of the store as she makes her last statement. As I disentangle myself from her hold, I notice that, unlike Crystal's hand, Emily's has no tattoo. I seem to be able to think more clearly when there's some distance between us. I realize I have ten minutes to find my text and get across campus to class.

"Oh, I've lost track of time. I've got to hustle. Excuse me." I head for the government section, grab my book, and head for the checkout counter. After paying, I glance around, but I don't see Emily, so I sprint out the door.

CHAPTER 31

COLORADO—LIAM'S NEIGHBOR
HAS A BREAK-IN

The officers are lined up on the couch
like good little guests at her tea party.

I discover that my neighbor works at the Servants' Center too. He's in charge of providing a safe place to spend the night for the overabundance of teens and young adults. There isn't enough housing to accommodate the surplus of hopeful students. The new government reissued the use of large gymnasiums to be used as Servants' Centers. The adjacent schools have been converted as hostels for one-night stays. Apparently there's a need for displaced young people.

Youth have descended upon college towns in record numbers. No linens or towels are provided, so the kids need to have their own. I'd rather serve the food. There's no conversation, and there is none of those "do you want to be my best friend" games. Some of these kids don't seem old enough to be teenagers. There's a short redheaded girl who comes through and asks me every day, "Do you know Jesus?"

There's no way I'm getting involved with some underage girl and losing my chance at advancement in the new government. Christianity is listed in the brochure as being one of the extremist religions and may be classified as a terrorist cell at a later date. The government has them on a watch list.

I glance around. "Please keep moving."

If Christians are willing to pledge their allegiance to the new government and receive their mark of loyalty, they'll be removed from the list. My mind revisits my earlier conversation with Crystal about the arrests of Christians. I've got to remember to call Mom tonight.

I pull into my driveway and notice my front door is ajar. I'm going to have to be more careful about making sure it's locked. I've never been the one responsible for locking things before. Even Gram took care of that in Kansas. Miss Lena's light is on, and I wonder how she likes the new wheels on her Dumpster. I move my Dumpster to the curb before entering the house. Streak jumps from the top of the china cabinet with a growl.

I yell, "Streak, sometimes I swear you must think you're a dog! What's wrong with you? Were you bored today?"

Streak immediately begins the meow-talking he does when he's excited. He rubs my leg and then heads to the library room next to the living room. I follow him and notice nothing out of the ordinary except that my computer is on again. I must've saved *never sleep* instead of *sleep after ten minutes.*

I check it, and it says it will go to sleep in ten minutes. Well, this is twice it's been on and hasn't put itself to sleep. I guess I'll have to remember to shut it down, or I'll burn out the monitor. I open my e-mail to retrieve Gus's messages, and my phone rings. It's Lena.

She asks, "Can you come over and help me for a minute?"

I hesitate a moment, and she adds, "It's important."

I answer, "Sure. I'm on my way."

As I approach the house, I notice one of the long door-length windows next to the front door is broken. I peek through the other window before knocking. I see Lena in the kitchen. She comes to the door.

"I'm so glad you could come. I came home this afternoon to find my window broken. All I can tell that is missing is some food. Can you help me put a board over this window?" Her hands are trembling as she motions toward the door.

I take her hands and hold them. "Of course I'll board this up. Are you all right?" I hardly get my question out and she is in my arms sobbing, scared to death. Hugging old ladies isn't something I'm comfortable with, so I awkwardly pat her with one hand.

She answers after a moment, "I'm not hurt physically, if that's what you mean. I'm scared. I don't feel safe any longer. I keep thinking about a stranger being in my home, walking through my rooms."

I ask, "Have you called the police?"

"No." She drops her head like a disciplined little girl.

I don't have the time or energy for this, but I think of Gram. "Let's call them now."

She nods. I dial, and we sit in the living room. The posse, Lena's cats, surrounds us on the couch. One strides back and forth on the back of the couch. Another sits in her lap, and one holds me down by sitting in mine. I think she keeps them around to anchor guests so she can have a captive audience.

"I don't have any family to speak of, and your aunt and I were very independent back in the day. We could hold our own, but now she's dead and gone, and I'm approaching ninety-five. I don't know what I'm to do."

I sure don't know how to help her figure out her dilemma. I silently sit stroking the tabby kitty perched upon my lap. Thank goodness the police arrive and take over. I slip out and come back with a board for the window. They finish checking the house for anyone who might be hiding. I hadn't even thought of that.

I finish my project and call through the open doorway, "I'm going home now. I'll call you in the morning before class."

I can't help but chuckle under my breath at the welcome the three policemen have received. Lena has fixed them tea and serves it in tiny fragile china teacups with matching saucers. The officers are lined up on the couch like good little guests at her tea party. Each of the officers has a saucer in one hand and cup in the other, but what sets the scene is the cat in each of their laps. One kitty is lying in his gentleman's lap, the next is trying to coax the officer to pet him, and Yeller is striding back and forth across the last officer's lap, rubbing on his chest, tickling the man's face with his erect tail.

I call to the officer with Yeller, "I hope you don't own a male cat." Then I turn to leave.

That officer disentangles himself from the cat and follows me out the door. "What is your name?" He notices he still has his cup and saucer in his hand. He quickly sets it down inside the doorway on an end table. He pulls his notepad and pen from his pocket and joins me on the front lawn.

"Liam White. I live next door. I just moved here this summer." I try to walk slowly toward my house.

The officer stops me. "Why were you over at your neighbor's house tonight?"

My smile leaves my face. "Lena called me as soon as I pulled into my driveway. She was scared. Can you drive by a little more often or something?" He may want to be accusatory to me, but I live on this street, and I've never seen anyone patrolling.

The officer takes notes. "Our protection forces aren't up to full capacity yet, but as soon as the first semester is over we'll be able to tell which students are here for the education and which ones are the dodgers. When we pick up the dodgers for the militia training, we should have things under control by the second semester. Right now, there're no curfews in the cities across the nation. It's one of the first freedom acts put into place by the new government."

I respond, "I think some of these kids are using the confused state of the union to disappear from their homes for whatever reason. These kids seem to be hidden by their sheer numbers. I've seen some of their faces on the television. The parents of those televised are looking for them, and they are labeled as runaways. I saw one of the boys from last night's news feed."

He asks, "What did you do? Did you call the police?"

I don't appreciate his tone. "I talked to the boy. You never know why they ran. I had a friend once who was beaten every night. I'd invite him to my house and give him a safe place to stay. My parents never knew." I begin to walk around the end of the fence to enter my yard.

Following me, the officer asks, "What did the kid you saw the other day say?"

I pause at the bottom stair of my front porch. "He wasn't chatty. He disappeared into the crowd." I turn and face the officer one more time.

The officer looks long and hard at me. "Next time call us."

I return his stare. "I will, Officer. Can I go inside my home now?"

He examines my home, scanning it and looking over to Lena's house. "Sure." He seems to have something on his mind but leaves it unspoken.

I climb the stairs, cross my porch, and lock my front door behind me. I'm exhausted, and I don't even make it upstairs. I collapse on the couch just a few feet away. Before sleep envelops me I think, *I haven't checked my e-mail.* Then as sleep draws closer, I think, *I'll do it tomorrow.*

CHAPTER 32

COLORADO—LIAM'S CHANCE MEETING

I think I've found a friend I can trust.

The next day I call Lena. "I'm leaving for class. Thought I'd check in with you."

She says, "Thank you, Liam, for fixing the window. You were right. I should've called the police first. I'll do that next time. Have a good day."

"Thanks. You too." I think about checking my e-mail, but I'm running late, so I sprint out the door, promising myself to check on the family tonight.

I'm walking from my last class when I see Emily sitting in the student union. I think, *I've got to talk to her again.*

I walk up, and I can't think of a thing to say, so I just stare.

She looks up, and her dimples deepen as a grin appears. "Have you been here long?"

I regain my composure and turn on the charm. "I've been here all summer." I laugh and continue, "I'd like to buy you lunch, but I don't know your schedule. When are you out of class?"

She says, "Now."

I ask, "Well, Emily, can I buy you lunch, or would it be supper? It's nearly four thirty. We could go somewhere and get something to eat or drink."

She hesitates only a second. "Sure, why not. And please call me Em."

We exit the student union and head directly to my car. She jumps into the passenger side of the Buick.

I ask through the open driver's side window, "How did you know this was my car?"

She avoids eye contact and states, "I didn't. Just a lucky guess."

I think, *That's odd,* but when I slide into the car next to her, I don't give it another thought.

We stop at a little deli that has outdoor tables and order a large nacho and drinks.

I pull out her chair.

"I think I saw you in one of my classes the first week of school. Did you change your mind and decide to take a different course?"

The waitress sets down a huge platter of nachos and two large drinks in to-go cups.

Em pauses this time, looking at me as if she is trying to decide whether she can trust me or not. I guess that would be a question a stalker might ask. She watches the waitress walk away, and then she decides to take the chance. "No. I'd like to, but I don't have any money. I sit in on classes I'm interested in and learn the subjects. I don't have to worry about taking the tests because I always offer to turn in someone's homework as I exit. The instructors see me hand in something and believe I'm legitimately enrolled." Then she digs into the nachos.

I'm impressed about her desire to learn. "Are there more kids like you who attend but don't spend?"

She smiles at the rhyme. "Yes, quite a few, really."

We eat and drink companionably, as I can see she is quite hungry. I don't bother her with more questions until our eating and drinking slows down. "If you don't have the money to go to school, where do you stay? Are you safe?"

She places her napkin down. "I live on the street. Where each night depends on the militia; they have us move from public areas, which are the safest, so the pickings are getting pretty slim. That other boy told you he had a group of kids just like him that had each other's back. Well, that's the way it is all over this city. There are lots of groups. Their reasons for grouping together are as varied as there are numbers of groups." She looks at the streets, which are beginning to fill with people. I follow her gaze and see them in their fragmented groups for the first time. They resemble ripened wheat blowing in the wind in Kansas. There's a section leaning one way while another leans the other.

I turn back to her. "I see what you're talking about, about the groups, I mean."

She is standing with her backpack over her shoulder and is soon walking away. "I need to get going. Thanks for the snack and drink. I'll be seeing you around." She jogs into the stream of people and swims effortlessly out of sight.

More confused than ever about this mystery girl who keeps appearing in my day, I smile. I think I've found a friend I can trust.

I head for home, my mind filled with possibilities.

CHAPTER 33

COLORADO—LIAM PHONES HOME

We're all looking for that peace that brings us understanding as to why we're here on this Earth.

I used to think living out of reach of my parents would be the ideal, but now I know my family protected me without me knowing it. I find my cell phone and call home.

"Hello, Mom. It's me, Liam."

She asks, "Why haven't you called? We were worried. Are you keeping up with the news?"

"I've been busy. I got a job near the campus, work during the day at the administration building, and started classes. I haven't been ignoring you, just busy." I stand at the top of the administration building steps.

Mom says, "Gus keeps us informed. He says he gets an e-mail from you almost daily. Would you like to talk to him?"

That's odd that Gus says I e-mail him daily. It couldn't be more than five e-mails. I see I'm going to be late to work. I lower my voice and keep an eye on my surroundings. "No, I don't need to talk to anyone else. I wanted to say be careful about telling everyone you're a Christian. This new government doesn't trust them. I wanted to say thanks for always having *my* back." I begin to choke.

Mom interjects, "Liam, we'll never bow to any religion that doesn't recognize Christ as God's Son. We want you to be careful. You know what you should and shouldn't do. Be safe. Gram said the last time we saw her that she thought you were very close to a decision of confession. I know

128

you've changed. I want you to know your dad and I love you dearly, and we believe in you."

The lump in my throat just got bigger. "I've got to go now. Love you too. Tell everyone hi. Bye, Mom."

I hate it when I'm weak like this. I glance around and make sure no one saw that weak moment. But no one noticed because they're all milling back and forth, eyes to the ground or focused straight ahead. Their thoughts seem focused on a definite spot somewhere out in the distance that they're walking toward. We're all looking for that peace that brings us understanding as to why we're here on this Earth. We search for something beyond this time and place, each in our own way.

CHAPTER 34

COLORADO—LIAM AND LEONNE

There are so many young people to save and so little time.

My shift ends, and as I walk to my car, I see my neighbor working on his car. I stroll over. "Hi. I think we're neighbors. Can I help?" I lean over and look under the hood too.

He looks up, smiles that guarded smile, and says, "I think it's this old belt. It's too loose to keep her running. I'll have to walk downtown and get a new one."

I offer, "Let me drive you. I know your feet have to ache as much as mine. You're always here before me and usually the last one to leave."

He suspiciously looks around. "Okay. Thanks."

I hold out my hand. "Hi. My name is Liam White." A peace I haven't felt since I lived with Gram moves up my arm as we shake hands.

"I'm Leonne. Nice to meet you, Liam."

I notice that as he shakes my hand he rolls it just enough to see if I have a tattoo. I can't tell if he has a mark proving his allegiance to the new government. He wears his work gloves all the time, and I've never seen him without his cap pulled down over his forehead. Maybe he's scarred or has some other deformity.

We pull into the auto parts parking lot, and we both enter the store. He makes his purchase and is out the door before I have time to decide what fragrance of air freshener to choose. I leave, deciding to come back when I've got more time.

"That didn't take you long."

"Nope. I need to get home. I'm very tired," he states without making eye contact.

We pull into the parking lot of the Servants' Center, and the young people are strolling in clusters like ripened wheat. They sway back and forth and from side to side. Sometimes the movement mixes for a moment, and then the rhythm begins, breaks, and is out of time again. As I'm admiring this epiphany, I realize Leonne has exited the car and is working on his car. He sure is a strange old man.

I'm not really around Leonne at work. He works with the clothing and young children. I serve food any time of the day depending on my schedule. We hardly finish with breakfast and it's time to prepare lunch, and the same for supper. That meal is the easiest. It's a sack lunch. The people are to take their meals and leave so we can leave early. The cleanup of the mess hall is the biggest job. You'd think if someone is feeding you, the least you could do is pick up after yourself or not make the mess in the first place. Sometimes it's awful. The gym floor has tables across the court, turning it into the mess hall. In the morning, the sun streams in the row of windows along the roof above the bleachers, waking all of us up.

I think repurposing the buildings is how we're able to get the new government up and running so quickly. They take the structures that are already in place and use them for different purposes. Between breakfast and lunch is the only time the showers are available for use by the public. I'm so glad I don't have to clean that area. By the time these thoughts travel through my brain and I stroll across to Leonne, he's finished and is closing the hood of his car.

I follow him to the driver's side as he tells me, "Thank you very much. I appreciated the lift."

He slides in behind the steering wheel. I'm standing there wondering why I followed him to his door. It seems I just didn't want this peaceful feeling to end. I reach out my hand one more time. "Sure, anytime. We should get together and have a cup of coffee some evening on the porch. I wondered if you knew my great-aunt. The house was hers."

He hesitates but shakes it. As soon as we touch, I feel that wave of peace, and Gram is so near for a moment that a lump forms in my throat.

Leonne withdraws his gloved hand. "Maybe sometime, but I'm usually exhausted when I leave here. There're so many young people to save and so little time. Please don't take it personally if I take a rain check tonight."

"Oh, I understand. I usually like to put my feet up and rest awhile too. There's something about you that seems familiar. You remind me of my family. I can't explain it. I'm sorry I'm keeping you. Good-bye."

Obviously he's ready to go home. Like a minirecorder, I play back what he said: *there are so many young people to save and so little time.* I think to myself what an odd way of looking at providing the services he does. I guess he is right though. Winter will be in full swing soon, and if these kids aren't inside and protected, they could lose their lives.

CHAPTER 35

COLORADO—LIAM RUNS INTO EM

A dark cloud blackens the horizon and moves silently across the edge of the town.

I make the highest grades of anyone on my midterm tests.

The arrival of cooler weather sends more kids indoors. Police arrest many as they try to find refuge in malls and grocery and department stores.

My hours at the Servants' Center change, and I'm even more ignorant about the news. It depresses me, and if I don't think about it, I can believe nothing is changing in my world. When I think about my day, my head spins. I go to work at four in the morning. I prepare breakfast and wake those sleeping by five. They're to be out or in line for breakfast by six. Breakfast is served from six to nine. The next shift of workers comes in, and I leave. Classes start at ten and run until four thirty. I work some afternoons from five until closing at eight o'clock.

There're four of us on the Work for the New World Program. We're paid an extra dollar an hour, and the government chooses the courses we take. They pay for the tuition, and all we have to pay for is books and housing. I'm selected to get a master's degree as a linguist and minor in government. The Work for the New World Program director thinks that with my current grades and aptitude I should reverse my major and minor.

I love my courses. These professors think the same way I do: that we're here on this planet not by divine intervention but that our destiny is in our own hands. There's a higher power, but it resides in us. We'll live in goodness and peace and plenty when we emulate those virtues. We don't have to worry about a thing; the government will help us sort out our thoughts and confusion about our futures. They assist us with programs of health, education, and welfare. We're to pay the same kindnesses forward.

I finish my last class before going home, and someone taps me on my shoulder as I exit the room.

"Hey, stranger. What classes are you taking next semester? I might want to drop by." Emily throws her head back and cackles.

I'm bewildered by her appearance and behavior. "Introduction to Humanities and the required hours of Peace and harmony classes. I'm limited by my days that are free to take a class." I observe Emily's eyes darting all over the place as I tell her this. Her face is flushed, and her pupils are dilated. I really hate to see her like this. I don't want anything to do with someone who dabbles in drugs. My plate is full enough.

She staggers a little closer. "I don't think I feel very well." Then she promptly vomits on my shoes.

I help her to the ladies room and go inside the men's myself. I wash off my shoes and return to the hall. She's sitting on a bench with her head in her hands. I walk over, squishing with each step. I place my hand on her shoulder. She jumps and stands up swinging.

"Whoa, girl. Take it down a notch. I'm not going to hurt you." I hold her arms and escort her outside. I don't want the campus police to haul her off to jail if I can help it.

She looks up. "Thank goodness it's you! I was trying to find you." She looks around and seems confused. Then she adds, "Where am I? My head is hurting. Did I fall or something? I can't think."

I'm more than a little confused myself. "You don't know where we are? You're on campus, and you came up to me. You got sick, and I took you to the bathroom."

Emily definitely isn't herself, but what would I know about how she normally acts? I've only spent one afternoon with her.

She listens, and then she says with tears in her eyes, "The last thing I remember is the militia dropping off a case of Starbuck's coffees at our encampment. They wanted to bury the feud caused by moving us all the time. They said they wouldn't bother us through the winter but that we'd have to find somewhere by next spring. Most of us grabbed a coffee. It was rich and smooth and warm. We *all* needed warm. Then we began to feel ill. The militia was still there, and they helped us to their cars and buses. I heard one of the officers say they were going to dispose of us so they didn't have to expend any more resources on constantly moving us. I jumped out of the car and ran. I think the car was moving. That would explain the huge knot on my head and my headache. They kept going. I looked for the greatest number of people and melted into their numbers. I've learned that's a great way to disappear."

I am not sure about what she is saying, but for some reason I believe her. "Can you show me where you were staying?"

She says, "I think so."

I suggest we go there. Emily seems confused and foggy. She seems to be retracing her last several moves as she tries to remember where she slept last night. I begin to wonder if the vomiting was caused by the drugs or a concussion. Within twenty minutes, we're on the outskirts of the city and at an old abandoned park. It gives me the creeps. I'd be scared to close my eyes in this place. It's remote and unkempt and looks like a battle zone. Boxes are thrown everywhere and belongings strung all over the ground.

I hear a quiet whimper of a cry, and I remember my rider. "Is this the place?"

She sniffles. "Yes, this is the right place. Why couldn't they just leave us alone? We weren't hurting anyone! No one obviously even wants this place." She begins to pick through a few things and finds a small jewelry box and clutches it to her chest. She continues to pick up a picture, a letter, and a few other things. She goes to a thicket and pulls out her backpack.

I stand dazed. "What will you do now?"

She throws her chin out. "I'll survive. I'll be stronger and smarter. I'll adapt." The old Emily I first met is resurfacing.

I believe her story, and I also believe she didn't take the drugs willingly, but I have to ask, "Emily, do you do drugs?"

"Are you crazy? If a person loses his or her ability to think clearly, he or she doesn't have a chance in this world. No, I don't do drugs. I didn't know that the coffee was tainted until it was *too late*." She stuffs the loose items in her backpack. "I immediately tried to make myself throw up before getting into the police car, but I couldn't."

The sun is setting behind the mountain, causing the temperatures to drop.

"Would you like to come home with me? You'll be safe, and you can get your legs under you. It's *too late* to get a cot at the Servants' Center. Since the temperatures dropped, the line to get a cot forms shortly after lunch. You can figure out your next move and find a new place to live. Maybe even find some of your friends."

I'm doubtful about ever seeing her friends again. If what she heard was true, then something has happened to those kids. They've been transferred, arrested, or worse.

She hesitates. "I'd like that very much, if you're sure I won't be any trouble."

A dark cloud blackens the horizon and moves silently across the edge of the town.

"It would be no trouble; it'll be nice to have someone in the house to talk to besides Streak."

"Who's Streak?" She hugs her backpack.

I pull away from the park. "He's my cat, I think. I may be his person."

Emily stares out the window as we wind our way back into the heart of the town. "I wish I knew where they've taken everyone. I'm worried about them. No one knows to ask about them because we live off the grid. If what I heard is a threat, the militia may want to harm them. I haven't told you this before, but I came here with my cousin. He and I were never very close, but out of necessity we found each other this last year."

I state my gang's self-first attitude: "It's over, and you need to look out for Em and no one else. You need to stay away from the militia. They know you can blow the whistle on them. You may need to stay with me for a couple of weeks until they stop looking for you."

She's livid. "I could blow a whistle all I want, but no one will listen to what I have to say."

I want to protect her and keep her safe, but I can't protect her from herself.

She calms down a notch. "This homeless group of people took us in and protected my cousin and me when we got here last May. They knew how to get the things we needed. They're like family now. I got to try to do something."

I have to state the obvious: "Where do you want to go?"

She thinks and then asks, "Do you know anyplace that's remote? They'd have to dispose of the bodies or make it look like an accident."

I answer, "I don't know anywhere around here. You're probably more familiar than I am. I work, go to class, and go home."

She leans over in the seat to look at the dials. "Do you have enough gas to take a drive?"

"Yes, I've got almost a full tank. Where are we going?" I ask.

CHAPTER 36

COLORADO—LIAM HAS A HOUSEGUEST

Then a thought crosses my mind. For all I know
she could be a serial killer.

She states quickly, "Down Flagstaff Road, but we better hurry. That fog is moving in fast tonight."

We wind back and forth on the switchbacks. We're out of time as the length of the trees' shadows becomes longer and the evening dissolves away. The fog is dark and foreboding. I turn onto the scenic drive at the edge of town that winds its way past steep rocky canyons.

"What are we looking for?"

She shifts forward in her seat and peers through the windshield and the passenger side windows. "Look for where they might've left the road in their cars."

It isn't long before we can't see the sides of the road well enough to tell if there are tracks.

"Where to now?"

She mumbles to herself something like, "He's got to be all right." Then she says, "To your house, I guess." She's quiet the whole way.

I pull into the drive and park the car in the garage tonight. "Here we are. You can go in the back door. I'll unlock it for you."

Her mood is lighter, and she states, "Take your time. I'll use your open front door."

I advance to the front of the house instead of the back. "Is my front door open?" Sure enough, the door is ajar. "I can't believe it. I'm going to have to get a better lock."

When we reach the steps, Streak is sitting at attention on one of the front porch pillar bases. Emily charges up the steps, and Streak takes off for the backyard. The garage is in the backyard, and he always walks with me to the house, chortling about the day's events. Today Streak takes off like a bullet when Emily surprises him.

She sees the bronze blur and asks, "What is that? Is it a wild cat?" She giggles like she is privy to a joke that's on me and then rushes into the house. "Hello, honey. I'm home."

I'm a little disturbed at her familiarity in entering *my* home. I state flatly, "I'll introduce you later." I'm beginning to regret my offer for the night. "You should've let me enter first. What if a stranger would've been hiding in the house?"

She laughs heartily, heads for the kitchen, and makes herself at home. She gets herself a glass and fills it with water. "I'm sorry. I should've let you come in first. I guess I'm still a little loopy from my spiked coffee."

I follow her into the kitchen, looking to see if anything is out of place, but who could tell? I leave a mess most days. I see a movement at the fence and realize it's Streak. I head out the back door to call him inside.

Then I address Emily: "Make yourself at home, and if you're hungry, get something to eat." Which I obviously didn't need to say because when she turns, she has two slices of bread and a knife in her hand. I continue anyway. "The washer and dryer are behind that closet door."

Emily stops what she's doing and asks, "Oh, do you live with someone?"

"No, I inherited this house from my great-grandmother," I answer.

Emily questions, "I thought you said aunt?"

She is quick at picking up the discrepancies for someone who is still loopy.

I begin to put things away. "Yes, I did. My great-aunt was my great-grandmother's only sibling. My aunt had no family, so she left her things to Gram, who left it to me."

Emily seems satisfied with that answer, so she proceeds to the laundry area. I assume she is fearless because she lives on the street. I put myself in her shoes; a stranger brings me home and then begins telling me stories that don't match up with each other. For all she knows, I could be a serial killer. Then a thought crosses my mind. For all *I* know, *she* could be a serial killer.

Emily's behavior puts me ill at ease. My exhausted mind has gone wild. I call Streak, and he comes in strutting like he owns the place. I've never seen him do that before. I half expect him to start marking his territory. He looks at Emily, and they both move away from each other as he heads toward the upstairs. I follow him into the living room. He goes upstairs, and I go into the library/office. I grab a blanket and pillow from the closet. My computer is on and opened to my e-mails. I pause to see that I've gotten a note from Gus titled *Help*. I quickly open the message and find that the contents have been erased, or they never made the trip through cyberspace. I'm too tired to think. I fire off a note: *Message didn't come through. Resend. Liam.*

I turn off the computer tonight and lay the bedding on the couch.

I call to Emily, who's rattling around in the kitchen. "Em, turn out the lights when you go to bed. I've laid out a blanket. Good night."

I hear a mumble like she has her mouth full as I head upstairs. I don't know what I've gotten myself into, but I'll figure it out tomorrow. I'm beat and in desperate need of sleep. I hear Emily flip on the television as I head upstairs. I fall asleep listening to the muffled news feed.

"News update from the One World Vision news stations around the globe: Your government is pleased with the overwhelming acceptance of its new policies. The retraining of individuals at the One Religion rallies has begun. No expense will be spared in making sure that all citizens make an informed decision to follow their new government in its views on peace, harmony, and religion. Space in the existing facilities was once an issue of concern. Now we know that there are plenty of areas to do this coursework by including the abandoned private prison systems. They're numerous and perfect for the structured teaching needed around the country. Those incarcerated without a high probability of reform were terminated to make room for individuals who can be saved.

"Foster homes have been set up to care for children until parents can complete their pledges and return to their homes. This is another example of success. We have pictures showing how happy and healthy the children are in the care of these excellent foster parents.

"The preschool through third-grade students are learning the principles upon which this new world will be founded. They're learning through rhythms and songs. They practice showing the correct respect to the world's symbols of government, religion, military, and money.

"The children in grades four through eight are receiving more formal instruction with an emphasis on reading, languages, mathematics, and science. The governmental core curriculum begun in primary school is continued through hands-on activities designed to illustrate services to others.

"In high school, all students will receive an expanded principles training of the core values of peace and harmony. Higher education will be offered free of charge to students who show the greatest aptitudes in the areas the government deems lacking. Students with drive and patriotism will be placed immediately upon graduation from high school in the areas of service. The first principle learned is one for all and all for one.

"We hope you've enjoyed the constant news and weather given to you free by this public station. You'll be enjoying more of these kinds of services when all aspects of the One World Government's visions are realized. We must speak the truth and lead people with the evidence given to us by the One World Media. You can trust us to provide you with the truth about your government.

"The donations of firearms and other weapons are breaking all records. In the areas they have been removed, there has been a drastic drop in crime. Remember, it's the responsibility of each citizen to relinquish his or her firearms voluntarily. If firearms are found in your possession, it will be considered an act of terrorism. Terrorists are dealt with swiftly and lethally.

"The new monies of One World currency are rolling off the presses as we speak. The emblem of the euro has been placed upon the existing new bills before circulation in nations that still had their own currencies. Existing currency without this combined symbol will be taken out of circulation and replaced with a new bill with common features of existing currency and the euro.

"Colleges and universities are bursting at the seams with young people eager to pass their harmony objectives. Upon passing those tests, students will take their pledges, proudly display their tattoos, and prepare for a life of service to the new government. It has been decided that all students in these institutions will become a part of the government's workers immediately upon graduation. They'll man the service areas such as sanitation, police, fire and rescue, transportation, communication, health, science and math, and of course, government. We're proud that so many of this country's brightest young people have enrolled.

"Those entering training facilities may also prove themselves worthy by exemplary grades and performance in the areas of recruitment of missing citizens. Students attending any institution will have the opportunity to tell us where we may find missing youth. They'll be earning merits toward higher-ranking government positions or college credits. Anyone helping to bring to our attention someone not bearing the mark of allegiance will earn merits as well. We must all be invested in this world to make it safer, happier, and more peaceful. So get off those chairs, get out there, and help us in finding the missing."

CHAPTER 37

OKLAHOMA—JATHYN'S FINAL PREPARATIONS

We'll worship God, protect our lives,
and provide food for our family.

Dad and Mom are headed for the state capitol. He says, "I want you to get your chores finished and no games on the television this weekend. Keep the television tuned to the news. I want one of you boys watching the news feed of how the rally is going at all times." Dad pauses, and I swear he chokes. "Boys, you know what I expect you to do." He stops and looks at each of us, gives us fist bumps, and is out the door.

Mom smiles, but it seems forced. "Girls, be good and mind your brothers. They're in charge. We'll be home, hopefully, tomorrow night. If not, we'll for sure be here by Sunday afternoon." She pauses and hugs each of us long and firm. "Why such sad faces? We're going to make our voices heard at the capitol. We'll be successful, and Christians will once again be allowed to worship together. I think of all the times when you were small and it was such a chore to get you ready for church." She stops and touches the family photo hanging by the front door. "I pray that you will one day be able to take your little ones. We love you, and we'll be home soon."

She steps out the door, and we all follow, standing on the front deck. We're still there as Dad pulls away.

We each silently step back inside the house. Malorie heads for the back door, grabbing a basket. "I'm going to gather the eggs early." Ever since she turned fourteen last spring, she's grown up. The folks don't have to fight with her to get her chores finished. She seems older as she exits the house.

Jaylie is behind her, pulling her jacket on to keep off the fall's crisp chill. "I'm going out too. I'll feed the goats." Jaylie isn't usually this responsible, but I figure at twelve, she can feel Dad and Mom's need for us to each do our parts without being reminded.

Little Lia dresses in rubber boots and a rain slicker. "I'm headed out to water the animals."

Lia looks for the opportunity to make a mess. It's no surprise we didn't have to tell her to do her chores. She can't wait for chores. She gets so distracted though. She'll get her chores finished, but she will end up taking an hour or two longer than anyone else. She sees something that makes her think of doing that and then hears something that causes her to investigate. I wonder if I was ever so susceptible to a wandering mind when I was ten.

Jax picks up his book about the history of Blaine County and begins reading. Since he found the outlaw's cave in Salt Creek Canyon, he's reading history books all the time. At eight, I hope he isn't feeling the impending danger the rest of us feel. I hope he can get lost in his reading and escape for a while. I know I wish I could.

I watch Masen clean his rifle and pack it in a heavy round plastic tube. I thought back to yesterday's conversation with Dad. He stated, "We'll never give up our right to bear arms."

I walk over to Masen. "But the new government said we had to turn them in or they insinuated they'd kill us. What are you doing?"

He continued preparing his rifle. "If someone comes to my home and threatens us, we're going to be able to protect ourselves. Dad said we're going to be able to provide meat for our family. What if a civil war breaks out because of the imposed authority of the new leaders? We have to be able to protect ourselves. There are still going to be people who want to take what they see because they feel entitled. There are others who want to cause harm for no reason, and we have the girls to protect."

I hand him the parts. "But the government says we aren't governed by our laws but theirs. We don't have the right to bear arms we once had as the United States."

Masen pauses and then sounds just like Dad when he says, "We'll worship God, we'll protect our lives, and we'll provide food for our family. End of discussion. We'll do as we're told."

I head to the gun cabinet and get my rifle. I start to clean it and put it in the tube too. Masen and I work on the guns in the living room while we watch the news. We have three rifles that are used for deer and small game. We provide practically all of our own food for our family. I gather all the bullets I can find to add to another tube. The government hasn't said anything about our compound bows and arrows, but I lay them out. "Do you think we ought to gather our bows and arrows for quick removal?" I figure Masen will make fun of me.

Masen's eyebrows drop a little as he thinks about what I just asked. "Definitely. That's good thinking, Jathyn. I need you to always be thinking ahead like that to help me."

I don't like the responsibility of thinking ahead, mainly because when I think ahead I see Dad and Mom arrested for firearm possession. And we're on the move. I mean, why in the world would the government want every citizen dependent upon it? Why would they want to take away a family's ability to provide food and protection for themselves? I shake my head and make my exit to start gathering the cases for the bows and arrows.

Malorie comes back inside from gathering eggs. She washes them and puts them away.

I ask her, "Where do you think would be a good place to hide the bows and arrows around the house until we can move them?"

She cocks her head. "The tree house Dad made us. The upstairs opening is too small for an adult to squeeze through. We could put them up there and cover them with something."

My little sister amazes me sometimes with how smart she is. "Amazing. That would be perfect. You're so smart. Here is a bow. Help me carry them out to the tree house." A smile beams from Malorie.

After storing away all of the bows and arrows in the upstairs portion of the tree house, we hide them behind some boards made to look like a bench. I come into the house.

"Bows and arrows hidden. What's next?"

He caps the end of the tube and hands it to me. "You should take Jax and go to the hills. Find a good place to store these weapons and the bullets."

I call down the hall. "Jax, come on. It's time to feed the cows."

"Okay, coming," is the response from my little brother.

I step down the hall to the bedroom and poke my head in the doorway. "Hey, do you have any books that have a list of hunting tools of the Native Americans? If so, bring them. I have an idea."

Jax finishes putting on his boots and walks over to the bookcase. He chooses two books and follows me out the bedroom door.

CHAPTER 38

OKLAHOMA—JATHYN FEELS THE WEIGHT OF PROTECTING HIS FAMILY

*My heart leaps to my throat when I realize
how easily she can be swayed.*

Jax bursts through the door first. "All taken care of, and we figured out several ways to catch game legally."

I come in behind Jax.

Masen is already standing. "Could you watch the news? I need a break for a little while."

Not waiting for an answer, he steps outside on the front porch. He has always liked to think things through all by himself before sharing any of his thoughts. I can never guess exactly what he might be thinking.

I take a seat and begin to pay close attention to what the news announcer is telling me.

"Our new government has established the ultimate One World Religion. It embraces all religions believing in one God, using the very best of each. It emphasizes the spiritual unity of all people. Humanity is evolving, as demonstrated by the need for all nations to join together to battle the cyberterrorism. Our need at the present time is for the establishment of peace and harmony. The voices of all people have cried out for justice and unity on a global scale. The government will provide this answer on the backbone of the new world religion."

There's a commercial, and I get a glass of water.

Lia states innocently, "That sounds like a nice religion."

I almost choke on the water in my mouth. I take a breath and will myself to be calm. "It does sound good, doesn't it? But there's one essential thing that's wrong with believing in an all-inclusive religion. Each time you make a compromise to give up one of your beliefs, God's Word—the Bible—is no longer pointing to the direct path to salvation and Jesus. It's like when you're on your air mattress on the lake. If you float without paying attention to where you're floating, you can drift from the shore. In this case, such a religion says that Jesus was only a man. Some say a prophet, some say a messenger, but none state the truth that Jesus is God's Son. Before you realize it, you've drifted away from the truths. Remember that, Lia. It's very important. If someone tries to tell you anything else, they're lying to you. Don't believe them, no matter what they say. Promise me?"

Lia listens carefully, and she states firmly, "I promise, Jathyn. I'll remember. Do you want strawberries for lunch?"

My heart leaps to my throat when I realize how easily she can be swayed. "Sure, that's fine, Lia." I pray we can keep our younger sisters and brother out of the training center. Their very souls could be stolen before they are even aware of it.

I return to the television, and they're showing the rally at the capitol. There's a huge turnout of Christians. They have one opportunity to voice their concerns and be cleared of being labeled terrorists. There was a grassroots attempt to approach our leaders before we merged with the rest of the world. At that time, it was the extremist Christian faction. The mainstream Christian believers didn't show up and didn't get their voices heard.

We want to keep our faith. Christians have this one last chance to make our collective voice heard. I know that's why Dad and Mom both went to the rally. Numbers of solidarity are very important in voicing this request to be taken off the terrorist watch list. Otherwise, one of them would've stayed with us, even though the government mandated that they both appear.

Masen silently comes in the back door, sits next to me, and says in a low voice, "I wonder if our cousins are watching the news, waiting, and wondering. Uncle Luke and Aunt Jennifer are there, along with Uncle Nic and Aunt Holly."

I glance over my shoulder and see the girls preparing lunch, deep in discussion of whether to have strawberries or brownies. "Do you think Jordyn will be able to voice her opinion now that she is twenty-one? Will she be able to do anything like a rally on a military base? Do you trust Ken to keep her safe?"

Masen leans against the couch. "I don't know. I hope our new brother-in-law takes good care of her. I miss her. I didn't realize how much she did around here."

It frightens me to think that Jordyn, my sister, is so far away and possibly needing us. We sit side by side watching the rally and listening to the announcer giving a huge sales pitch for the new government. He has a panel of experts singing the praises of how ideal our world will be when all of us live in harmony.

Masen states flatly, "It's so scary to think about how many people will be fooled if they don't know what the Bible says, warning us about things just like this."

I shift my legs. "What things are you talking about?"

Masen whispers as he leans toward me, "Doesn't it sound like an ideal place to live? A world that believes in one God, all humanity acting as one big, happy family, men and women equal, prejudices are bad, science and religion are harmonious, economic and family problems are results of not seeing things the new religion's way, and we all need world peace. Now to achieve this we need a One World currency, One World Religion, One World Government, and a One World leader who will appeal to all of the people?"

I turn to look him in the face. "My head says that sounds good, and my heart knows something is wrong with what you're saying. I think the Holy Spirit is heading me off from disaster, just like Dad said it would. I believe in one God, but the deceit is in the fact that they don't recognize Jesus Christ as God's only Son. Am I getting close?"

Masen smiles. "Yes. Go on."

I continue tentatively. "One big, happy family would be ideal, but they're God's children and Satan's children and the undecided children. They can't live together as one happy family because they don't recognize Jesus for who he is. Prejudice *is* bad, but *to see* the good in Satan is *not* possible. There's evil and good, right or wrong. Science living harmoniously with religion may be possible, but we live by faith, not because we have to be able to explain it according to man's calculations. We do need peace, but as long as Satan has reign over the Earth, the Bible says that's impossible."

Masen smiles. "What about our economic and family problems being a result of not acknowledging their religion?"

I answer, more sure of myself this time, "Satan controls the chaos of the world, not their religion."

Masen nods. "You're right, little brother. It's up to us to keep our sisters and Jax safe from the government. We can't let them fall into their hands and the brainwashing that is going on around the world."

We look over our shoulders at the girls and Jax. Malorie is stirring the macaroni, Jaylie is spooning the brownie batter into a pan, and Jax and Lia just ran off giggling with the beater blades to lick the chocolate. Jaylie has her pouty face on and is hot on their heels.

Something stirs inside me, telling me I need to have my entire family close. I need to call my cousin, Zayne. He and Jax were born a week apart eight years ago. When Jax returns to the kitchen with clean beater blades, I call to him, "Jax, come here."

He comes over. "What's up? Do you need me to take a turn watching the news?"

Smiling at the brownie batter on his cheeks where the beater bumped them, I say, "I need you to call Zayne. I need you to invite him over for the weekend. I'm sure someone is babysitting him, but he might like to be with us."

Jax immediately starts dialing, and within a few minutes he hangs up. "Zayne is with his grandmother. Her mom fell, and she needs to take her to the hospital. She says it's a great idea for Zayne to spend the weekend, since she may have to stay with her mom. We can pick him up at Weatherford's Hospital."

Masen sighs, stands, and says, "I'll have to go. I'm the only one with a license. You have yours but barely. Mom and Dad would agree that I should go. I'll be back in a couple of hours."

The news is back on: "News update from the One World Vision news stations around the globe: The preliminary reports are that all is going well at the individual state rallies. There have been no outbursts by extremists. Day one heard all of the citizens' concerns of how their individual religions will be included."

CHAPTER 39

RAMSTEIN, GERMANY—JORDYN'S LONELY, WORRIED, AND SCARED

I rise to protest, but the man steps between me and my disappearing electronics.

I hope Mom responds this time. I've sent her dozens of e-mails and texts in the last twenty-four hours. I get nothing back from her. I don't know what's going on, and I promised Ken I wouldn't call home. I'll have to ask him again to see if I can't at least make one call this week. I send one more text.

Ken works longer and longer hours. He is flying officials of the One World Government all over the world for their meetings. We have so little time to talk or discuss anything of substance. Our conversations have been reduced to "What would you like to eat tonight?" and "Do I have a clean shirt?"

Mom, I know you say we should work through this ourselves, but I'm in over my head. I don't know how to be the good wife Ken needs when I'm the only one talking. Love, Jordyn.

I walk through the living room, glancing out the window as militia approaches my door. Panic grips my heart that something has happened to Ken. I stand stock still, rooted in place as my doorbell rings. They begin to pound on the door, and one man looks in the window at me. When our eyes lock, I know I must move. I stroll over to the door and open it. "Can I help you?"

The man who addresses me has mesmerizingly blue eyes. They're a deep-midnight blue, almost as dark as the pupil, with cornflower-blue flecks.

"Are you refusing to answer?" he shouts at me.

I stammer, "I'm sorry. Could you repeat the question?" I can't believe I was so immediately hypnotized.

He asks, "Where is your husband? We demand to speak to Herr Hartman."

I collect myself and answer with confidence this time. "He's not at home. He's away this week."

The officer nods, and two men head to the back of the house. "We will come in now and check."

He pushes me aside and struts into the room. His presence fills the room. He nods again, and three more men spread out, searching the house.

I'm relieved that their visit wasn't to tell me about a plane crash, but I'm more than a little upset at their intrusion. "What do you think you're doing, bursting into my home?"

He levels those once-warm blue eyes at me, and they seem dark-gunmetal gray now. "My duty!"

I realize I'm not in Oklahoma anymore, and I keep my mouth shut and sit in a chair as far away as I can get from him. The men return with my computer and cell phone, and they march outside with them.

I rise to protest, but the man steps between me and my disappearing electronics. "If there are no transmissions of questionable loyalty on these devices, they shall be returned to you. But if we find that you and Herr Hartman are traitors of the new government, then other actions will need to be taken." He smiles, cocks his head to one side, and gives me a nod before adding, "Good day, Frau Hartman." He leaves as abruptly as he arrived.

I pull the curtains in the house. I go to the bathroom and run water and begin to cry. I feel weak, and I immediately know that I'm not alone. I know God is with me. I begin to pray silently. I hear someone at the door. I turn off the water and listen at the closed bathroom door. I turn the tumbler to lock it. I look for anything that can be used as a weapon. I wish

I was home in Oklahoma. I'd have a gun to protect myself. We couldn't bring any kind of personal weapons on base. Guns are frowned upon by the new government. I hear footsteps coming across the living room. They walk up the hall and pause outside the door. I don't hear anything as I press my ear to the door. The knob begins to turn. The tumbler lock holds and prevents entry. I step back one step at a time to the opposite wall, which isn't five feet away.

"Jordyn! Are you in there?" Ken calls out.

I dive across the room in one step, fling open the door, and leap into Ken's arms, sobbing. He holds me close, and all my fears and doubts melt away. I can feel his warm breath in my hair and hear his quickened heart beat as I lay my head on his chest.

He holds me and asks quietly, "What's happened? Is something wrong back home? Is someone hurt?"

I shake my head *no* on the last question, and I look into those eyes that will forever hold my heart. I have to tell him how I've endangered both of us by not listening to him. He specifically told me to refrain from talking to my folks about the government. I breathlessly say, "Hold me a little longer please!"

He gathers me into his arms protectively and ushers me into the bedroom across the hall. We sit on the bed and lean against the headboard. He wraps us up in a cocoon with the comforter in the chilled room. The events of the day distracted me, and I never turned the thermostat up. My body trembles from the chill, nerves, and fear.

"Are you warm enough? Why is the house so cold?" he asks.

I mutter, "I forgot to turn the heat on this morning."

He leaves my side and adjusts the thermostat. The heater fires up, and the fans kick in by the time he returns to my side. I know I must tell Ken everything and quick before I lose the nerve.

I begin, "I had visitors today." My voice is small and weak. I don't even recognize it.

Ken's alarm is shown on his face, but he remains calm and asks, "Who was it, and what did they want?"

I drop my gaze from his eyes, and I focus on a small flower on the comforter as I tell him about the militia.

Ken responds, "Why would they want our computer and your phone?"

I take a deep breath, look him in the eyes, and confess, "I don't know, but it has my e-mails and texts to my folks and family. I'd just sent Mom a message this morning about helping me to be a wife who knew what to do and when to do it for her husband. I complained about your working with the government and how it is robbing us of our time together. I'm sorry…"

Before I can complete my sentence, Ken pulls me close and kisses me long and gently. We slide deeper into the comforter, and he pulls it over our heads as if closing out the world. I smile. There is enough light showing through the fabric of the comforter that I can see that he isn't smiling back. Mine fades. His stare is foreboding. Slowly his arm reaches around my back. He pulls me to him gripping my arm opposite his body just below the elbow. I begin to panic because my arms are pinned down. I can't move anything but my legs.

As if he reads my mind, he throws his leg over mine, and now he takes his free hand and clamps it across my mouth. Tears come to my eyes, causing my nose to run and making it difficult to breathe. I try to scream, but he has his mouth at my ear, hoarsely hissing instructions.

"Don't fight! I'm not going to hurt you. I'm sure the house is bugged. We *are* in danger. We mustn't say anything more about today. We'll take a walk and try to find a safe place to discuss how much damage you've done. Nod if you understand."

I nod, and his grip loosens. I gasp for air.

CHAPTER 40

Colorado—Liam's Tattoo of Allegiance or the Mark of the Beast

I look down and see my tattoo on my right hand.

Em tugs on my arm as we weave our way into the high school cafeteria. We've been inseparable these past two weeks. At first, it was convenient to do some things together. Then I found that I was extremely lonely without her. She made sure she was by my side every minute of every day. Most nights we fell asleep on the couch, reading. When we did go to bed in our own bedrooms, Em made sure I knew having separate beds was my idea and not hers.

I couldn't go against Gram's wishes in her will. I respected Gram even if I didn't respect myself. I would lose much more than my home if I gave in before marriage. The terms of the will were specific, but more important was the reflection of me that I saw through Gram's eyes. She always looked at me as if she was sure I had *already* made the correct choice. Her pride in me is all I have that is good in my life. I can't lose that memory. It's the best part of me.

Em is so excited to make her pledge. "This is so surreal to be a part of the new world order. You've no idea how pumped I am to be valued as a woman and have the power of a man. When I get my tattoo, I'll look at it every day as a reminder of how men and women are going to be treated as equals and the financial security *that* will bring to my life. I'm going to learn all I can about how to promote and protect our new government. I'm going to be the best patriot they've ever seen. I'll do whatever they require or request. I'll sell my soul if that's what they want." Her enthusiasm is infectious.

She drags me forward. I apologize for stepping on the foot of a man trying to leave. "Slow down. The government officials aren't going anywhere," I tell her.

Em stops tugging. "You're right. I'll slow down, but it seems like I've been taking a lifetime to come to this decision. I know it's going to be the most important decision I'll ever make in my entire life. I want to thank you for letting me stay at your house. It afforded me the opportunity to watch the video feeds of the One World Religion and allowed me the time to investigate religions without any preconceived ideas."

Her comment about the most important decision of her life sounds familiar, but I can't place where I've heard it before. I find a place for us to sit after we're given a number. We sit next to the flat screen television that is tuned to the news. I listen to the news as we wait for our number to be called. Em snuggles close, and I like the contact of another human being. When she's this close, I can't seem to think about anything but her. I hadn't realized how withdrawn I'd become in the last year.

They call our number, and we go forward to take the Patriot's Pledge of Allegiance. To take the pledge today is Em's idea. I've been so busy taking on extra shifts to pay for the extra mouth to feed that I haven't had time to really think. She seems to eat enough for two people. She was hungry for so long that now she can't eat enough. I haven't finished looking over what the new government stands for or against. I've headed down here a dozen times before I met Em, but something always seemed to stop me. Em has one arm around my waist and my other arm over her shoulder, where her fingers are entwined with mine. We move as one. I feel exhilarated that there'll be no stopping me today. It'll be one less thing I have to read, research, and take care of in my busy life.

Then I say, "I'm glad you're staying with me until you get on your feet. You know how I feel about you, and I'd do just about anything for you and with you."

Em smiles and gives me a kiss. "I feel the same way."

The room is full of people milling around. I see the redheaded girl talking intensely with a group over by the trophy case. She has her Bible open, and they're very engaged in their conversation. A man tries to take her Bible from her, and she kicks him in the shin and runs out the door. The group discusses something and then slips out in three different directions.

I bet she's witnessing to them like Gram used to do with me. I'm glad they could make a choice they feel comfortable with and that will make them happy. That's the one part of the new religion I agree with completely. We each get to make our own decisions. I enjoy researching and deciding with Em what we should do about honoring the One World's Religion.

With a heart full of love, I watch Em as she reads her paperback. I agree with whatever she wants to do. I see another couple leave before their turn. One of them is consoling or comforting the other. It looks like one is ready for this decision and the other one isn't. I feel like I've been searching all my life for God and I've finally found him. The ideology of this religion's god is *I don't have to take responsibility for all my missteps in life.* Repentance is not required to go to heaven. This religion is living and breathing with the times. It changes to meet the needs of the people. I know God is out there; it's the confessing of my sins that I can't wrap my mind around.

Em interrupts my fanciful thoughts. "Come on!" She drags me across the room again.

We raise our right hands, pledge our allegiance to the One World Government, and line up to get our tattoos. A man grabs my right hand and begins the tattoo. I see a group of kids; it's the same ones who left after the redheaded girl ran out. They drift across the room and surround one girl in line for her tattoo. They whisper to her. She begins to softly sob, and they disappear together into the crowd. The group bands closely together as if protecting her as they exit the double doors. When I look back at our line, the girl is gone. They must've left with her.

I look around, and I see so many people. I feel helpless in stopping this crush forward. I don't think some of them are ready to make this decision. The momentum has started, and there's no stopping it now. I feel like Em when she said she feels like this will be the most important decision of her life. I watch the line march forward, and I think of how we're marching to the end of one age and looking to start a new one. A better time that is peaceful, with everyone living in harmony.

The tattoo artist tells me to move. He's finished with my tattoo. I look down and see the tattoo on my right hand. It is a world of green and blue with 666 stamped across the equator. The symbolism of the number from Revelation is not lost on me. Now I remember who first said I had a decision to make and that it would be the most important one of my life. It was Gram. After a moment of sheer dread, I look for Em.

She is twirling round and round, looking at her hand as if she's wearing a wedding ring. It's like a veil has been lifted from my eyes. I'm seeing everyone and everything for the first time. I can see them for who they really are and who it is that we serve.

We return home, and Em, *I mean Emily,* is psyched! She no longer seems like a close friend. She plops down on the couch and crosses her legs under her. I'm not the neatest person, but this furniture is going to have to last. If she treats everything so casually, it won't be long and it'll look dirty and tattered, matching my life. I'm angry with myself and the world. I know I've rushed to a decision that I'll regret, and I have no one to blame but myself. I find fault in everything about Emily now. I'd love to place all the blame at her feet, but I made my own decision, or did I?

Emily opens one of the Peace and harmony textbooks. "I want to pick a branch of the government where I can do the most advancement. Do you realize for the first time in our lives that women will truly be treated as equals? We'll not only be able to get the same jobs, but it says right here in the bylaws that the same wages and advancements will apply. I think I'd be best in the field of surveillance. I love watching people, which reminds me, I need to make a call." She jots down a phone number from the text and then looks up. "I want to watch for corruption and those who could threaten our peaceful world. When they found all of those homeless kids frozen to death in the canyons, you and I both know it wasn't an accident. If someone had been watching and reporting, it might not have happened." She leans toward me and gives me a big kiss and then bats her eyelashes. "I'm so glad I'm here with you. How about fixing me some supper? I'm starved."

I'm getting used to her overzealous displays of affection when she wants something. She hasn't fixed one meal since I brought her into my home and gave her free room and board. I seem to see everything for what it is. She is using me, but when she kisses me like that, I'll do anything for her.

"Which would you like, leftovers or a sandwich? I'm beat after pulling a double shift."

She says, "I want to celebrate. Fix me a steak, a baked potato, and salad. Doesn't that sound good?" She puts both arms around my waist and snuggles my neck while kissing it.

Before I realize it, I'm in the backyard, grilling steak. I stay outside, visiting with Streak. We haven't had much time since Emily moved in with us. I say to him, "I think I made a big mistake, buddy."

Streak chirps a sad meow tonight. I haven't heard that from him before. He sits close and watches me but doesn't jump into my lap like usual. I reach down with my right hand to pet him, and when I touch him, static flies from my fingers to his fur. He takes off like a scalded hound, yowling that same mournful yowl he made when we first came to Boulder and thought he'd been abandoned.

I keep one eye on the house for Emily to show up and one on the steak. I want to honor Gram's will and not have shenanigans going on in this house. I know I own it but only if I conduct myself with the propriety Gram expected. It was her family values. I'm a part of that family, and I know that now. Sometimes I wonder if it was a mistake asking someone to stay with me who wasn't a family member. The will inferred that the house is to be used like a huge dorm room for family only. Every time a doubt enters my mind, Emily does something like squeezing my thigh that makes me forget my resolve to remain separated from her at night.

Emily bounces out of the house. "What field of study did you say you were interested in when you moved here?"

I find my voice. "I've talked about it. Didn't you listen?" I know I shouldn't have snapped at her. As soon as it's out of my mouth, I rush on, "I'm working toward a field of service to others. I'll have a major in linguistics and a minor in government. Working at the Servants' Center will look good on my resume."

Emily crinkles her nose as if she smells something foul. "That's okay but a little unambitious, don't you think? I'm going for what I can get for me. I want things in this world, and now I'm on my way up. I'll do whatever it takes to get to where I'm going."

I defend myself out of old insecurities of being thought of as a weak guy. "No, I don't think it's unambitious. There are advancements in every field, including the ones in the service industries." I'm beginning to regret my offer of giving her a roof over her head more and more.

Streak follows us into the house as we carry the steaks inside. Emily goes to the table and waits for me to bring her supper. Streak walks by the table, sees Emily, and hisses his disdain. He gives her a low growl and runs upstairs. Streak doesn't just stay scarce when Emily is around; he has been giving me the cold shoulder as well. He definitely doesn't like her, but he'll have to learn that there'll be others in my life besides him.

She states with loathing, "I hate that cat! He'll soon learn who the boss is." Smiling, she resumes filling her plate.

I felt so close to her at the high school as we pledged our allegiance to *our* new government, but now I want to ask her to leave. I felt connected as a couple, but now I don't know. I see us as two strangers under the same roof with a strong physical attraction.

I say flatly, "Streak is my cat, and he stays. When you get your new government job, you can live in a cat-free environment." I leave the words *somewhere else* unsaid but implied. I decide I'm past tired and I need to not say another word tonight.

She smiles and plays the part of sweet, innocent homeless girl. I can almost see her morph into the girl I was so taken with on campus, and my heart softens. She feels the difference and this time kisses me for a very long time.

The next morning, I wake up and smile when I see Emily lying on her side next to me with her back to me. I reach over to squeeze her shoulder, and I see the 666 tattoo on the back of my hand. I stop before touching her. I get out of my bed, go to the bathroom, and vomit. I stare at the numbers, and I can't breathe. I look into the mirror and see Harrison's red eyes looking back at me. I'm lost, and I have no idea how I got here. I used to look at my reflection and imagine the man Gram had seen in me. I know now he's gone forever. My brain shuts down.

I go through the motions of getting dressed. I go to the kitchen to start some coffee, and Streak is there to greet me. But as soon as he sees me, he acts like I'm a stranger and hisses. He runs to the door but keeps one eye on me. I open the door, and he growls as I try to pet him on his way out. He runs away and disappears within seconds. Lena is in her backyard, raking some leaves.

I call over the fence, "Good morning."

She smiles and walks to the fence and says cheerfully, "Good morning. You've been awfully busy lately."

I rest my arms on the top of the fence. "Yes, too busy I think." I remorsefully think of yesterday and the pledge, tattoo, and now Emily. I find it hard to swallow. When I look up I see Lena staring at my tattoo. Instinctively, I pull my arm down from the fence. I search her face for the kind old woman I called friend, but she's gone. I think probably forever. Lena's face wears a mask of sadness and fear.

She steps back from the fence. "I have to get back to work. Have a good day."

She doesn't even wait for a response before returning to her raking. I stand there watching her as the old woman looks even more vulnerable and feeble. She stays next to the back door, raking the same place over and over again. She fugitively looks in my direction to see what I'm doing. I turn to go back inside, and I hear her door close and the locks click into place.

I'm observing the world around me this morning without my usual filter of preoccupation of what tomorrow may bring. I report to work early because there's no need to stay at the house until Emily wakes. She waits for me to fix her breakfast or to go buy it. As I think back, I realize she could've at least made breakfast. I pay for the food. She never picks up after herself and always leaves the bathroom in shambles. I'm not perfect, but I don't like to live in filth. All of the things I'm seeing now have flaws and faults. I'm discouraged at everything I see. I arrive at work just as the teens are leaving the showers area, carrying their small parcels of clothing. They head straight for the breakfast line. As I put on my apron, I contemplate how so many young people are destined to return tonight.

Leonne says, "Morning, Liam. You're here early this morning, aren't you?"

I jump at the sound of a friendly voice. All of the voices in my head aren't very friendly today. I finish tying my apron. "Morning to you. I thought I'd get a jump on the day." I pull the latex gloves on, and the numbers on the top of my hand ache. I see Leonne watching.

His demeanor and body language illustrates his sadness. "I better get back to serving the kids. There's surely a few I can still help before I go home this morning."

I feel like someone has kicked me in the stomach. I go through the motions of serving breakfast and then lunch without ever making eye contact with anyone.

"God loved you, you know?" Startled, I look up to see the redheaded girl looking at me with a single tear running down her cheek. She takes her tray and disappears into the crowd.

I look at the line, and there seems to be no stopping the constant flow of young people. I've never felt so helpless in all of my life, not even when the bullies surrounded me in the bathroom and tormented me. My helplessness seems to come for the vision before me of the endless groups of youth. They need so much. They need food, clothes, a place to sleep, and something as simple as a bathroom with a shower. But they need God more than all of these things. I know the end of the ages is coming soon. It's upon us.

I continue to hand out trays of food and think of the constant stream of people before me as a river. They're marching the wrong way. They're marching to the end of the ages, and they aren't ready. I can't turn them around. I can't help myself. I have no words that can talk them out of their movement forward. Time is determining our pace. It's traveling faster, out of control. It'd be like trying to talk a swollen river out of its flow to the ocean. I can't tell the river to go back to where it began as raindrops in a cloud. The journey has begun, and only God knows where it ends.

CHAPTER 41

OKLAHOMA—JATHYN,
I CAN DO ALL THINGS...

*I never thought about what my thoughtless
outburst might do to the youngest kids.*

We decide to watch the news on Friday and Saturday nights by using shifts of four hours each. The second day of the rally was much like the first. The exception was that the government seemed to seriously consider each of the points that the Christians brought to the discussion. As the sun comes up Sunday morning, my heart is lighter than it has been all weekend. Dad and Mom will be home today, and all will be well with our world.

Jaylie comes into the living room and curls up on the couch. "Have you been up all night?"

"No. Masen shared the night with me, along with Jax and Zayne. Zayne and I took the first shift of time until midnight, and Jax and Masen stayed up until four this morning. That is when I came back in here. I couldn't sleep. I didn't see any sense in waking Zayne. Nothing that affects us happened last night."

Jaylie yawns and stretches. "Do you want some cereal? Mom said we should take good care of the kitchen duties so you boys could concentrate on the things Dad told you to do."

Looking at my little sister, my heart swells because I want to protect her and the others. "Thank, you, Jaylie. I'd love some cereal."

Jaylie bounces off the couch and heads to the kitchen. "What kind would you like?"

I chuckle at the insignificance of such a decision. I know it's important to her because she is trying to do her best. "Surprise me. You girls have done a great job of taking care of all of us. You prepare our meals, clean up the kitchen, and I haven't heard a single argument. I should've told you before now"—my gaze falls upon the television—"but I was preoccupied."

She steps into the kitchen and comes back with a big bowl of Cocoa Puffs with marshmallows. "I gave you a surprise just like you asked. Hope you like marshmallows."

I grab the spoon and begin to eat ravenously as I mumble with my mouth full, "This is great!"

She giggles so loudly that we soon have Lia, Jax, and then Malorie awake with us. I love to listen to their laughter. It's so infectious, it lightens the heaviest of hearts.

Masen and Zayne join us at about ten o'clock. The final stages are set up for the rally, and we all gather around the television. Even Jax puts his book aside for a while when the familiar news banner appears.

"News update from the One World Vision news stations around the globe. News update, Oklahoma state capitol rally. The One World Religion says all concerns have been resolved with the various religious groups. These entities realize that the One World Religion believes in the same core values. However, extremists such as the Christians have turned out in force this weekend. They do not have the same agenda for peace. They've remained argumentative and will remain on the terrorist watch list.

"As a symbol of good faith, the Christian alliances have been invited to be first in line to take the pledge of allegiance to the new government. They shall receive their tattoos as they exit through the capitol building. There are booths set up all the way around the rotunda. They'll enter the south entrance and exit on the north. Those voluntarily pledging shall be allowed to go home and worship in the privacy of their homes. Collective groups of people meeting to worship Jesus will be viewed as terrorist cells. They'll be dealt with as such."

The news helicopter shooting the footage for the rally pans out, and we see people gathered for blocks. Large jumbo screens are used to give all the people a view of what is happening on the capitol's steps.

"Just as we suspected, the Christian groups have no intention of conforming and becoming a peaceful part of the new religion. People on the outer circles of the group are beginning to leave. They're choosing to leave and not take the pledge, but the militia has stepped in, and they're forcing anyone who doesn't take the pledge to board buses. Let's see if we have someone in the studio who can tell us why there are so many buses and what they're going to be used to transport."

The news helicopter widens his shot even more, and we see our parents. They're running, trying to get away. They run through a yard, and Dad helps Mom over a fence. The militia is in a solid line on the other side of that fence. They take Mom roughly toward the buses. Mom stumbles, and the officer jerks her. She grabs her shoulder as if it hurts. Uncle Nic breaks free of his officer long enough to punch the officer dragging Mom. The other officers step over to help and hit Uncle Nic in the back of the head with the butt of their rifles. He falls to the ground and lies there motionless. They load Mom, who is kicking and screaming. Then they carry Uncle Nic to another waiting bus with bars on the windows. Dad and the others are loaded onto the buses too.

"We have explanation of the buses now. They're here to transport terrorists to the nearest training center. If a terrorist is found to have had malicious intent, he or she will be imprisoned. If not, the person shall have the opportunity to be retrained by entering the program for no less than one year and possibly two."

I scream at Masen, "Where are they taking them? They can't do that, can they?" I never thought about what my thoughtless outburst might do to the youngest kids. I've got to remain in control of my emotions if they're to feel safe. Dad drummed that into my head, and what is the first thing I do? I create more stress.

Jax and Zayne begin to cry, and Malorie holds on to them. "It'll be okay. We're here for you. We have chores to do, boys. You have to help us."

Lia breaks out in bright red splotches from nerves. She is wheezing, unable to breathe. *I'm such an idiot!* I put my arm around her.

"Where's your inhaler? Let's go get it together."

We leave, and she takes a puff and puts the inhaler back into her backpack.

Masen looks at me as if he could kick me. Then he says ever so calmly, "They're taking them to their motels, I'm sure. Uncle Nic just got excited, so they'll need to get medical help for him first. That's why they put them on different buses."

Everyone looks at him hopefully. "We need to get our chores done, and we need to put extra food and water out for the animals. I'm sure we'll be so excited to see the folks that we won't want to have to do chores tomorrow. So do an extra good job. Now hop to it, everyone."

Everyone seems relieved to have something familiar to do. They head out the back door.

Masen turns to me, and I think he's going to knock my head off, but instead his eyes fall on the television screen. It goes black. There's no picture at all. He steps over to it and checks the outlets, the antenna cord, everything he can think of to do. Maybe God gave him this distraction to keep him from tearing me limb from limb.

I speak first. "I'm sorry! It won't happen again. I promise. I see what Dad was talking about now. I've got to remain calm, and the kids will feel safe and calm. By the way, you did a great job. Masen, say something."

He steps over close to me and grabs my shoulders. "We've got to get out of here as soon as it's dark enough. Get whatever you need and load the truck. *This is not a drill.* Dad and Mom aren't… coming home."

The pause between *aren't* and *coming home* almost sends me into a panic, but I know I have to remain calm. Masen needs to see me in control.

I say with a calmness that deceives my nerves, "I'm on it. We won't have too long to wait. Dad and Mom will know where we are and will come for us when they think it's safe. They'll be all right." On the last sentence, I squeeze his shoulder as I leave the room.

If we're caught, they'll surely take Masen and possibly me into custody. He's old enough to take the pledge. Malorie, Jaylie, and I will be separated from the little ones. We'll end up shipped off to a training center. The little ones will possibly stay here with foster parents, attending schools that will brainwash them. We have to get away safely. Dad was right: the lives of my brothers and sisters may rest in my hands.

I pause and say a prayer. "Please, Lord, watch over Dad and Mom and our aunts and uncles. Please direct me no matter what we face. Please show us the way and keep my family safe. Amen."

When I come through the front door, Masen is telling everyone that we'll wait for Dad and Mom at the cave. We've practiced, and we're ready. Then our cell phones ring at the same time. We each have a text. It's from Liam. It says, *Stay put and I'll come to get you as soon as I can. I'm leaving now. I saw the news, and I'll come and help you.* Then the side post says one minute ago in Boulder, Colorado.

I look at my phone in disbelief. Then I say what we're all thinking. "Can we trust him?"

Masen wets his lips with his tongue. "He is our cousin, and he seemed so sincere about turning over a new leaf when he left. Maybe we can."

Jax speaks up, "I know how we can tell."

"How?" I ask.

Jax moves between us and looks up at Masen. "Call his brothers, Gustin, Eli, or Fuller. They talk to him once in a while."

Dialing from the house phone, Masen calls.

Eli answers on the first ring. "Are you all right? We saw the footage of the militia arresting our parents. We've been listening on our Dad's old ham radio, and we're picking up some skips of information. It sounds like they're taking the women to one training facility and the men to another. We haven't heard from our parents yet. How about you guys?"

Masen flips the phone to speaker. "No news on this end either. How did you know it was us calling? You've got to be careful."

Eli hesitates and answers, "Caller ID, but you're right. It might not have been you calling from this number. I'll be more careful."

Masen paces back and forth as far as the cord allows. "Have you heard from Liam?"

Eli replies, "Yes, now that you mention it. He texted us not long ago. He said to stay put, and he was on his way to us from Boulder." Eli stops when Masen doesn't say anything right away. "He's changed, you know. His time with Gram seems to have reformed him."

Masen sounds upbeat. "Yes, he seemed sincere at the reading of the will. I talked to him before he left for Colorado. Well, I just wanted to check in with you guys. Stay in touch and let us know if you hear from anyone."

Eli clears his throat. "Sure. As soon as our parents or Liam gets here, we'll be over to get you guys and coordinate our next move." His voice cracks. "We'd come now, but we have strict instructions to stay put until someone shows. If it's a stranger, we'll head for the cave over by the pond. If not we'll stay home. We know the drill."

The blood drains from Masen's face. "That's a good plan." He drops his gaze and voice. "What if when you see Liam he's back to his old self?

166

What'll you do then?" I know having to say this kills my brother. To voice out loud something so potentially hurtful to our cousin pains us all.

There's a long pause, and then Eli replies softly, "Don't worry, Masen. If Liam is the one to come, we won't bring him to the cave until we're sure he is right with the Lord. I understand why you'd be worried. He doesn't have a very good track record, but he *is* my brother, and I trust him with *my* life."

Masen shakes his head and looks at the ceiling. "Sorry I doubted him. Our world has been turned upside down, and we can't afford to make even one small mistake. Hope you understand and can forgive me?"

Eli is quicker to respond this time. "Of course, I understand. It's not just about you. You're responsible for your sisters and brothers. I have to think about Fuller and Gustin. I *needed* this call as much as you needed to make it. We'll stay on our toes, and you do the same. Good luck to you."

Masen states, "Luck has nothing to do with it. Our lives are in God's hands now. I pray I hear his voice and respond correctly. Take care, and we'll see you soon."

Masen hangs up the phone and unplugs it from the wall. He wraps the cord around the phone and places it in a large trash bag.

Malorie asks, "What are you doing?"

Masen begins to unplug all the electronic devices and places them in the bag. "Jax, run to the shed and get two plastic bins. Jaylie you go with him. Be quick." He turns to me and says with a panicked look on his face, "We forgot the electronics. The GPS, the ability to see who we call. They can still tell, but they'll have to go to the phone office. We don't want to lead someone to family. In the meantime, it might buy us days, maybe longer. Do you think you can take the GPS tracking chip out of our phones? If you can't, we'll dump them."

I don't bother to answer and begin working on my phone's chip. Then I work on Malorie's and then Masen's last. I have him send me a text, and it comes through, but it doesn't give the location from where it originated anymore. "I think we're good. The sun is down, and it should be dark enough to leave anytime. How about we load up?"

Malorie slips into her jacket. "Girls, go to the bathroom and be quick about it." She runs to one bathroom while the other two head the other way.

We drive slow, taking the well-worn path by the elm grove. We have a mini trash dump started with things we can't put in the Dumpster. There is a hot tub. We place the computer bin on the ground and flip the tub on top of it. Then we drive along the fence of the irrigation field.

The night sky is full of stars tonight as we head to the place in the pasture to stash the pickup. I review with everyone how important it is that we be as quiet as possible. "So if you feel a spider's web, Lia, what will you do?"

She wiggles. "I won't scream. I promise. I'll be brave because I can do all things through Christ who strengthens me."

I praise her, and we all thank her for reminding us that we aren't alone tonight.

CHAPTER 42

RAMSTEIN, GERMANY—JORDYN PACKS A BAG

Remember I love you and everything that happens
in this world is not my fault!

Ken and I take the trash out together in the hopes of talking freely. Our Dumpster is in the alley next to a transformer that hums and buzzes all the time. We hope no one can pick up our conversations. We found at least two bugs in the house, and we're paranoid about saying anything inside.

Ken begins to flatten boxes to fit them into the Dumpster. "Do you remember when you told your mom that if she argued at every turn and went against your dad's decisions it would sabotage the success of what he'd planned for your family? Your mom doesn't ever assert herself over your dad's wishes. The responsibility rests on his shoulders, and she *trusts* him. You have to trust *me* that same way! I can't explain everything, but *know* I'm protecting us the only way I know how."

I throw one sack in. "I remember." I'm humbled that he has to use my own words to make me see that I have to trust him explicitly.

Ken smashes a box, throws it inside, and states clearly and flatly, "We're leaving this week. Pack a small bag to take with us on the plane, and the militia will move the rest of our belongings. We leave on Wednesday. I'll be working late every night until then. You need to be ready Wednesday morning. I'll come for you, and we'll be stateside by this time next week. Then we're going to visit your family in person."

I throw my last sack into the Dumpster. I study his eyes. "I'll be ready."

We return to the house hand in hand. I fix a light supper. We curl up on the couch and watch a movie. I snuggle into his strong, protective arms, knowing everything will be all right. Ken has been under such extreme stress that he hasn't slept. He sleeps now. I hold him around his waist, resting my head on his chest. I hear his heart beating as the minutes of the night tick away.

We wake to a dark house and the television streaming a monologue of news.

"News update from the One World Vision news stations around the globe: We have breaking news from across the ocean. The United States has finished their grassroots attempt to convince the Christian factions to abandon their efforts of insisting that Jesus is the Messiah. To proclaim any of the religions' heroes were anything other than prophets, seers, or spiritualists is detrimental to the peaceful efforts of this new government. As a last resort, those Christians who refused to pledge their allegiance to the government have been transported to retraining centers. They may have up to two years to reconsider their positions and take the pledge. If at the end of two years they still refuse to take the pledge, they shall be terminated.

"Any organized meetings of these groups will be considered an act of treason resulting in immediate disposal. We'll not jeopardize the movement of the world toward total harmony and peace. The children of these individuals will be sent to boarding schools across the nation to learn the Peace and harmony objectives. Young children are staying in their homes with foster parents assigned by the new government. These adults have been displaced because their homes have been confiscated for one of the many needs of the new One World Vision. Areas around the globe will be used as hospitals, schools, and militia housing. Other areas may be stripped of their current structures to make way for airstrips and police, fire, and rescue stations. We'll be back after this brief message."

I look at Ken. The television's glow flickers on his face. I'm terrified for my family. I haven't heard from them because the militia still has our computer and my phone. I'm assuming no news is good news, but now I'm petrified. What if they contacted me? What if the militia intercepted the message of where they might hide?

Ken holds my stare as if willing me to stay calm and not say a word in the house, where we might be overheard. He must expect me to break down and cry, because he hands me a tissue. I push his hand away and stand defiant in front of him. He stands, and I pull myself up to my full height of five feet eleven. Normally I slump slightly out of habit to make my appearance shorter. When I stand proud and confident, I'm almost as tall as Ken's full six feet.

He says softly, "Careful! You might hurt yourself in the dark going to bed."

I answer loud and fearlessly, "I can take care of myself! You'd better watch your step. You're the one who is groggy from sleep." I add the last sentence for those outside who might be listening. I march to the bedroom, grab my carry-on bag for traveling, step into the bathroom, and lock the door.

When I hear the front door close, I assume Ken has left. I step out of the locked bathroom and head down the hall toward the kitchen. I'm grabbed from behind and lifted off the floor. I kick and shriek. I'm spun around to face Ken. I'm shocked, scared, and relieved all at the same time. My head spins in the confusion.

He says loudly, "Surprise! You didn't think I'd leave you without a good-bye kiss, did you?" Then he kisses me softly, gently coaxing me with his lips to respond. My lips have a mind of their own, and they eagerly kiss him good-bye.

He whispers, "Remember, I love you, and everything that happens in this world is *not* my fault! I'll be home to pick you up Wednesday morning. I'll not be home again until then. Everything has to appear normal." He releases me.

I give him a long, sincere hug. "I'll miss you. Hurry home." The depths with which I feel these words shock me. I watch him exit the front door, and I choke out, "I love you too." I know he doesn't hear me. Only the walls with ears hear me.

CHAPTER 43

COLORADO—LIAM'S THOUGHTS OF MURDER

The stranger walks past me asking softly,
"Are we square?"

A veil seems to have been lifted from my eyes. I watch Emily in her self-absorption. She is addicted to power and the thought of getting more. The fact that she rules our house isn't enough.

I put thoughts of her aside. I fall asleep in the tiny recliner downstairs for the third night in a row. I ache all over. I refuse to share a bed with her, and she refuses to get out of it. I've got to tell her to move out, but I can't seem to do it.

I don't care about anything. I head to the kitchen for a cup of coffee. There isn't any coffee in the canister. I guess I'll go to the store. I think back to last night when I was ready to talk and she wasn't. She was pouring over those stupid books as we sat in the living room, watching the news.

I pick up the books she has left strewn about the living room, closing and stacking them neatly. I'm holding one in my hand as a police car pulls up to Lena's house. I step out to the front porch to get a better look. I hope nothing is wrong. The militia knocks. They talk to her for a moment, and she begins to cry.

I step off the porch, and I'm at the curb when I see them put cuffs on her. Why would they need to cuff this little old helpless woman? What could she have possibly done? I turn to go back into the house. I see a flyer on the floor of the living room, where I picked up the book in my hand. It is a detailed plan of how to round up all nonpatriots. The first suggestion is to get to know your neighbors. If they don't have a tattoo, it says to report them. There is a check mark in red, crossing this off as if it has been finished. The police have a minibus waiting across the street at the flophouse. They escort at least fifteen youth to the bus in handcuffs just like they did Lena.

"*Hmm*, it's about time they got here," Emily states from directly behind me, making me jump.

I ask her in disbelief, "What have you done?"

"I'm only doing what any conscientious patriot should be doing. I'm assisting the government in being more efficient. There's no way they can be everywhere at once," Emily states smartly as she pivots to march to the kitchen. She whines from the kitchen, "There's no coffee made."

I can't believe she's so cavalier about handing over our neighbors. They did absolutely nothing against us or the government. I fold the flyer and stuff it into my pocket. I grab my keys.

Emily tramps across the floor in my house shoes, which are two sizes too big for her, and accuses, "Why didn't you make me some coffee?" She produces her empty cup under my nose.

I flip on the television while I tie my tennis shoes. "Because someone didn't pick up any groceries while I was working and at school. We have no coffee."

"News update from the One World Vision news stations around the globe: We apologize for yesterday's interruption to your state's video and audio feeds. All states went off-line temporarily. We won't have that problem today because we have resolved all issues."

I want to see some news feed from yesterday. Some of the students from Oklahoma said there was an incident at Oklahoma's capitol. I was hoping they would rerun the incident. They loop other information numerous times. I guess if there had been any news, they would have opened with that story.

"The One World Government is announcing that the rallies at the capitols across the nation were a success. There were many compromises made to the One World Religion, pleasing all who attended."

As I watch, all that is televised is broken clips of people talking, smiling, and shaking hands. The propaganda video loops over and over again as the announcer continues.

"There were the isolated incidents in which Christian terrorists tried to disrupt the peaceful assembly. It's being reported that the majority of those attending insisted upon taking the pledge of allegiance to the new government, and they received their tattoos yesterday. Those choosing to wait were bused to the nearest training centers before making their decisions. It's the fervent hope of the new government to make sure *all* of its citizens are at peace with their decisions. At the end of their training this year, those individuals will be given another chance to accept the all-inclusive religion and new government. The citizens around the world are expected to submit and honor their nation's part in creating a better world."

I can't stand to hear any more. Ambling to the back porch in search of Streak, I find a couple making out. I didn't mind giving Emily a place to stay, but sometimes I feel like she is taking advantage of the situation by allowing strangers into my home. I return to the living room. I wonder where Streak has disappeared to so early this morning.

I ask Emily, "Who is the couple on the porch, and have you seen Streak?"

She answers sweetly, "They are new patriots. They needed a place to crash last night, and I knew you wouldn't care for one night. As for that stupid cat of yours, I haven't seen him." She smiles broadly and sways across the room like she's queen. "I hope he's all right. I did go out back early this morning to look at the beautiful stars. You don't think he got out, do you?"

She is at the stairway, turns, and looks at me with her fake pout upon her lips. I can't believe she was out of bed before ten. I used to think she looked so innocent when she did this, but now she looks as guilty as sin.

"I'm sure if he did go out, he'll be fine. I'll be back in a jiffy. I'm going to the convenience store to pick up a couple of cinnamon rolls and coffee. Would you like anything?"

She smiles. "One of your cinnamon rolls might be nice."

I call for Streak, but he doesn't show up. I jog to the store, and Crystal is working. I haven't seen her for at least two weeks. "Hello, stranger. I'd like two cinnamon rolls, please." I begin to fill two large coffee cups.

She grabs the rolls. "What have you been up to lately? You don't come around here much anymore."

"I'm working, going to school, and trying to keep up. How about you? What have you been doing?" I reply.

She hands me my change. "The same, except I've been getting to know the homeless in the neighborhood." She winks and adds, "Did you know that you can earn merits toward credit of college hours?"

I pocket the change. "No. How does it work? I might be interested."

She wipes coffee drips from the counter. "I thought you might be interested, so I took an extra pamphlet. It explains it all on this page. I'd love to talk, but I better get back to work."

The flyer looks identical to the one stuffed in my pocket. I'll read it on my break at work. I can't believe I can make such poor choices in friends. It's obvious that Crystal also feels it's okay to sell out the homeless to the government.

I call and watch for Streak all the way home. I know Streak and Emily don't get along, but he didn't like me either at first. He's a one-person or one-family kind of cat. I step into the house, and Emily is standing with her back to me. A stranger is talking to her and facing me. I'd seen this guy across the street. He was never very friendly, so it seems odd that he'd be in my home, especially after the roundup by the militia. I notice he doesn't have a tattoo and wonder how he escaped the bust. Emily turns, and she's holding Streak's limp body.

The man with her says, "I knew this was your cat. I've seen you two together. I found him in the street. I guess he got run over or something."

I drop the sack of cinnamon rolls as I move to take Streak from Emily's cold hands.

The stranger walks past me, asking softly, "Are we square?" before the door closes.

My focus is on the lifeless body that's still warm. I walk to the back porch, crying like a baby. It's like losing Gram all over again. I don't see anywhere on his body where fur is missing from skidding on the pavement. The only thing I can see is that his neck lies at a right angle to his body. His neck is broken. I guess the car must've clipped him.

My life is out of control! I know exactly how to get it back. Harrison may've been my worst nightmare earlier in my life, but I know in my heart he has prepared me for this moment. I won't care about anyone or anything ever again. As far as I'm concerned, I'm alone on this planet. I'm going to take care of number one—*me*.

I bury Streak and return to the house. I go to the bathroom and wash my hands and face. I change my clothes and head downstairs for my cinnamon roll and cold coffee.

"Emily, where's my roll?" I ask.

She calls from the living room, "Oh, I gave it away. I didn't think you'd want it."

I walk to the back porch and the couple that was making out on the couch earlier now has friends with them. I explode, "Get out of my house!"

They jump and look up. They begin moving, keeping their eyes on me. They start to go through the house, but I block their path. They quickly exit through the back door. I lock it as soon as they're through it. I spin around. I'm ready for that conversation with Emily now. I march through the house to the living room, where Emily sits wide-eyed.

I address her as if she is a bug to be squashed. "Emily, you're no longer useful to me. You've overstayed your welcome. Tell your friends to stay away. Get your things now! I want you out of my house." I aim each sentence at her to inflict as much pain as possible. My old habits of knowing people's weaknesses and hitting them verbally and physically raises its ugly head.

She takes on the little frightened deer posture and runs upstairs. She returns shortly with her backpack and the trash bag of things she'd brought with her. She gives me one of her sultry looks, and I meet it with my own emotionless stare. I'd learned to master it years ago, playing the parts needed to get what I want.

Her demeanor changes to the heartless vixen she is. "It was the best *trade* I've ever made." She walks to the front door, opens it, turns, and then waits with pleasure dripping from her pouty pink lips.

I remain across the room from her. "What trade?"

She smiles as she holds the door wide open to walk through. She had been setting the scene for her departure, so I let her have this moment.

She answers with disdain dripping from each word, "I traded a friend a tip-off about a raid for a little favor."

I take a step toward her, ready to slap her as she finishes.

"The favor was to snap that fool cat's neck!" She leaps through the door and runs down the steps.

I can't comprehend what she has just said, but the stranger's whispered words, *Are we square*, now make sense. I see her stop a car and motion toward me, and she begins to cry on cue. The car speeds away as I reach the sidewalk. I return to the house, slam the door, and swear to never show weakness again as a picture crashes to the floor.

I'm so angry, I can't see straight. I grab my keys and leave the house. As I'm backing out, the police are at Lena's, leaving with her cats. This surreal scene leaves me unfazed. Nothing matters any longer. All I can think of is finding that car with Emily inside.

I pull the car into the drive a little after midnight, and I let out a long sigh. I'm glad I didn't see Emily. I think I might've snapped *her* neck if I had found her, and she's not worth the trouble it would rain down upon me. I insert my key to unlock the front door, and the door slides open. I step over to the car, pop the trunk, grab the tire iron, and enter my home unafraid. I flip on the light and find that nothing appears to be out of place. I check both floors. I guess I was so furious that I left without locking the front door. I lock the front door and prop a chair under the doorknob. Then I go to the back porch and do the same with that door.

I check my e-mails and Facebook. I see nothing I didn't already know: rally riots and nonsense. My littlest brother has sent me at least a dozen messages. I don't have time to read the drivel of an eight-year-old, so I don't even open them. I just delete them. I can't allow my family to be my weakness. I shut down the computer and sit watching the screen fade to black. I decide to unplug the computer tonight.

In the morning light, things seem clearer. I go downstairs and check to see if both chairs are in place. I lock the front door behind me and check it. It's locked tight. I move a planter pot enough that if the screen door is opened, it will tip it over. Then I jog to the store. I find an empty table and eat a bowl of oatmeal and fruit. If only I could rewind my life back to the first time I sat here like this. Melancholy images of Streak and a hopeful future fade to black before my eyes.

Out of nowhere, as I'm lost in my thoughts, the redheaded girl steps up to my table and says, "Nightly, God watches over them. He moves in the hearts of others to feed, clothe, and protect his children. They may harm each other, but no one else will harm them. They'll go until the end of their journey." Then she leaves the store with her Bible tucked under her arm.

I hope she is talking about Gram's God. I hope she's right for *their* sake.

CHAPTER 44

OKLAHOMA—JATHYN AND THE OUTLAWS

What outlaws?

Adrenaline helps us make it to the curve on the railroad tracks by midnight. We stop when we're around the bend and out of earshot of anyone on the road. We huddle together, sitting on the rails, facing each other, and resting. I sit next to where Masen remains standing.

"We need to talk."

Masen answers in a whisper. "Talk about what? We need to be in that cave before sunrise. We need to head down the ditch now." He begins his decline down the earthen bridge built up through the canyon to carry the railroad track. The fence is across the ditch at the bottom of the berm.

I speak softly this time. "Wait!"

Masen stops, and I catch up to him.

"We had a hard time on this part when we were with Dad. We've got more of us, multiplying our chances of someone getting injured. It was breaking daylight, and we could see. It's pitch-black down in the bottom of that ditch. The trees block out any of the starlight. Let's go down to the old original road that crossed the tracks connecting the two pastures. We can walk on the grass and not leave any tracks across the pasture and the dam. We'll make better time. What do you think?"

Masen looks up at the tracks, where our motley crew sits watching hopefully for instruction. "Good thinking, Jathyn. Let's do it." He marches up the bank and informs them of our decision.

They don't say a word and begin to follow us. We're at the pond, and we cross the dam within twenty minutes. At the pond, four deer getting a drink leap into action when we approach. They gracefully leap and lunge up the embankment to the caprock above. We all take the time to admire the beauty surrounding us. The thin sliver of a moon is reflected on the motionless glassy water, along with the shadows of the cattails and chubby cedars at the water's edge.

We turn on our flashlights only long enough to descend the path from the top of the dam to the cliff's edge. The natural spring cut a deep scar into the landscape, leaving behind an ever-widening canyon. The spring continues to flow down the canyon by running through the overflow pipe of the pond. Our great-grandfather built the pond by damming across the canyon at a narrow area. The two walls were ten yards apart at that point, and he filled it with earth, stopping the water and thus creating a pond. When the natural spring had the pond filled, he put the pipe in to keep the water from flowing over the top and eroding the dam away. Then he added more earth across the dam, making it high enough to handle heavy rains. The overflow would always bring the extra water level down to the pipe.

Masen stops. "Wait while I enter the cave and look for snakes. We have to be careful."

I don't argue. I appreciate not being the oldest at times like these.

Jax whispers, "I wonder if the outlaws knew of this cave too."

Zayne asks, "What outlaws?"

I nearly jump out of my skin when he hisses his whispered question directly into my ear. I was imagining that I was crawling inside that cave with Masen and thinking of rattlesnakes. "I have no idea."

Jax whispers, "I wonder if while they were on the run they had to whisper. Do you think their hearts were pounding like ours are now?" He looks around at the rimrock above.

Zayne does the same and whispers in Jax's ear this time, "What outlaws?"

Jax whispers, "The bad ones!"

My eyes follow his gaze up through the tree's shadows. "Devote yourself to prayer, being watchful and thankful."

Jax steps closer and holds my hand. "What did you say?"

I bring my gaze down to their shadow-filled faces. "It's a Bible verse from Colossians 4:2. It just popped into my head. I was thinking out loud to calm myself and to give myself some moral support." I'm glad I voiced these words. The little boys need the peace God's Word brings as much as I do.

Masen gives us an all clear, and we begin our crawl into the cave. I bring up the rear and make sure no one is left behind. Masen and I decided in the pickup that he would lead and I would follow tonight. I look around and flash my flashlight back and forth on the ground to see if we've dropped anything. I don't see a thing, but the weeds look a little trampled. I try to fluff them as I back toward the cave, brushing away any possible footprints that might be on the dust of rocks. Then I enter as well. The group is already beginning to make their way up the rope ladder when I get to the pit.

The order we're traveling through the maze of tumbled rocks is Masen, the oldest at eighteen, and then the eight-and ten-year-olds, Jax, Zayne, and Lia. Next in our line are Jaylie at twelve and Malorie at fourteen. I'll bring up the end of our parade. I get to the top of the rope ladder, and I reach up to grasp a rock as I pull myself over the edge.

This part of the cave twists and turns around boulders. The glow of the group's flashlights have rounded one such turn, and I'm thrown into darkness except for the tiny light of my own flashlight. I lay my flashlight on the path ahead of me and begin to climb over the edge. My ribcage rests on the edge, and I see a movement from the corner of my right eye. It's a snake slithering directly toward me. He came from a crack in the craggy crumbling gypsum rock. I remember my cousin saying that when one snake crawls out, it isn't long and more venture out as well. I quickly jump to the path and begin to make my way between the tumbled boulders. I call out as quietly as I can and still be whispering, "Masen, wait for me!"

No one hears me, and I can't see their lights any longer. I flash my light forward and back. My eyes are torn on whether to look forward or turn to see what might be behind me. My shoulders brush the tumbled boulders, and I move away, only to have my ankle brush past another rock. My imagination of what might be in the darkness gets the better of me. I feel the dark breathing in and out on the back of my neck. I whirl and look behind me, shining my light and expecting my mind's vivid picture of snakes dripping from every crack and crevice.

I see nothing, but the thoughts take on a life of their own. I come to a fork in the pathways. I call again, this time a little louder. I whirl around and scan the ground after doing a 360 degree turn a few times first, scanning the floor and then the walls, the ceiling, and lastly the piles of rocks and crevices between rocks. I'm totally confused by this time. I stop looking for snakes, and I don't know which way to go. *Please, God, help me!*

I scream, "Masen!" I know it will echo, but I need help.

I'm worried sick, and I begin to get claustrophobic. I can't breathe. I can't take the chance that I'll go back to the pit, because the snakes are there. My flashlight's glimmer becomes faint. I'm wet with sweat. The cool breeze sucking through the cave causes me to shiver. I shake my flashlight, and it burns brighter momentarily. Then I think I see a dim light down one of the pathways. I hear a distant rattling, a crackle of the raspy buzzing. The echoes make the sound of snakes appear to be coming from all directions at once. As my light becomes more yellow than white and dims, I think that I hear footsteps. The rattling is becoming louder, so I assume the snakes are coming closer. I face one of three possible paths.

I squeeze my eyes tight to block out the lack of light and yell, "Masen! Help me!" I *will* my foot to take a step forward.

A hand firmly grasps my wrist and jerks me around 180 degrees. Masen says only loud enough for me to hear him, "Follow me quickly."

He doesn't let go of my wrist, and he begins to fast-walk down a maze of pathways. We step from behind a large solid rock of gypsum, and we're in the large room that was quarried decades previously. I run to the opposite side of a large irregular-shaped room, putting as much distance between me and the snake-infested tunnel as I can. Large pillars of rock rise from floor to ceiling.

I lean against the wall and feel the coolness of the rock through my wet shirt. I slump onto a rock nearby, and after I'm sitting, I feel the muscles in my legs begin to quiver. I think about how I was about to burst into a dead run down the pathway I was facing—the very path that led back to the pit and would've placed me in the den of the deadly rattlesnakes. I see Lia approaching me.

She places her hand on my shoulder. "You can do all things through Christ who strengthens you." My nerves fail me, and I sob.

Masen is squatting beside me. "Are you all right? Did they bite you?"

Trembling, short answers are all I can manage. "No bites. Scared!" My brain is still frozen back in the labyrinth of pathways. I find my voice. "How did you know which way to go?" I begin to feel tears well up in my eyes, and I look away from Masen's concerned face. "I didn't know the way. I lost my sense of direction. I'm sorry I cried out; I didn't know what to do, and my flashlight was dimming."

Masen places his arm around me. "It's okay. You're okay. We're okay."

We all sit quietly in the room made from solid rock. I can't stop the vibrations that begin from deep within, so I walk to the gated entrance of the room. My mind is numb. I can't think. I stare out at the thick cedars hiding our entrance. My head bobs slightly from the tremors racking my body.

The dawn breathes light into the air, appearing nowhere at first and then everywhere. I feel better in the light, and my breathing returns to normal.

I jump as I notice Malorie beside me. "Are you feeling better?" she asks.

I nod. "Yes, now that the sun is coming up."

She squeezes my arm slightly. "Masen would like all of us to come away from the entrance because he wants to call a family meeting and doesn't want the risk of someone hearing us."

She heads back into the quarried chamber. I'm filled with dread and near panic with each step deeper into the hill, which now feels like a mountain upon me. The cold pressure builds against my ears. The icy weight upon my chest grips my heart and makes it pound harder against the frozen walls. I think about returning to the cave entrance and the warm light of day.

Masen has made a small fire where a previous occupant had made a fire pit. Its warmth nourishes my body with what it needs. I hadn't realized how cold I was in my damp clothes, and I begin to shiver uncontrollably. Masen sees me and touches my arm. He's alarmed.

"You're freezing. How did you get your clothes so wet?"

I stutter, "I… I… was sweat… ing."

Masen motions for the girls to turn. "Turn around. We need to strip off these damp clothes." Zayne and Masen remove my clothes because I can't do anything except shake. My shaking scares me, causing me to shake that much harder. Jax brings some dry warm jeans and a sweatshirt. He wraps his sleeping bag around my shoulders and leads me to a place in front of the fire pit.

Masen commands, "Girls, join us."

We sit in a circle around the fire. Our faces glow with the dancing flickers from the fire. The flames of yellow and orange reflect the seriousness upon our minds.

Jax makes an observation. "We're running from the new government, so we're outside of the new law. Technically, we're outlaws sitting in our cave, making our next plans."

I think to myself that I should tell him that to romanticize a lawbreaker is wrong. But he's right. I keep quiet and wonder if we're doing the right thing.

Zayne pulls on Jax's sleeve. "What outlaws?"

Jax turns slowly and places his hands on Zayne's shoulders. He leans in, holding eye contact, and then in a voice just above a whisper, he explains, "The Isaac Black and Dick Yeager gangs. Dick, also known as Zip Wyatt, used the caves in this area. The posse found them on a Thursday, August 1, 1895, in these Salt Creek canyons just a little ways from here. With guns blazing, they chased them north, where they had another gunfight across the road from our great-great-greatest grandma's house north of Longdale. I don't remember her name."

I interrupt Jax. "You shouldn't make it sound cool, because it's not! Black was shot through the head! Yeager was shot in the chest but still managed to get away on foot!"

Jax takes over again. "Let me finish! I told *you* the story in the first place, Jathyn. Yeager made a boy driving a horse-drawn cart take him to somewhere. He kept running through Friday night. I don't remember when, but he stole a fresh horse. About five miles south of Enid, his horse gave out, and he was on foot again! He escaped through a cane field and took a man and his two old horses with him while he looked for food. Outlaws had to live on the run, sometimes not eating. They stopped at a lady's house, and she gave them cornbread and milk, and he tried to pay her, but she said no. He dug in his pocket and found a fifty-cent piece and gave it to her boy. It's said that the family still has that coin."

Masen stands next to the fire, facing us. "That's enough talk of outlaws. We need to make plans. We did pretty good last night as far as getting away unseen. I don't think anyone has any idea where we are."

Jaylie asks, "But?" and nods her head up and down like a bobble head in a car, impatient for him to continue.

Masen adds, "But I think we need to brainstorm about the things that went well and how we can improve. If any of you can imagine a scenario that could cause us a problem, we need to talk about it."

I've thawed out enough to stop my teeth from chattering. "I want to say I'm sorry for yelling. I could've jeopardized everyone's safety." I'm still not in control of my emotions, so I look down. Lia pats my hand.

Masen faces me. "Since you brought it up, I think you did the correct thing in calling out to us. The first yell I heard let me know we had a problem, so we ran the rest of the way to this room. I had to clear the pathway of people before I could come after you. I was on my way when I heard the second call for help. You knew it looked like we'd not been seen. You knew we were alone in the pasture or else the deer wouldn't have been present. They would've been spooked if someone was around. You may not have realized it at the time, but inside you were pretty sure we were alone."

Jaylie interrupts and states the obvious. "So we all need to be aware of what nature is doing around us. We can tell if there's danger by watching the animals."

Masen nods. "That's right. We need to all be watchful. Not just Jathyn and I but everyone. I think we should have designated partners in case one of us is in need again. If we hadn't been so close to the end of the tunnel system when the first yell came, I don't know what we would've done. It didn't make sense to take everyone back. Neither could we ignore the fact that someone needed to go help."

Malorie scoots back from the fire. "How do you want to pair up?"

Masen walks closer to her. "I'm open for discussion, but I'm thinking an older sibling with a younger one. Maybe me with Jax and Zayne, Jathyn with Lia, and, Malorie, you with Jaylie. Does that sound okay with everyone?"

All heads nod in agreement.

He continues. "Let's think this through. How will this be helpful?"

Jax is first to chime in. "Well, if something happens to you, another man will take your place, me and then Zayne." We all can't help but grin at this comment from our little eight-year-old brother. He obviously doesn't notice because he continues to seriously state his position. "Dad has included me in the discussions and plans of taking care of everyone. I know I'm young, but I think when we regroup, the strength is in our staying together."

Zayne grumbles, "I'm a week older than you; I should be the next man in line."

Masen moves behind the boys and squats down between them. "That's using your head, Jax. And, Zayne, point taken. What would all of you do if your partner was suddenly disabled somehow? Take a minute and talk it over with your partner, and then we'll share."

We each share "what if" scenarios. Lia and I use the rattlesnake episode to begin our discussion. Soon she says, "If you are down, I can't carry you. The other pairs can each manage their partner. I'm not going to be much help to you or the group." She quickly becomes discouraged.

"No, I think you're wrong," I say with confidence and continue my thought. "You and I are the strongest team. You're the one who reminded us all to put God first. You helped us all to see that we needed to let the Lord guide us. You're bringing the greatest asset to the problem—the Lord."

She quotes, "Psalm 32:8, I will instruct you in the way you should go; I will counsel you with my loving eye on you. With three brothers and two older sisters, I use lots of verses." We laugh, and it's time to share our plans.

It's decided that we each bring strength to our partner as well as the group.

CHAPTER 45

COLORADO—LIAM'S INTERLOPER

I put everything back the way it was; and,
I unscrew the lightbulb as I formulate a plan.

I notice Leonne checking the oil in his car and puttering around outside his house as I drive into my driveway after working all night. I call out to him, "Good day, neighbor."

He nods. "Good day to you." He acts extremely focused on wheeling the trash bins to the curb.

I step to my side of the fence. "Thanksgiving is coming up, and I volunteered to work overtime to earn extra money for Christmas. I'm buying me a new recliner and computer. Do you know your hours yet?" I think about my broken chair, and I become angry with Emily again. She insisted on sitting on my lap when I sat in it, and the extra weight broke it. She was in my life for a short time, but she totally turned it upside down.

Leonne stops and walks over to the fence. "I volunteered too. There'll be lots of kids who'll need food, clothes, and a safe place to hang out. We're opening the auditorium early Thanksgiving and showing the football games. Has something happened to that cat of yours? I haven't seen him in a day or two. I like him."

I miss Streak so much it hurts. I can't let myself think about Emily and her calculating ruthless actions. I don't want to tell him the truth. "He got run over and killed by a car."

Leonne states, "I can't believe that. Your cat was so careful around cars. I guess something distracted him. I'm very sorry for your loss. I know you thought a lot of him."

186

Steeling myself, I stand straighter. "Thanks, but that's life. I better let you return to your work."

As I approach my house, I think about school. I'm going to focus on my studies. Emily was right about one thing: I need to plan my future with a definite purpose in mind. I think I might focus on an overseas assignment when I finish college. I've been surfing the net to find out what jobs are out there in my fields. I'll have a major in five languages and a minor in government. Emily will undoubtedly manipulate her way through college. She's ambitious, and I won't let her get ahead of me on the advancement ladder to success. I want to be at the top of that ladder when she comes along so I can be the one to kick her off backward. I feed my rage on a daily basis. I'm beginning to feel like my old self before the church thing.

I'm to my front door before I see the planter overturned. I look, and the door is ajar. I go directly to my office, and the computer is on. I look at every room much more carefully this time. I know someone has been here because the computer was unplugged. I do a search to see what the last places visited on the Internet were. I see that someone is watching where I go on the Internet. They've been in my e-mail account. I log off my e-mail account after I check my mail. I also clear the history on where I've been looking.

I've been up all night, but I'm not going to sleep until I'm sure my doors are secure. I go to the hardware store and buy two dead bolts and a new locking doorknob for the front door. I install them, lock them, and collapse on the top of the covers in my room. I'm exhausted.

The next morning the computer is on. All of the places I visited are back on the computer's history, and my e-mail is open. I check the doors, and the back door is dead bolted, but the front door is open. A shiver runs up my spine, causing me to look over my shoulder. I check every window and find only the bathroom windows unlocked. They are so small I never dreamed anyone could gain access through them.

I pour myself a cup of coffee, and as I'm standing in the kitchen, I think there has to be somewhere I haven't looked. Then my eyes fall upon the basement door. I stand frozen in time, staring at the door. It's as if the demons from all the horror movies I've ever watched are about to erupt through that portal.

I step into the living room and get my baseball bat. Then I turn the knob slowly on the basement door. I flip the switch for the light, but nothing happens. I go back to the catch-all drawer in the kitchen and get a flashlight. I stand on the landing and shine the light around the basement. Squatting down, peering under the ceiling of the room, I realize I've never gone all the way to the bottom step before. I've put the thought of having a basement out of my mind because the very thought of it creeps me out.

There's an old boiler system standing in the corner. There's a workbench with old cans of paint sitting on it. There're some boxes that have deteriorated and collapsed, spilling their once neatly packed contents onto the floor. I shine the light on the steps one at a time and see at least one large man-size foot print on a step. There's one step that has a heavy layer of dust on it. Why are there only a couple of steps that have dust?

I walk down into the basement and shine my light directly above these steps. It seems to be where the washer sits. I guess when it spins, it must cause dust to fall. I replace the burned out lightbulb, and the room becomes brightly lit. I see where someone has walked across the floor. It's the same large footprints, and they lead beside a large shelving unit. I look behind it, and the unit is pushed away from the wall far enough for someone to squeeze by it. I move the shelving unit farther and find stairs that lead to the outside of the house. I forgot about the exterior doors I discovered when I cleaned up the yard. I put everything back the way it was and unscrew the lightbulb as I formulate a plan.

I spend the morning gathering supplies that I'll need. I head to work as if nothing has been discovered. I'm alert at the soup line at lunch and supper, watching for a guy I've gotten acquainted with by serving him every day. He is from Nebraska and about my height and build. Finally, at the end of the supper line I see him.

I call out, "Hey, Burt, can I talk to you after supper?"

He shrugs. "Sure." Then he makes his way to the tables.

I pass off my job to a newbie. I go over to the same table and sit down with Burt. We eat in silence, and then when he's finished, he asks, "So what's up?"

I say to him, "Let's go somewhere a little quieter. I have a question for you." He follows me to the long hallway that was once lined with trophy cases. Now it holds lockers for the homeless to leave a few things in while they live on the street.

I pull up a straight-back chair, and he does the same. "I was wondering if you needed some winter clothes. I have some at the house, and we're about the same size. I was going to bring them to the Center and give them to you, but I feel bad about not having something for some of the others. We seem to have hit it off, and I want to do something for you."

He seems totally surprised but very appreciative. "I'd love to have some warmer clothes. I only have the summer clothes I came here with in July."

I ask the next question that I really need to be *no* for my plan to work. "Do you have anywhere to stay tonight?"

Burt answers, "Nope. I got here *too late* for a place in the auditorium. I've gotten a job, and sometimes I don't get off in time to get in line."

I clear my throat. "Why don't you come home with me tonight and try on the clothes and crash on my couch? I'm not to bring anyone from the Center home with me, but it's just for tonight. I won't tell if you won't."

He hesitates. I can tell he'd rather refuse. I quickly interject, "I'm not weird or anything. This is strictly a place to crash and about the clothes. Let me be totally honest. I think someone has been breaking into my house while I'm gone. I need someone to be leaving my house in the morning like they're going on a hike. I'm sorry if you feel used."

He relaxes with the truth. "Sure, I'll do it."

I grab my stuff, and we leave the Center. In the car, I tell Burt my plan.

"I'm going to let you off about a half a block from the house. I'll park in the back of the property in the garage, and the intruder leaves usually by the front door. I'd like for you to watch for someone to leave my house. Once he's gone, come to the house, and ring the doorbell, and I'll let you in."

He says, "Sounds fine with me. Do you want me to tackle the guy or anything?"

I answer, "No. I'm not sure if he's dangerous, and I don't want you to get hurt."

Burt says, "If you don't mind my asking, why don't you just tell the police?"

I try to choose my words carefully, and then I give up and decide the truth is better. "I don't trust some of the police, and I'm not sure who'll come to investigate. I knew a group of kids who were homeless, and I think that the police helped them to…"

He finishes my sentence, saying, "Freeze to death."

I say, "Yes, how did you know?"

He states, "I live on the streets most nights. It's one of the many things we hear from survivors. Some are Looney Tunes, but most are as sane as you or me."

I pull over and point to my house. I tell him to be safe. Burt gets out and sinks back against a tree, and soon I can't even tell where he's standing. I pull up to the house and park in the garage. I look at the cellar's exterior entrance as I walk to the front door. The door is ajar, and I enter like nothing is out of the ordinary. I search the upstairs and basement. I'm finishing the ground floor when the doorbell rings.

It's Burt. He enters, and we lock the door. "I didn't see anyone leave. I guess he left early today."

I thank him and show him the pile of clothes. He tries on clothes, and I give him a backpack to put them inside. We visit fairly late into the evening. I don't have anyone here to talk to, and I guess I was in need of a conversation fix.

"Here's a pillow and a blanket. I've shown you where the bathroom and kitchen are, so rest well. I'll see you in the morning."

Heading up the stairs, I hear him say, "Thanks, Liam. You don't know how nice it is to be in a house."

I go on up the stairs without commenting. I think to myself of how I should've brought him home a long time ago. Something kept telling me to help someone, and who did I help? Opportunistic Emily. I shake the thoughts of her from my head as I make my way to bed in the dark. I don't want anyone knowing there're two people in the house tonight.

The morning rolls around, and I tell Burt, "If you could wear my hoodie and jog to the convenience store on the corner. I'd appreciate it. I'll give you money for a breakfast and a sandwich. If anyone is watching, they'll think I'm hiking today. Keep your hood up, and the only one who'll know you aren't me will be Crystal, the clerk. I really appreciate this. Thanks."

Burt says, "Anytime. Hope you catch the guy."

Then we turn off the lights in the house, and he closes the door and pretends to lock and check it before jogging off toward the store.

Now I get my bat and go to the basement to sit in the shadows.

CHAPTER 46

RAMSTEIN, GERMANY—

JORDYN HEADS HOME TO OKLAHOMA

I fly down the ramp and see the stewardess
preparing to close the door to the plane.

Wednesday arrives, and Ken comes through the door, visibly excited. He throws his car keys on the table where a dish once sat, but it is now in a box. He neatly hangs his military dress jacket on the chair. As he strides across the room toward me, I can't help but think that he's the most handsome man in the world. He's so striking in his dress military uniform. He scoops me up, twirls me around, and gives me a very passionate kiss.

He succeeds in taking my breath away, and that is when he chooses to speak. "Jordyn! It's happened! I got the job to fly the figureheads of the United States back and forth to their meetings in the Middle East. We can live here or stateside." He pauses for effect.

I jump into the conversation with, "Stateside, of course! Oh, I can't wait to see my family. I knew I'd miss them; I just didn't realize how much."

Ken smiles. "I knew this would make you happy. You've seemed so distracted and sad lately that I felt like I had to do something."

I kiss him all over his face while saying, "Thank you, thank you."

He takes me by the hand and leads me to the couch. We sit down. "We're scheduled to leave by noon. I hope you left a change of clothes out for me. I need to take a shower and shave."

I nearly scream, "You bet! I thought you might want to do that."

He pauses and squeezes my hands. "There's one catch. *Both* of us need to take the pledge of allegiance to the New World Government. It won't take long. We're only pledging not to cause any dissention while the world government is trying to make all the different cultures gel together."

My mouth drops open to protest, but he rushes on. "I've read the pledge, and it says we promise to do our best to bring peace to this war-torn world. We promise to look at others with differing views with a broad lens of acceptance. It states that our allegiance is to the One World Vision of harmony among its people. We are to focus on our similarities and not our differences. If we see someone or something happening to prevent peace or harmony from growing, we're obligated as good citizens to report it."

I see the sincerity in his eyes, and I feel the love that's in his heart. I know Ken believes we can make a pledge of allegiance and that's all that'll be demanded of us. I hope he's right.

"Fine."

He hugs me tight. "Thank you. I'm trying to do what is right for all of us."

We jump up from the couch. I head for the closet and lay out the one set of his clothes I hadn't packed.

He calls out, "I brought home my duffle of dirty clothes. I'll go outside and get them."

I take this time to fire off a text to Masen on Ken's cell: *Ken and I are coming stateside. We'll be in United States by tomorrow. When I know where we arrive, I'll text you. Love, Jordyn.*

I have my bag packed with the extra passport in the bottom lining of the bag. I have a separate suitcase for Ken. That way if he has to stay on base, he'll have his things and I'll have mine. Ken returns and kisses me on the top of the head and heads for the shower. I smile, but I think to myself that something isn't right. I can't put my finger on it, but I feel that Ken is uneasy about something.

The car arrives to take us to the base. Ken and I are so excited to be heading home. We giggle and snuggle in the town car's backseat all the way to the base. We park in the high-rise parking garage and go to the office number given to us to take our pledges. I put it out of my mind that I'm pledging my allegiance to anywhere other than my United States. I still can't believe the United States is a part of the larger group called the One World Government. I can't read the German newspapers, and the television is in German as well. I suppose my brothers and sisters will fill me in when I get home.

Ken and I walk into the room, and I'm smiling so big I can't stop. There's a captain or something behind the desk and a man in the corner with some boxes. I give my attention to the captain and Ken as we say our pledge. Then the man says something in German, and Ken turns white as a sheet.

I whisper, "What's wrong?"

Ken smiles and locks his eyes with mine as if willing me to stay calm as he relays in English what was said. "Jordyn, you won't believe this. They've thought of everything. We get our tattoo before leaving today. This gentleman is the best at world tattoos. I was told we'd have to do that part when we were in the United States. Can you believe our luck?"

I smile, but I feel like I'm going to lose my breakfast. I giggle and clutch the driver's arm and ask him, "Excuse me, but where is the restroom? I'm liable to have an accident if I don't go to the restroom first."

The junior officer points to the hall, and I exit before Ken can argue or grab my arm. I saw that our driver placed his keys in his jacket pocket. I slipped them out when I asked for directions to the restroom. The officers stop my escape, and I giggle, cross my legs, and say *restroom* in English. They point to the bathroom. There's a window. I climb out, and I'm on the top level of the parking garage. I run to the elevator and hit number ten. We parked three levels below this one. I find the town car, and I'm backing out when I see Ken driving down the ramp on the aisle opposite me in a matching town car. I don't know where he came up with a car unless they sent him after me.

There are two rows of cars between us. He is racing to cut me off. In order to beat him to the next level division, I'll have to drive backward. To take the time to turn around will give him the advantage, and he'll be able to cut me off. *Thank you, Lord, for preparing me for this moment; you gave me practice chasing the cows and bulls that got out back in Oklahoma. I drove in reverse more than in drive.* With the gear shift in reverse, I floor the accelerator. *Please, Lord, don't let anyone back out of any of these parking spaces.*

Ken and I are flying parallel to each other, Ken traveling forward and me backward, both of us trying to reach the exit first. I hear his engine change a gear as I push the accelerator harder. I stop looking at Ken and start watching the exit opening. I'm upon it. I'll have to slow up just enough so that as I brake, turn the wheel, and spin the car, I'll be facing forward. I glance as I leave this level and see Ken get cut off by a car backing out. He hits them head-on. *Lord, thank you, but please keep Ken and the other driver safe.*

I race to the bottom of the parking garage. I drive straight to the airport. I park the car and run to the ticket counter. "When is your first available flight to the United States?" I grab my bag, and I reach into the false bottom and pull out my old passport with my maiden name and my ticket. It was a ticket I could use anytime as long as there was a seat available. I send another prayer, *Lord, let there be a seat for me, please.*

The man at the ticket booth eyes me skeptically. I only have my backpack.

I add to my request, "My father is ill, and I must get home as soon as possible. Please, can you get me a flight?"

With the explanation of my lack of bags and disheveled appearance, he begins to search rapidly. He looks up. "There's one boarding now at gate thirteen. If you run, you can make it." I hand him my ticket. He stamps it, and I take off. I weave in and out of people. Hearing the last boarding call, I sprint faster.

I hand my ticket to the gate personnel just as he is beginning to close the door to the ramp. He opens the door and calls, "Hurry!"

I fly down the ramp and see the stewardess preparing to close the door to the plane. She sees me, smiles, and steps out of my way.

Huffing and puffing "Thank you" is all I can manage.

I'm escorted by another stewardess to a seat at the back of the plane. I collapse next to a grandmotherly woman, buckle in, lay my head back, and concentrate on breathing. I feel the plane begin to taxi into position. I keep my eyes closed, and if I didn't need oxygen so desperately, I'd hold my breath until we take off. We begin to pick up speed. I grab the armrests. The plane accelerates more, and we lift off. I hear the landing gear click into place as I open my eyes. The stewardess is staring at me.

"Take-offs and landings scare me a little."

She doesn't smile and hands me my ticket stub. I watch her take her seat at the back of the plane close to me. I wonder if the air force flagged my name before I was aboard the plane. I may be picked up at the airport when I touch down in New York. I'll cross that bridge when I come to it. *Lord, thank you for watching over me and getting me this far. Please help Ken too.*

I don't think he knew about the mandatory tattoo. I have to believe that, but why did I run from him if I trusted him completely? I wish I could talk to him. I don't know how to function without a phone. I feel totally vulnerable and alone. I look in my pocket wallet, and I have my credit cards, driver's license, and about two hundred dollars. I know I can't use the cards because that will alert everyone to my whereabouts. *Lord, help me to somehow get to my brothers and sisters.*

CHAPTER 47

OKLAHOMA—JATHYN FACES
HIS GREATEST FEAR

*If it was one of you, would you give them
more time and wait on them?*

Masen pulls me aside as the rest of the kids are sleeping. We step to the gated entrance.

"We haven't heard from Dad and Mom, and I'm worried. We need to find out where they've taken them and try to help them."

I stare out the barred doorway to keep from making eye contact with my brother. "Dad told us both that if they were arrested we were *not* to try to find them. We were to be patient and wait for things to settle down. It might be a long time."

Masen faces me; I can feel it. I keep my eyes glued to the horizon. He takes a step close and whisper-shouts, "I know what Dad said, but we have to do something!"

I inhale a big breath of air. "We are. We're watching over the family. If you want to worry about something, where are Eli, Fuller, and Gus? They should've been here by now."

Masen breathes out a heavy sigh. "You're right. It's crossed my mind too. They live the closest, so I thought maybe they were watchdogging it for all of us."

I face him now. "Watchdogging? What are you talking about?"

Masen swings his head and dips it to the right, motioning me to move farther around the corner for this conversation. "You know, keeping a watch for *someone* to show up. Eli said he'd be careful and not take chances. You know as well as I do that Liam should be here by now."

I stare at the floor, step around the boulder, and peek at the group. "I know. I thought of the same thing. Do you think we should go check out their house? Maybe something happened. Maybe one of them got hurt and the others refused to leave him?"

Masen says, "I'm going to the arrowhead pit. The snakes should be back to bed by now. If they came in after the snakes were awake, they could be waiting at the pond for the snakes to settle down before coming inside."

I can't believe I hadn't thought about how dangerous it would be for them to come into the cave behind me. "I hope they're okay. Do you want me to go with you?"

Masen says, "No, I'll take my partners. I think it's too soon for you to go back there."

I'm so grateful that all I can do is nod in agreement.

Masen walks over to the little boys and tells them his plan. They grab their flashlights and head to the tunnels.

They return after what feels like an eternity. They have Gus with them but no one else. By the look on their faces, something is wrong.

Jaylie runs to them. "What's wrong? Where's everybody?"

Masen directs Gus to the fire pit. He sits down. Jax and Zayne flank Gus on either side. These three cousins are the closest of all of us. They were born within a month of each other, and our families have lived within five miles of each other all their lives. Masen turns to the rest of us as we all take a seat, forming a circle.

Masen leans back against one of the pillars supporting the ceiling. "Gus is the only one coming. The militia came to the house and took Eli and Fuller with them. Gus was in the attic of the garage, looking for some camping equipment. I'll let him tell you the rest of his story when he's ready."

Jaylie says to Gus, "I'm so sorry your brothers aren't with you, but we'll find them. I know we will."

Gus meets her gaze. "Thanks. If Liam would hurry up and get here, then he could help me. I thought it was him arriving when the militia showed up. It was about the right amount of time for Liam to have driven to Oklahoma. *If* he started when his text said he did." He stares into the fire without blinking and continues his thought. "He should've been here at the latest this morning. When he didn't come, I came out of the garage attic and began making my way over here. I was waiting at the pond for him. These guys made me come to the cave when we heard a helicopter."

Jax gets up and moves around the fire, pacing. "It wasn't safe. They could see us, and it might jeopardize all our safeties. If they have heat-sensing devices, they could see you even if you hid under a tree."

Zayne puts his arm around Gus's shoulders. "I'm sorry. We'll go look as soon as the helicopters are gone. I know how much you love Liam. He'll be here."

Masen barks, "No, he won't; he ratted us out. None of us are safe! Liam must've told them about the cave. Why else would they be circling this area over and over again? Gus, you've got to *man up* and help us by being a contributing member of *this* group. We need you as much as *you* need us."

Gus fires back, "I don't need you. I need Liam. He'll be here. He texted me. He e-mails me often. We can trust him." Gus begins to tear but wills himself to not cry. I can tell because of his body language. He's stiff as a board, with his fists clenched and his jaw set.

Masen states quietly, "We're keeping everyone safe. Everyone knows the drill. If we become separated, we head to one of the safe spots and wait."

Gus fumes, "That's what I was trying to do at the pond. I was waiting. Liam *will* come, and he won't know I'm here. If he goes into the cave and the snakes are active, he could be bitten."

"Jathyn, can we get to the pond over land?" Gus asks, ignoring everyone else.

I look at Masen and the others. "I don't know for sure, but I don't think so. You have to go to the road about a half a mile away, follow a road one and a half miles west and then north a mile, and follow the tracks across the pasture and come in the only way we know to get here."

Gus pleads with us, "If it was one of you, would you give them more time and wait on them?"

Lia immediately pipes up, "Sure, we would." When she realizes it's only her voice to say this out loud, she doubts herself. "Wouldn't we?"

I stand next to Gus. "Of course we would. We would never abandon any one of you." I turn to Masen. "Were the snakes active when you came through a while ago?"

Masen eyes me skeptically. "What are you thinking?"

"I'm thinking that Gus and I can go back and stay out of sight at the pond. We'll be careful to duck back into the cave if we hear the helicopters," I answer.

Masen broods. Lips paper-thin, he stomps off to the gate. Jax follows and touches his sleeve. "Let's pray." Masen looks at him and relaxes.

Masen walks back to the group. "Let's pray. Grab a hand." We gather in a circle. "Lord, please give us direction. Give us peace with our decision. Please protect Liam until he can make it to us. Amen."

Masen tells Malorie, "Find us some of the checker tokens that are black on one side and white on the other." She returns with the black-and-white disks. Masen tells us, "Everyone take one token. Now pray for God to show you which color to choose. White, Jathyn and Gus go to the pond. Black, we stay hidden."

We all turn our backs to the center of the circle. Then we turn to face the center of the circle. When the last one has turned, we open our hands at the same time to show our votes. They are all white. Now I say a silent prayer for God to keep us safe through the tunnels and the snake pit. I replace the batteries in my flashlight with fresh ones. Jax gives Gus his flashlight because he left in such a hurry that he didn't bring anything. I caution Gus, "If you need to say something to me, whisper it. The cave echoes. People can hear us for up to a quarter of a mile. Remember, I'm the boss. You have to do what I say, no matter what. Do you understand?"

Gus says, "Yes, I understand. I appreciate what you are doing for me and my brother. Thank you, Jathyn. I know he hasn't been nice to you in the past."

Masen walks us to the tunnels. "Remember to look for the notches at the top of the openings to tell which way to go. Hope you bring back Liam."

I doubt I'll ever forget the notches again. We take off, and my light is much brighter this time. We don't see or hear a thing. It's dark when we get to the opening. We sit in the cedars overlooking the pond, not saying a word. We are in our own world, hidden from prying eyes. Gus never takes his eyes off the pasture road. It's as if he thinks he can *will* Liam to come.

By morning, the helicopters are in the sky and circling the area. We head back to the cave before they're within range. I go first, looking for snakes. It's been good to face my fear. We make it back in great time. Gus is sullen and withdrawn.

Zayne goes over to him. "I know what it feels like to be the only cousin without a sibling here."

Gus looks up. "Thanks for the thought, but I don't feel like talking."

CHAPTER 48

COLORADO—LIAM IS TAKEN CAPTIVE

I have to warn Gus and save myself
as well as the family.

I don't have to wait long before I hear the door to the cellar open. Whoever this is has been close enough to see my house. I'm ready to swing, and what little conscience I have begins to eat on me. I grip my bat and move to the shelving unit that covers the entrance from outside. I hear the crunch of heavy footsteps on the concrete stairs. Whoever this is hasn't stolen anything but some food and Internet access. The brush of material scrapes the wall and the shelves as the person squeezes between the two. It could be a kid who wants to stay connected with home and is hungry. Then the figure steps into the room. I can take this guy down with one swing, but I know better than anyone a person can die from a blow to the head.

I call out, "Stop!"

The person turns and faces me in the dark. "It's me, Harrison."

I flip on my flashlight and see my worst nightmare standing before me. A part of me is glad to see him because he brings something familiar to my life. But another part of me wishes I'd have beamed him and knocked him out so I could figure out what to do without him twisting my thoughts.

I command, "Go upstairs to the kitchen, slowly."

He turns and begins up the stairs, talking all the way. "I've missed you. I'm sorry I've been sneaking into your house. I needed a place to stay, and you were the only person I knew. My folks are in jail, and I've been staying with my cousin in Texas. When we read in the paper your grandma left you a house in Boulder, we headed this way. I saw the picture you posted on Facebook, and we were able to find it. I figured you wouldn't help me since I wouldn't help you after the church deal."

Then I think I hear a creak of one of the steps behind me, but before I can turn, I'm struck from behind, and *my* lights go out.

I wake on the couch on my back porch. Harrison and Emily are enjoying a cup of coffee at the table and staring at me. I'm immediately filled with rage at the very sight of Emily. I try to jump up, and my head throbs so severely that I vomit.

Harrison says, "Settle down, Liam. Lie down and listen to us."

He said *us*! He is with this demon woman? It makes sense that the devil in my life is with her. I lie down as my head throbs with each beat of my heart.

Emily speaks this time. "Liam, I want you to meet my cousin."

I close my eyes and feel extremely weak. I want to say something, but I can't. I know I'm passing out again because everything is going black.

When I wake again, the house is dark, and I hear the television in the other room. I try to focus. I don't see anyone on the porch with me. It's cold. I'm shivering. I think to myself that they could've at least covered me with a blanket. I can hear them talking.

Harrison says, "Don't worry. I'll send an e-mail to the Servants' Center stating that Liam has the flu. It's his account, so no one will doubt that it's not him. The old man never comes over, and we had the old lady picked up."

Emily asks, "What about Liam's classes? He never misses a class, so the New World Program monitors may check on him."

Harrison says, "Stop worrying. Nothing is going to go wrong. After turning in that militant homeless group for not conforming to any of the government's demands, we're way ahead of schedule for a pay promotion. If we can figure out the exact location of Liam's family, we will meet our goal."

Emily asks, "What's happening in Oklahoma?"

Harrison answers, "I've been in constant contact with Gus, Liam's younger brother, and he told me he was going to meet the rest of his cousins at the pond. I know where the pond is. I just don't know why they're meeting there. Maybe there's a hideout of some sort. I've asked Gus to be specific about where he'll meet me."

Emily asks the question that troubles me: "Won't this Gus be a little leery of you?"

My thoughts exactly. Hearing this makes my lying still and pretending to still be knocked out that much harder. I'm freezing on the outside and burning up with anger on the inside.

Harrison says, "I told you not to worry. I've been using Liam's e-mail account and texting him with his phone. I erased my messages so Liam would remain in the dark as I tightened the net around his family. I know they'll never pledge, so they'll all be eligible for merit pay. Gus is the only one who may pledge just so he can be near his beloved Liam. He loves the fact that I, the fake Liam, always tell him the truth about himself."

There's laughter from the kitchen, and then I hear footsteps. I close my eyes and try to remain limp, but the shaking keeps my body in motion.

Emily says, "Aw, he's cold. Do you think I should cover him up?" I bet she's smiling.

Harrison says, "No. If he dies out here from natural causes, that will be best. If he's still alive by morning, we'll figure out what to do then. You need to stay up and watch him. He may try to run. That'll decide what we do for sure. I'll relieve you at about one o'clock tonight, and I'll take the rest of the night. I'm going to get some shut-eye."

I hear steps retreating but only one set. I know Emily is in the room. I can hear her breathing. She is so close I can feel her brush against me. I'd like nothing better than to jump up and break her neck like she did Streak's. But I have to remain in control. I have to warn Gus and save myself as well as the family.

CHAPTER 49

OKLAHOMA—JATHYN'S HIDEOUT IS FOUND!

What have you done? Who are you texting?

Lia and Jaylie are playing Old Maid at the back of the quarried room. Malorie is looking through the choices of canned goods for lunch.

I'm at the gated opening with the rest of the boys. The topic of conversation is how safe our hideout is. We all hush at the same time and listen as the sound of the rotary blades of the helicopter cease.

Masen is first to voice our collective concern. "I think it landed at the pond."

I look at the girls playing their card game at the tunnel entrance opening. They're giggling and talking in their normal voices. That isn't unusual, but we now have reason to believe someone can hear us. I sprint to the back of the room and whisper to them, "*Shhh*. I think we could have company. Pack up in case we have to leave in a hurry."

Lia looks terrified and stares at the tunnel as if waiting for someone to come through. I motion to Jaylie to get moving.

"Okay, buddy up. Help each other brainstorm on what we'll need to take."

I gently help Lia stand. I turn her to face me. "Tell me the scripture that will help me. I need my buddy more than ever."

The fear begins to leave her face. She whispers back, "You can do all things through Christ who strengthens you." I am so glad to see my brave little sister isn't going to go to pieces on me. "Thanks, I needed that. Let's get ready. Can you pack your own bag?"

She nods and turns her head to the tunnels as we hear voices echoing into the chamber, "Hey, bring me a flashlight! I've got a cave here." She sprints off and begins packing as I run back to Masen.

I whisper, "Did you hear that?"

Masen nods. "We'll head for the outlaw cave that's in Salt Creek. Get packed. We don't have much time."

Everyone has at least a large bottle of water and one can of food. Whatever we deem necessary. We check the packs for weight and find Lia's to be way too heavy for her to make it that far. We unload a few things, oil the hinges, and remind everyone to try to not leave a footprint.

Masen motions for us to huddle close. "We'll stay on the caprock for as far as we can. Then we'll make our way down into a ravine that leads to the bottom of the gypsum hills. We'll follow the heavily wooded bottom to Salt Creek and make our way up the canyon. Everyone find your buddy and remember our order: my group first, Jathyn's group last, and everyone else in between. Do your best to help each other and keep up. I'm going to set a fast pace."

We line up with Gus off by himself, texting. I jump to his side and grab his phone. His text reads, *Moving to new hideout. Come to cave on Salt Creek Canyon.*

I explode in a loud whisper, "What have you done? Who are you texting?"

Gus is taken aback by my outburst, and he stammers, "I… my… brother, Liam, of course. How will he find us? If we leave, he'll have to know where we went."

Masen is by our sides. "What's going on here? We have to leave now!"

Gus fills him in and begins to protest aloud when I rip his phone open and begin to pry the GPS tracking chip out of the phone. I grind it with my foot and then scatter it in the portable toilet. Masen clamps his hand over Gus's mouth.

We hear echoes from the tunnel. "I think I heard someone. This way."

Gus's eyes widen, and he stops struggling. Masen keeps his hand in place and whispers softly into Gus's ear, "Your texts and e-mails are the only thing that told anyone where we were hiding. We know you believe and love your brother, but think about it. You're endangering all of our lives when you aren't truthful. You have to believe us. We'll talk when we're safe." He releases his hand, runs to the front of our line, and exits at a trot.

I grab Gus. "You're in my group. Stay with me, and you've got the mountain pack with the sleeping bags. If you need help carrying them, I'll trade you my pack, but it isn't much lighter."

Gus doesn't say a word and follows. I put the pieces of his phone in my pocket to assemble later. I stop long enough to lock the gate. When whoever is following us gets this far, they'll have to go back to the pond because they can't get through the gate. My crew brings up the end.

CHAPTER 50

NEW YORK—JORDYN ARRIVES STATESIDE

*The only family member who's in a town
where he could disappear is Liam.*

The stewardess at the back of the plane eyes me suspiciously.

I'm sick about Ken. What if he was trying to run away with me? What if I left him hanging all alone? I don't know what's happened to him, but I know he'll find me if he can. I can't believe he'd turn his own wife in to the government. As we unload, I slip by passengers lingering with their belongings whenever I can. When I get to the ramp, I hurry until the end and peer out to see if the police are waiting.

I don't see any, so I exit with a group of exchange students. I mingle with them until we're in the crowd in the terminal. I don't have any luggage, so I head for the nearest exit. I see some police running to my gate. As I'm leaving the building, I see them talking to the stewardess who was so skeptical of me. I see her scanning the crowd.

I don't wait to be seen but jump into the first cab and ask, "Can you take me to the Empire State Building? I'm to meet my fiancé there. We're going to meet on the top floor just like from the movie."

The cabbie says, "Sure, lady. It'll be about twenty bucks."

I straighten my clothes and fuss with my hair. "Fine."

He asks, "You don't have any luggage you need to pick up?"

I grin at his reflection in the mirror. "We're pretending I just came back from Paris. He dropped me off earlier. I didn't really go anywhere on a plane. We live in Brooklyn. It's silly, I know, but I wanted to do something special for my birthday."

He asks sarcastically, "Okay, are we in a hurry in your pretend world?"

I give him my best pouty face. "Yes. I'm meeting the love of my life."

I worry that if they're looking for a fugitive, they'll ask the cab companies for the ones who took fares to bus or train stations. I looked up the Greyhound bus station address before Ken picked me up this morning. I wish I had my cell phone. The bus station is about a half a mile from the Empire State Building. I figure if I jog I might be able to get out of town before the net closes around me. I shake my head and think to myself that I've lost all touch with reality. I just ran away from my husband. What was I thinking?

The cab pulls to the curb. "Twenty bucks. Enjoy your birthday."

I look bewildered, and then I remember my lie. "Thanks. Hope you have a great day." I look up at the building and watch him pull away. When he's out of sight, I check my bearings. I jog down Fifth Avenue, turn on Thirty-Third to Seventh, and then hurry up to the station. The lights are all in my favor, and I don't have to slow down at the crosswalks.

The first thing I do is find a pay phone and call the house. A stranger answers and says the people who used to live there were found to be terrorists and are in a training center. I get the same thing when I call Uncle Nic's, but there's no answer at Aunt Jennifer's house. I try Masen's cell, but I get no answer to any of the family members' phones.

Lost, I blend in with a group from the Midwest. I pick up an old newspaper and read that since the restructuring, young children are in schools managed by the government. My stomach does a flip. *What if they have my brothers and sisters?* It says they are being trained in the basics of peace and harmony. My brothers are old enough to be in jeopardy of being forced into service of the government or, worse, arrested for not conforming. They won't denounce that Christ isn't God's Son. And I'm sure they wouldn't receive the tattoo, so they may have been shot! This government isn't going to mess around with anyone who doesn't obey them.

Where would the kids go? Think, Jordyn. The only family member who's in a town where he could disappear is Liam. He inherited that house of Gram's in Boulder, and it's a college town. There will be lots of kids. That has to be where they would go.

I jump up and ask the first window when the first bus to Denver leaves. They tell me in the morning at nine thirty. I take it and glance around to find an out-of-the-way place to avoid the camera's eye while I wait.

Morning arrives before I know it, and I board the bus headed to Denver. I remember my last text to Masen was right after Gram's will was read. I hope Masen knows what he's talking about when he says Liam is a changed man. I know my brothers and sisters are in hiding. I'm sure they have probably met up with our cousins by now as well. My folks and aunts and uncles are in prison, or as the government would like me to believe, retraining centers. If I go home and begin looking at all of the possible places the kids are hiding, I might inadvertently give away their hiding place. If things heat up, they'll make their way to Liam because he has a house and likes his privacy off the grid. Also, it's a town with lots of college students. They would blend in and be hidden among the masses.

I almost miss my first bus transfer daydreaming about Ken. I'll have five more to go in the next two days.

My stomach growls, and the lady sitting next to me offers, "Would you like a cracker?" She holds out a sealed peanut butter cracker pack.

I lick my lips. "Thank you. Do you have some for yourself? I don't want to take your last snack."

She pats me on the right hand with her gloved one. "I'm fine. I don't have far to go. I get off at the next stop."

I gobble the crackers down. I hadn't realized how hungry I was. When I added the hours from my house to the air force base to New York to my present position, it's been thirty-one hours since I last ate.

We stop to transfer to another bus and a short pit stop. The lady says, "Take these. You may need them before you arrive at your destination. God bless and keep you safe." She shoves three more packets of crackers into my hand.

I'm shocked that she added the blessing. I notice she didn't have the tattoo of the world either. She slips on her gloves again and bids me, "Good-bye."

I finally find my tongue. "Thank you and same to you." I make eye contact and nod slowly to affirm that I too am a believer in Christ.

She pats my right hand again and is gone. I look down and notice that my lack of a tattoo sticks out like a sore thumb. I must be more careful to conceal that I don't have the mark. I slip my hand into my pocket, and it remains there whenever I'm around people. I look for some cheap gloves and find some for a dollar. I use the last of my money to purchase them. I watch a little girl who has a water bottle. When she throws it away, I scoop it out of the trash and take it to the restroom. I wash it with soap and water and fill it with tap water before returning to my bus.

There are police asking to see everyone's identification as they board the bus. I catch up with a group that has just pulled in from another bus and walk with them as they enter the terminal to refresh themselves. I make my way through the building and out the opposite door.

CHAPTER 51

COLORADO—LIAM FAKES AMNESIA

I hear the shuffling of footsteps
retreating down the upstairs hall.

When I'm sure Harrison is upstairs and sound asleep, I pretend to wake up and have amnesia.

"Emily, what happened? My head is killing me. Did I fall? Thank you so much, baby, for staying with me." I sit up and act weak. I can tell I'm stronger, but I have a terrific headache.

Emily plays along like I thought she would. "Oh, Liam, you had me so worried." She begins to kiss me all over my face. I return her kisses and vow to myself that this will be the best performance of my life. Harrison taught me to lie and deceive people with my actions. It's war when you pick on my family, and I'm ready to do battle.

I repeat, "What happened to me? Why am I on the porch?"

Emily thinks quickly on her feet. "You thought you heard someone in the basement. You fell, and this is as far as I could get you before you passed out."

I ask innocently, "Why didn't you call an ambulance?"

She states, "You wouldn't let me. You made me promise not to call anyone. I don't know why."

I say, "Let's go up to bed. I want to feel you by my side. I'm freezing." I stand and start for the kitchen door.

She's at my side and helps me. "Oh, baby, I'm so glad you're okay!" she exclaims loudly as we make our way across the room. She brushes a plate, sending it crashing to the floor.

I stop and ask, "Are you all right?"

She looks past me up the stairs, and I pretend not to notice. "I'm fine. Let's get you to bed."

I hear the shuffling of footsteps retreating down the upstairs hall.

Emily tucks me in. "I'm going to get ready for bed. I'll come to bed in a little while." She closes the door.

I look around the room for my phone. I can't remember when I last saw it. I listen, and I can hear hushed whispers, but I can't understand a word they're saying. I go back to concentrating on where my phone might be, and it comes to me—in the basement!

The doorknob turns slowly; I roll over and pretend to be asleep. The door opens and then closes. Soon I feel Emily's warm body next to mine. I close my eyes and will away the yearning I have to roll over and hold her in my arms.

The next morning, I'm up early and fix breakfast for us. I check on her once, and she is sound asleep. I dress for work and set the table. Then I slip down into the basement. I hear my phone vibrating, and I find it under the steps.

It's under the stairs. The incoming text is from Gus. I quickly open it and he says. *We're moving to Salt Creek Canyon.* That's all it says. I'm so thankful that they at least have a fighting chance. I fire back a reply: *Phone and e-mail jeopardized. Not me. Don't trust written communication. Don't contact me again. It's not safe. Someone stole my identity, and I'm going to get it back. Trust messages with our secret word only. Love you. Be safe.*

I dump all texts, and then I decide I need to destroy this phone. I hear footsteps coming down the upstairs staircase. I rush into the kitchen just as the woman of my nightmares appears around the corner.

I smile. "Thanks for keeping me warm all night. I hate to run, but I made your favorite for breakfast. I need to get to work. I can't afford to have a smaller paycheck now that we're a couple." I give her a long kiss, and then I exit the house.

I leave in the car without anyone stopping me. I think about telling the police, but I know Harrison wouldn't hesitate to tell them about the death of the preacher. No, I've got to keep close to Emily in the hopes of keeping track of what they're up to so I can head them off. I have to make sure my family is safe. This is war now.

I hold off destroying my phone in case they need to contact me, and I forward to Masen the same text I just sent Gus.

I send Gus an e-mail.

Hey, Gus, I forgot to ask you to check Scruffy's shots record. He may need to go to the vet soon. Your bro

CHAPTER 52

OKLAHOMA—JATHYN GETS READY TO GO TO COLORADO

I'd like to go with Jathyn. After all, he's my partner.

We get to the outlaw hideout, and it's cramped compared to the quarried-out chamber room. Masen calls a family meeting.

"Everyone sit down, please. We need to brainstorm about our next move."

Gus is the first to say something. "I'm sorry, everyone. I never thought about leading the police to our hideout. I don't think it was my brother who turned us in though. I trust him, I *know* he loves me. I'm all he has. He told me so!" Gus gets up and leaves the group and turns his back to us. We all know he's probably crying, and none of us wants to embarrass him, so we leave him alone.

Masen goes after him and brings him back to the group. "You're right, Gus. Liam is on our side. I just got an e-mail from him that said not to trust communications from him unless he used a secret word that only you and he knew. Someone is impersonating him." Gus gives Masen a huge bear hug.

I agree, "It wasn't Liam. I think it was the GPS in Gus's phone. The police have Eli and Fuller, and so they put a trace on his phone, obviously."

Gus looks at each of us. "I'm so lucky to have all of you."

Masen says, "Well, we can't be sure of anything. If they were watching his phone, then they know his last transmission. That told that we were coming here. This is a little-known cave, but folks from around here know about it. It's been in stories forever. It was in a published book. We have to assume our safety here is limited."

Malorie asks, "Can we go get the pickup and drive somewhere next time?" while she massages her sore feet.

Masen and I both look at each other with the same expression. "Malorie, you're right. We need to get the pickup. If no one has found it, we can drive to Boulder and hide out at Liam's. What do you think, Gus?"

Gus returns to the group. "You'd go to Boulder? You'd let Liam prove himself?"

Jaylie looks at him with furrowed eyebrows. "Duh? What does he have to prove? He's family, isn't he?"

Zayne asks, "Where is Liam's address?"

Gus looks panicked. "I don't know his address."

Jax asks, "How will we find him? Boulder is huge. It probably has a million people living there."

I look out the opening of the cave. "You're right, Boulder is big, but not a million people, only about a hundred thousand maybe."

Masen stands beside me. "That's still too many. Can you fix Gus's phone? We can call for directions once we get there."

Gus says, "I remember Liam told me he works at the Servants' Center on campus. He serves the homeless."

Masen says, "I'm impressed. It sounds like Liam is just the guy we need right now."

Gus asks, "Can I tell him we're coming? Please."

Masen says, "Sure, but you need to use my phone. We can't risk that your phone may be being monitored. Make it a short text and be sure to use that secret word before you tell him much."

Hi, Liam,

It was good to hear from you. I'll take Scruffy first thing in the morning. Keep your eyes peeled Scruffy and I might drop in to see you. I think if we started now we could make it by morning. Watch for us. LOL. Gus

Lia has been reading her Bible all this time, and she reads aloud, "Luke 12:52–53, from now on there will be five in one family divided against each other, three against two and two against three. They will be divided, father against son and son against father, mother against daughter and daughter against mother, mother-in-law against daughter-in-law and daughter-in-law against mother-in-law."

We're all silent, each of us deciding what that means to us personally.

Lia looks up and sees the confusion on our faces. "Yes, there will be some families that turn on each other, but those who are a part of God's family will bind together and stand firm. We'll stand together united and focused on Christ. We'll let Christ lead us like Daddy said, and Jesus *will* lead us home."

Masen mumbles, "Out of the mouths of babes. All of you rest until dark because we'll have to walk all the way home to the pickup. It'll be quite a long walk."

I step back into the cave. "Why can't I go alone and bring the pickup to the group? There's less chance of seeing one person than eight. I can do this, Masen. You need to stay with the group in case I don't make it back. It'll either mean that the truck is gone or that someone caught me. Either way, we won't have so many people vulnerable if it goes bad."

Gus chimes in, "I'd like to go with Jathyn. After all, he's my partner."

Lia steps forward and insists, "Me too."

Masen puts his hands on Lia's and Gus's shoulders. "Your sentiments are duly noted, but Jathyn can make better time alone. Gus, I'll need you and Lia to make up the last pair of our group when we move out. I'll be counting on you guys to take care of brushing out our tracks. Can you do that for us?"

Gus and Lia exchange glances and seem satisfied. "Sure," they say in unison.

I climb to the top of the caprock to get my directions down before nightfall. As soon as it starts to become twilight, I take off as fast as I can across the pastures. I know I can't risk a fall, so I slow down as the night becomes darker. I realize that I can see pretty well even without my flashlight. I look up, and a full moon is riding high in the sky. I think, *Thanks, Lord.*

I keep jogging. It takes me a little over two hours to reach the timber where the pickup is parked. I approach slowly, and then I see it. A reflection off the windshield breaks through the trees. I look around for any sign that someone is out tonight. I see nothing, so I climb into the pickup, reach under the seat, and grab the waiting keys.

I look one last time and then turn the key. She fires right away, and I pull out slowly and carefully. I make my way across the pastures. I turn at the irrigation field and drive along the fence to the main dirt road instead of going by our house. I'd love to see how the animals are doing, but I can't. I check my gas gauge and find it's full. I guess no one has bothered anything since we left. I pause to call Masen.

"On the way. Will pick you up at the highway."

He answers, "Okay. We'll be there."

We hang up, and even if our phone numbers were being watched for use, we weren't on long enough to be traced. I pull up to an oil lease road when Masen pops out from behind a tree. Masen and I hook up the lights on the tailgate so we aren't stopped, and we head toward Colorado. Everyone settles in to take a nap under the pickup bed camper shell. Masen and I are the only ones up front.

I take the passenger's side. "We ought to be in Boulder by sunrise. Gus said Liam almost always serves breakfasts."

Masen pulls away. "Yep. Lord willing, we should be there by morning. You did a great job, Jathyn."

"Thanks, but what about our little sister? Lia blew me away with her insight of what standing firm truly means." I beam with pride almost as bright as the full moon.

Masen adds, "We're so fortunate to know who to believe in and from where our strength comes."

CHAPTER 53

St. Louis, Missouri—Jordyn Trusts the Holy Spirit

*God wouldn't have brought you here unless
there was someone who could help you.*

I step into an abandoned church that's door is ajar, sit in the last pew, and bow my head as I begin to pray. *I can't do this alone. I'm out of money, and I'm in a town I don't know. I don't know what to do next. Please, Lord, help me!*

I look up, and a priest is standing before me. "I'm sorry. I needed a place to rest and pray. I'll be on my way." I get up to leave.

He holds up his hand. "Wait. You came for a reason. Rest awhile, and we'll talk. You're safe. If we hear someone approaching the church, follow me quietly, and I'll get you out safely. Who is it you run from, girl?"

I correct him, "I'm running *to* my brothers and sisters. They need me. I feel it. I know it. I ask God to show me a way."

He sits in the pew in front of me. "Do you know anyone in the area?"

I answer quickly, "No."

He patiently says, "Are you sure? God wouldn't have brought you here unless there was someone who could help you."

I never thought about my movements as God-driven. I knew he was protecting me. Jesse pops into my head.

The priest notices that I sit up straight. "What has the Holy Spirit told you?"

I stay with my thoughts of Jesse while the priest talks. I remember he went to train school. He was training to be an engineer or something. "Where's the nearest train terminal for freight?"

He smiles. "It's quite close. It's two blocks north and four blocks east. Be watchful. I'll pray for your safe passage."

I squeeze his hand. "Thank you." I make it to the door and ask, "Which way is north?"

He points, and I sprint away. I enter the train yard and see men in uniforms from the different railway divisions. I walk up to a group of men and ask, "Can you help me find a cousin? His name is Jesse…"

"Jordyn, is that you?" Jesse asks as he approaches the group.

I turn, and there's Jesse. I almost cry. *Thank you, Lord.* "Yes, it's me. I'm so glad I found you." I turn back to the men. "Thank you but it looks like he found me." They nod and go their separate ways, leaving us all alone.

Jesse asks, "What are you doing here?"

I never thought about what I'd say. So I just tell him the truth. I tell him the whole story from Germany to now. Then I finish with, "I don't understand it, but I know God has sent me to you for help. I have to get to Liam, your nephew, in Boulder."

Jesse takes his cap off. "That's quite a story. I'm honored that you trust me this way."

I answer quickly, "It wasn't my plan. I mean, I didn't pick you. God did. He has faith in you, so I do too. I don't even know where you stand on the new government's mandatory allegiance, but I trust God."

He has gloves on and doesn't offer to take them off. He nods, thinks a minute, and then asks, "How can I help?"

I move closer and drop my voice to a whisper. "I need to get to Boulder. Do you know Liam's address?"

He whispers back, "No, but I know he works at the Servants' Center serving the homeless on campus. I think he works almost every morning."

I put my hands together. "Can you get me there? I mean, I have no money left, and the airports and bus terminals are watching for me now."

"You mean you want to hitch a ride on a freight train?" He looks at me like I'm crazy.

I nod.

He paces. "I could get fired if they find you. You'll go to jail." He slaps his leg with the cap in his hand and then puts it back on, all while pacing.

I plead, "Please help me."

He pauses directly in front of me. "You don't really know me. What makes you think Liam will help you?"

I hold his gaze boldly. "Because I believe that's where God is leading me. Masen says Liam has changed, and he *is* family." I think I had his help at the word *family*.

He nods. "Okay, I'll get you on board, and you have to promise to act like you don't know me if you get caught. Is it a deal?"

"It's a deal. Thanks, Jesse." I give him a quick hug.

Jesse reaches in his pocket and pulls out his billfold. "I'll be up at the engine, so when we get to Boulder, you'll have to let yourself off. Here's some money for a taxi or whatever. Good luck. I hope you hook up with everyone. Tell them I love them."

We rush to the engine at the end of the train. He puts me aboard and says, "Stay low and don't touch things. They usually never check this engine. It's turned on remotely to help push us over the steep passes. I've got to do my final check. I'm due to pull out any minute. I guess God is behind you, because if you'd been a little later, I'd have been gone. When we take off, it'll be about six hours tops, and then we'll be in Boulder. I'll lock the engine from the outside, but you'll still be able to get out when the time comes. Watch for signs that we're approaching Boulder."

I sit in the corner out of sight of the windows, but I hear his boots crunching the rocks, running toward the other end of the train. I do some figuring and guess I'll be to Liam's place of work by sunup.

CHAPTER 54

COLORADO—LIAM AT SONRISE

Go on, Gus. It's too late for me!

I call Emily. "Honey, I'm sorry, but they're shorthanded here at the Center, and I'm going to pull a double shift. I won't be home tonight, but I'll be home after class tomorrow afternoon."

Emily states, "What am I going to eat for supper if you're not here?"

I roll my eyes but remain calm. "I'm sorry. I'll make it up to you. You know where I keep some extra money. Get some and take a girlfriend with you and have supper on me. I've got to go, baby. Bye."

I'm nervous all night. I help Leonne, and I see why he likes the evenings. He helps the youngest kids feel safe by preaching to them. When someone is frightened, he begins teaching them about Jesus. He comforts them and watches over them. He sits with the ones who wake to nightmares and tells them of God's love. I see why Leonne is so secretive. I know I've taken the pledge and where my allegiance should lie. I know I waited until *too late* to make my decision, and the top of my right hand reminds me constantly of my choice.

The morning comes, and I begin to serve the breakfast. I like this time of the day. I've become a people watcher. This morning I watch the air force guy who has shown up the last two mornings. He's the first one here. He's polite but distant. He sits as near to the door as he can. He watches the door like a hawk. He's a pleasant distraction from my mundane duties. Sometimes I imagine him as a spy and the militia is searching for him. Other times he's a man hiding out in a uniform to trick people. Red, the girl with the Bible, comes in and sits down and starts a conversation with him. She opens her Bible. I think, *She sure is gutsy today.* She's witnessing to him in the main hall, at the front door. He seems interested. She pleads with him to go with her, but he shakes his head and stands by the door. She mills to the next group.

Leonne has remained this morning as well. He must be pulling a double shift. He pulls some kids aside who he'd been talking to the night before. They're crying and praying. I think the whole room has gone crazy. There's an urgency in the air that's electric. Then when the gymnasium is almost full to capacity and the sun begins to rise, the light spills into the room, vanquishing the darkness. I look back at the crowd and see some really young girls who look like Malorie, Jaylie, and Lia. I've never seen these girls here before. They have their backs to me and they mingle as if one unit, talking to other young people about their ages. I know I'm homesick, and I must be imagining things. It's so crowded, people can hardly move.

Leonne and his merry band of crybabies have moved to a larger group of young kids. They each take a kid aside and talk intensely with them. Before long, a few are crying. It must be one heck of a story they're hearing.

I return to my task of serving oatmeal. My serving tray is low, so I go to the kitchen to refill it. When I return I think the room has gotten even brighter. The light hurts my eyes and makes my brain ache. I look up from serving and see Masen and Jathyn. I must've really seen the girls earlier. I search the group as Gus, Jax, and Zayne step out from behind Masen and Jathyn. The light is getting so bright, it's getting hard to see. I wish those windows faced some other direction other than east. The shafts of light are shining down on the crowd of young people, bathing them in a warm caress. I envy the people on the gymnasium floor.

A tall girl bursts through the door. It's Jordyn. She sees Masen and makes her way to him. It's like she is swimming upstream. She stops and talks to two girls who've asked her a question, I guess. They visit and bow their heads. The air force man comes out of nowhere and grabs Jordyn's arm and spins her around. There's a moment when I think Jordyn is going to break and run. She leaps into the officer's arms, kissing him. Hand in hand, they work the crowd as one, now pulling people aside and talking to them.

I stop serving, and I try to find them. I call out, but my words are lost amid the many voices. I see Gus with Leonne's boys, and they bow their heads. When Gus looks up, he's smiling. He turns his head and sees me. His face lights up, and he tries to make his way to me, but the crush of people pulls him away. They're moving closer and closer to the bright beams of light streaming through the windows. I'm smiling back at him and realize I haven't smiled in a very long time. I can't even remember the last time I laughed. *When I get to Gus, we'll laugh until it hurts.*

The shafts of light streaming into the room seem to have substance because they are so brilliant that they block out everything else. The walls seem aglow in the presence of the morning light. It's as bright outside the door as it is in the building. My eyes ache from the brightness. I see Red and my family mingling and talking as they move farther away. They're talking, pleading with people. Jordyn and the air force guy join them.

Suddenly Harrison and Emily walk between me and my family. They are like a heavy black cloud. The light happy feeling I had is gone. I ignore their presence. I want to see my brother. I call out, "Gus!"

Harrison and Emily follow my gaze, and they make their way toward my family. I have to stop them. I fight my way through the crowd. Harrison is almost to Gus. Gus is smiling at me and doesn't realize Harrison is dangerously close. Gus wouldn't even know why Harrison is dangerous. Gus tries to move toward me, closing the gap between Harrison and him. I have to get Gus to go the other way with the rest of the family. Gus waves at me.

I motion for him to go on with the others. "Go on, Gus. It's *too late* for me! You go on!" I yell at him, but he can't hear me.

Emily is within an arm's length of the girls. The air force guy has his arm around Jordyn. She doesn't notice the danger approaching her sisters. Many from the gymnasium floor look up toward the windows at the same time. I can't believe they can look directly into that light and not be blinded.

The light bursts forth through the windows like a blinding blast. The pain to my eyes is excruciating. I double over in pain. The pressure of the bodies pressing against me lessens as if a third of the people left the building. I open my eyes, and we are all on our knees. The room isn't nearly as full as it was a moment ago. I stand and spot Harrison. *Does he have Gus?* I don't see him. Maybe he got away. Masen and Jathyn have vanished. Maybe they took Gus. Jordyn and the air force guy are gone. I look at the doorway, but I don't see them there.

I look for Emily and find her whirling around, looking for something or someone. My little girl cousins are gone. Emily missed them. They're gone, all of them. Jax and Zayne, the whole family is gone. Harrison and

Emily are looking around as if the missing people are hiding. I look for Leonne and Red. They're gone too, along with the groups that were with them.

I have a lump in my throat. I want to rejoice, but an overwhelming sadness envelops me at the knowledge that Christ came and I wasn't ready. I long for the bright white light that filled the room. I want it in my soul, but there's only darkness—deep, heavy, suffocating darkness.

Harrison grabs me and snarls at me, "Where are they? What did you do?"

I throw my head back and let out a forced, bitter laugh. I laugh to keep from crying. I'm happy for my family but in the depths of despair for my own soul. My tears are hot and heavy upon my cheeks and my heart now. Emily slaps me. I laugh that much harder.

I finally say, "You're *too late*! They've gone home."

They rush away into the crowd, searching for my family. The light streaming into the room moments ago is now gone, and darkness has filled the heavens. The smile fades from my face as the reality sets in that I'll be forever separated from all I love. The lights automatically turn on.

There is a God! He came, and I missed him because he didn't know me! I never acknowledged him. I hear someone reading scripture from the Bible. It seems to only be playing in my brain, because no one else stops what he or she is doing.

First Thessalonians 4:15–17: According to the Lord's word, we tell you that we who are still alive, who are left until the coming of the Lord, will certainly not precede those who have fallen asleep. For the Lord himself will come down from heaven, with a loud command, with the voice of the archangel and with the trumpet call of God, and the dead in Christ will rise first. After that, we who are still alive and are left will be caught up together with them in the clouds to meet the Lord in the air. And so we will be with the Lord forever.

Fights begin to break out across the room. Lights are broken, throwing that part of the gym into shadow. More people stumble into the building in horror of the total and complete darkness outside. There are tortured screams from the depths of the darkness. As the last light in the building goes out, Gram's words ring in my ears: *Jesus Christ is the light of the world, without him is complete darkness.*

The inky vacuum permeates my soul and fills it with hopelessness because I know God never wanted this torment for me, but now it's *too late.*

NOTE FROM THE AUTHOR

Thursday night, May 3, 2012

I'm alone in our family home on the farm. I have a dream. I'm awakened by my Lord saying, "Write it down so you won't forget it." I grab my notebook and pencil and glance at the clock. It's four thirty. Then with early morning grogginess, I write down what I saw and felt as the fog of the dream rapidly recedes.

When God burdens my heart to write, he supplies the topic to be covered. Then if I hesitate and don't get started, he sends me a story. The images and words always tumble out rapidly. The dream's details are becoming more vague, and I can hardly keep up, so I jot down phrases instead of full sentences. The phrases below are the exact notes of that night. Only one word was changed—the word *man* needed to be *young adult* in the next to last line to match the images I remembered:

- Large masses of boys and girls
- That were ebbing and flowing
- Living on the streets out of the reach of their parents
- Some searched for
- Most not
- Teens on their own curfews
- Living on the streets, parks, yards, campuses
- In mass for protection, searching, growing in number
- Gathering together; banding
- Some aligning themselves to the masses to witness, comfort, and console
- Others searching for him
- Searching for the One they know to be there

- Young adults mingling in the nights
- Seeing how they live
- They offer food, shelter
- Teens eat, bathe, and are on their way tomorrow
- To repeat all over again
- Our young adult mixes the morning's breakfast
- The large "hospital," the "institution," "college" giving them refuge
- Wake them at 5:00 a.m. to move on
- Meals at 5:30 a.m., baths, out by 6:00 a.m.
- They do their daily lives, destined to return in the night hours
- Server sees there's no stopping them
- Knows he's helpless
- Helpless to change it
- It has begun
- He serves the food, provides what he can in clothes and facilities
- He knows he's watching the march to the end of ages
- But can't turn them around
- Talk them out of their movement
- It would be like trying to talk a swollen river out of its flow to its destination
- To tell the river to go back where it came from
- The drops in clouds
- The journey has begun and only God knows where it ends
- The man knows
- He must help them to get to the end safely
- He must stay with them
- Preaching, teaching, helping them down the path
- Nightly he watches over them
- He moves in the hearts of others to feed, clothe, and protect his children
- They may harm each other, but no one else will harm them
- Until the end of their journey
- The (sun) Son is coming up in the east
- Day will shine upon all of them
- The ones searching will reach him first
- The others will tarry too long
- Seeing only what's involved in their daily survival

- They won't see the (sun) Son coming up
- Only the ones looking skyward
- Don't stop for the food, the clothes, the baths
- Come as you are
- Come now
- Don't wait
- Look up
- He's here
- Go home
- Go home with him
- The search is over
- Some teens see him
- They try to convince more before they are to the end of the line
- They plead, beg, cry
- But the distance is getting too great
- The numbers behind them too large
- The teens are between the masses and the (sun) Son
- The masses stop to talk, mill, walk in groups
- One following another with no one knowing the direction
- So they search aimlessly
- The man knows the direction
- The young adult serves them but doesn't help them with directions
- He and others tend only to the teens' physical needs

God said, "No. Write Son, not sun!" I crossed out the word *sun* and wrote *Son*, and the message took on a whole new meaning.

This was my prayer immediately following this dream: Lord, help me to always feel this urgency to remember the helplessness of my inadequate actions. Show me the way, the words, Your words, and actions that I might witness for You and tell the lost and wandering teens the message before it's too late. Amen.

This book was inspired by this dream. I didn't realize how much until one day I was two-thirds of the way through writing it, and I thought this sounded familiar. I looked up my notes from the dream and found my story was following the notes.

My books' topics are divinely chosen. This one is to cover the persecution of Christians and how to stand firm in faith. God chose the message. I chose to put bullying in as a type of persecution because it's so relevant to young people. The young adults are the ones who burden my heart.

Liam is a character from Falcon Feather, my second book. His family accepts Jesus as God's Son, but he refuses. He chooses to follow his own desires and the world. Having grandchildren, it broke my heart because originally the character Liam was instead named after one of my grandchildren. I rewrote the end of that book with my grandchild saved. For the next two weeks, each time I closed my eyes, God said, "No, some will wait too long. They'll be too late. They need to know what will happen. This ending is not what I told you."

I put Falcon Feather's original ending back the way it was given to me the first time from my Lord and Savior. Once I was obedient, God said, "Change his name." I had peace, and now this is the rest of Liam's story.

RESOURCES ON BULLYING

Statistics, Scripture, and Solutions: Strength

Statistics
- Two-thirds of those bullied will become bullies. "The Bullied Become Bullies," accessed August 29, 2013, http://www.examiner .com/article/the-bullied-become-bullies.

Scripture
- *Philippians 4:13:* "I can do all things through Christ who strengthens me."
- *Psalm 18:32:* It is God who arms me with strength and keeps my way secure.
- *Psalm 22:19:* But you, Lord, do not be far from me. You are my strength; come quickly to help me.
- *Psalm 28:7a:* The Lord is my strength and my shield; my heart trusts in him, and he helps me.
- *Isaiah 12:2:* Surely God is my salvation; I will trust and not be afraid. The Lord, the Lord himself, is my strength and my defense; he has become my salvation."
- *Isaiah 33:2:* Lord, be gracious to us; we long for you. Be our strength every morning, our salvation in time of distress.
- *Isaiah 40:29:* He gives strength to the weary and increases the power of the weak.
- *Isaiah 40:31:* But those who hope in the Lord will renew their strength. They will soar on wings like eagles; they will run and not grow weary, they will walk and not be faint.

- *Isaiah 41:10:* **So do not fear, for I am with you; do not be dismayed, for I am your God. I will strengthen you and help you; I will uphold you with my righteous right hand.**
- *Ephesians 3:16:* **I pray that out of his glorious riches he may strengthen you with power through his Spirit in your inner being.**
- *2 Thessalonians 3:3:* **But the Lord is faithful, and he will strengthen you and protect you from the evil one.**

Solutions
- Defend yourself by not being an easy target. Be brave! Rely on divine strength when you have none of your own! Never believe the bullies' lies. Always tell someone about the abuse. If the person you tell does nothing, find another until someone listens.
- Body language and tone of voice can make a huge difference.
  o Display your confidence by standing tall, speaking up loudly and clearly when confronted, and walking with deliberateness. Bullies want someone who is timid, insecure, and weak physically or mentally.
  o Buddy up with someone. Bullies would rather pick on one person at a time. There is strength in numbers. Speak up and defend each other. Strengthen each other by memorizing one of the above verses together. Be ready to quote it to encourage each other.

Statistics, Scripture, and Solutions: Be Aware, Observant

Statistics
- Thirty percent of students admit to being a bully or doing some bullying.
- Thirty percent of those students who reported that they had been bullied said they had at times brought weapons to school.
- A bully is six times more likely to be incarcerated by the age of twenty-four.

- A bully is five times more likely to have a serious criminal record when he or she grows up. These statistics are from "14 Facts and Statistics from 'The Bully Proof Classroom,'" accessed August 29, 2013, http://info2.thertc.net/blog-0/bid/300979/14-bullying -facts-and-statistics-from-the-bully-proof-classroom.

Scripture
- *2 Thessalonians 2:8:* **And then the lawless one will be revealed, whom the Lord Jesus will overthrow with the breath of his mouth and destroy by the splendor of his coming.**
- *1 Peter 5:8:* **Be alert and of sober mind. Your enemy the devil prowls around like a roaring lion looking for someone to devour.**

Solutions
- Defend yourself by not being an easy target; arm yourself with God's Word. Tell someone if you are abused in any way. Don't listen to the bullies' lies. Find someone who will listen and help.
- If you know someone has a weapon, tell an adult immediately!
- If you witness bullying, don't settle for being a spectator. The bully usually feeds off his or her audience. Laughter at the victim's circumstance adds fuel to the bully's torment. It's like the law of supply and demand: If the general population doesn't demand the need to see or hear about the victim's misfortune, then there's no need to supply a victim. You can make a difference! Walk away, tell an adult. *If* you don't think the adult is taking the report seriously, tell someone else. Keep reporting no matter how many times or how many adults it takes. Tell someone until he or she listens. Write down exactly what you saw and heard immediately so there is no variance in your reporting. Do not fabricate a more intense drama. If the bully has an audience, he or she may take bolder actions, or if he or she feels you want a more sensationalized act, he or she will accommodate. He or she needs to feed *his* or *her* hunger for power and authority over others.

Statistics, Scripture, and Solutions: Thoughts of Suicide

Statistics

- Suicide is the third leading cause of death in young people. Youths who are bullied are two to nine times more likely to attempt suicide. According to studies by Yale University, "Suicidal Thoughts and Attempts Higher among Young People with General Medical Illnesses, Yale Study Shows," accessed August 29, 2013, http://news.yale.edu/2000/06/05/suicidal-thoughts-and-attempts-higher-among-young-people-general-medical-illnesses-yale-s.
- One hundred sixty thousand young people stay home from school every day out of fear of bullies. Found at the National Education Association site, "Pennsylvania Schools Stand Up to Bullying," accessed August 29, 2013, http://neatoday.org/2011/12/12/pennsylvania-schools-stand-up-to-bullying/.

Scripture

- *Psalm 139:14:* **I praise you because I am fearfully and wonderfully made; Your works are wonderful, I know that full well.**
- *Psalm 140:4:* **Keep me safe, Lord, from the hands of the wicked; protect me from the violent, who devise ways to trip my feet.**
- *Psalm 34:7:* **The angel of the Lord encamps around those who fear Him, and He delivers them.**
- *Psalm 9:13:* **Lord, see how my enemies persecute me! Have mercy and lift me up from the gates of death.**
- *Psalm 56:13:* **For you have delivered me from death and my feet from stumbling, that I may walk before God in the light of life.**

Solutions

- Defend yourself by not being an easy target. Your strength is in God's infinite power, not your own. Always find someone you trust to tell what a bully has done. Never believe the bullies' lies.
- Tell an adult about the abuse—someone who believes you and can help you understand that it's not your fault. Tell a parent, a pastor or clergyman, a counselor, or an adult relative.

- Talk to someone right away!
  - o   If you can't talk to an adult, go to an emergency room.
  - o   Call the suicide hotline: 1-800-273-(TALK) 8255.
  - o   The website http://suicidehotlines.com/ has listings of suicide hotlines by state.
- Remember that bullies are wrong, they tell lies, and they abuse power.
- Don't listen to them, and don't dwell on their words or actions.
- Don't isolate yourself with your own thoughts, focusing only on the words of liars. You are smart!

Statistics, Scripture, and Solutions: Lies and Cyberbullying

Statistics

Resources on cyberbullying:
- "Enough Is Enough: Making the Internet Safer for Children and Families," http://www.Internetsafety101.org/cyberbullyingstatistics .htm#_ftn1.
- Cyberbullying Research Center, http://www.cyberbullying.us /index.php
- Codirector of Cyberbullying Research Center. Additional information available. http://www.uwec.edu/patchinj/webvitae.htm.
- Codirector of Cyberbullying Research Center. Additional information available. http://wise.fau.edu/~hinduja/.
- National Crime Prevention Council, http://www.ncpc.org /cyberbullying

Scripture
- *Job 5:21:* **You will be protected from the lash of the tongue, and need not fear when destruction comes.**
- *Psalm 25:21:* **May integrity and uprightness protect me, because my hope, Lord, is in you.**
- *Proverbs 14:3:* **A fool's mouth lashes out with pride, but the lips of the wise protect them.**
- *Job 11:15:* **Then, free of fault, you will lift up your face; you will stand firm and without fear.**

- *Psalm 3:6:* **I will not fear though tens of thousands assail me on every side.**
- *Psalm 23:4:* **Even though I walk through the darkest valley, I will fear no evil, for you are with me; your rod and your staff, they comfort me.**
- *Hebrews 13:6:* **"So we say with confidence, 'The Lord is my helper; I will not be afraid. What can mere mortals do to me?'"**

Solutions
- If you burn your hand every time you place it in the fire, you learn to not put it in the fire. You can wait for the flames to die down and warm your hands over the coals. Waiting or having patience doesn't mean you will have to remain cold.
- If your heart is broken and your self-esteem shattered each time you open a social media site, learn to stop opening it. You can wait for the firestorm to subside. Patiently wait for God to work on you and perhaps others. Use face-to-face conversations with only trusted and true friends. Avoid the world in its wickedness. Stand with like Christian sisters and brothers, drawing strength from one another.

ADULT RESOURCES

A note to the parents: In *Too Late!* Liam's family didn't recognize the signs of his bullying. He chose to do it because he wanted to be on the side of the bullies to stop the torment he felt.

Does your child exhibit any of the following behaviors?

- becomes violent with others
- gets into verbal or physical fights
- makes frequent trips to the principal's office or other disciplinary situations
- shows up with money or stuff and can't explain where it came from
- blames others quickly
- denies responsibility for his or her own actions
- hangs out with other kids who bully
- must win or dominate in activities

According to the US Department of Health and Human Services, "The Roles Kids Play," accessed August 29, 2013, http://www.stopbullying.gov/what-is-bullying/roles-kids-play/index.html, the above items are bullying behaviors. If these behaviors are repeated to cause harm or hurt the victim as a show of superiority or power of the other individual, this is bullying. Saying, "It was a joke" or "I was teasing," doesn't make it okay for the victim.

To help your child stand firm and draw strength from his or her faith, remind your child of his or her strengths, whether it's physical, intellectual, emotional, or spiritual. Be specific, give examples, and don't just say, "You're a strong boy or girl." Describe what he or she has already done to *demonstrate* those areas of strength. Physically act out scenarios in which he or she has to scream, deflect blows, and practice defensive moves. Encourage him or her to move faster and scream louder than your child believes he or she can. Show your child and others by *their own examples* how strong they can be in Christ when they believe in themselves and not the words hurled at them to make them doubt that divine strength.

Visit my website for additional resources for my books: www.pamelajeanhoffman.com.

REFERENCES

ABC's 20/20. "Why Does a Kid Become a Bully." *ABC news 20/20*, October 15, 2010. abcnews.go.com/2020/video/kid-bully-11896438 (accessed August 27, 2013).

"About us—Cyberbullying Research Center." Home—Cyberbullying Research Center. http://cyberbullying.us/about-us/ (accessed August 28, 2013).

"Alarming Bullying Statistics in the USA." Bullying Facts | Bullying Definition | Bullying Articles. http://bullyingfacts.info/bullying-statistics/ (accessed August 27, 2013).

Audience. "Cyberbullying â€" National Crime Prevention Council." Home â€" National Crime Prevention Council. http://www.ncpc. org/cyberbullying (accessed August 28, 2013).

"Bullying Statistics—Youth "Ambassadors 4 Kids" Club (A4K)." Ambassadors 4 Kids (A4K) Club | Bullying Resources For Kids | Reporting, Stopping & Preventing School Bullying | Cyberbullying Information Organization—Youth "Ambassadors 4 Kids" Club (A4K). http://www. a4kclub.org/get-the-facts/bullying-statistics (accessed August 27, 2013).

"Bullying and Suicide—Bullying Statistics." Bullying Statistics—Teen Violence, Anger, Bullying, Treatment Options. http://www. bullyingstatistics.org/content/bullying-and-suicide.html (accessed August 28, 2013).

Burns, James. "14 Bullying Facts and Statistics from "The Bully Proof Classroom"." Regional Training Center. info2.thertc.net/blog-0/ bid/300979/14-bullying-facts-and-statistics-from-the-bully-proof-classroom (accessed August 28, 2013).

Charles, Kristin. "Author archive on Ministry-To-Children—Part 6." Ministry-To-Children: free children's ministry ideas. http://

ministry-to-children.com/author/kristin/page/6/ (accessed August 28, 2013).

"Home—Cyberbullying Research Center." Home—Cyberbullying Research Center. http://cyberbullying.us/ (accessed August 29, 2013).

"InternetSafety101.org: Enough Is Enough." InternetSafety101.org: Home. http://www.internetsafety101.org/abouteie.htm (accessed August 28, 2013).

"Justin W. Patchin, Ph.D." University of Wisconsin-Eau Claire. http://www.uwec.edu/patchinj/ (accessed August 29, 2013).

McKenna, Paul. "bullying facts and statistics 2013 | Mr Bullyproof." How to be Confident | How to build Confidence | Mr BullyProof. http://www.mrbullyproof.com/search/bullying-facts-and-statistics-2013 (accessed August 27, 2013).

"NEA—Our Position & Actions." NEA—NEA Home. http://www.nea.org/home/19535.htm (accessed August 28, 2013). Putting an end to bullying in bullying statistics. "Bullying Statistics USA | Bullying Statistics." Bullying Statistics 2011/2012 and more!. http://ebullyingstatistics.com/bullying-statistics-usa/ (accessed August 27, 2013).

"NEA—Our Position & Actions." NEA—NEA Home. http://www.nea.org/home/19535.htm (accessed August 28, 2013).

"Sameer Hinduja—Florida Atlantic University—Books, Journal Articles, Presentations, Reports, Grant Work." Welcome to Florida Atlantic University. http://wise.fau.edu/~hinduja/ (accessed August 28, 2013).

Skindzier, Jon. "The Status Of The Bully—AskMen." AskMen—Men's Online Magazine—AskMen. http://www.askmen.com/entertainment/austin_500/558b_the-status-of-the-bully.html (accessed August 27, 2013).

Smith, Maria. "The bullied become bullies—Fort Worth Parenting | Examiner.com." Welcome to Examiner.com | Examiner.com. http://www.examiner.com/article/the-bullied-become-bullies (accessed August 27, 2013).

"SuicideHotlines.com—When You Feel You Can't Go On—Let Someone Know Your Pain." SuicideHotlines.com—When You Feel You Can't Go On—Let Someone Know Your Pain. http://suicidehotlines.com/ (accessed August 28, 2013).

"The Roles Kids Play | StopBullying.gov." Home | StopBullying.gov. http://www.stopbullying.gov/what-is-bullying/roles-kids-play/index. html (accessed August 27, 2013).

"What Makes a Child Become a Bully | 2KnowMySelf." 2KnowMySelf | The Ultimate Source for Understanding Yourself and others. http:// www.2knowmyself.com/what_makes_a_child_become_a_bully (accessed August 27, 2013).

"Why Do Children Bully?." Ministry-To-Children: free children's ministry ideas. http://ministry-to-children.com/why-do-children-bully/ (accessed August 27, 2013).

"Why Does a Kid Become a Bully? | Video—ABC News." ABCNews. com—Breaking News, Latest News & Top Video News—ABC News. http://abcnews.go.com/2020/video/kid-bully-11896438 (accessed August 28, 2013).

"YaleNews | Suicidal Thoughts and Attempts Higher Among Young People With General Medical Illnesses, Yale Study Shows." YaleNews. http://news.yale.edu/2000/06/05/suicidal-thoughts-and-attempts-higher-among-young-people-general-medical-illnesses-yale-s (accessed August 29, 2013).

Chicago formatting by BibMe.org.

CPSIA information can be obtained at www.ICGtesting.com
Printed in the USA
LVOW08s2354141013

356845LV00001B/3/P